Back Home

Back Home

by Irvin S. Cobb

Copyright © 6/24/2015
Jefferson Publication

ISBN-13: 978-1514694183

Printed in the United States of America

All rights reserved. No part of this book may be reprinted or reproduced or utilized in any form or by any electronic, mechanical, or other means, now known or hereafter invented, including photocopying and recording, or in any form of storage or retrieval system, without prior permission in writing from the publisher.'

Contents

PREFACE 3
I. WORDS AND MUSIC 4
II. THE COUNTY TROT 17
III. FIVE HUNDRED DOLLARS REWARD 28
IV. A JUDGMENT COME TO DANIEL 39
V. UP CLAY STREET 49
VI. WHEN THE FIGHTING WAS GOOD 61
VII. STRATAGEM AND SPOILS 73
VIII. THE MOB FROM MASSAC 89
IX. A DOGGED UNDER DOG 102
X. BLACK AND WHITE 112

PREFACE

AFTER I came North to live it seemed to me, as probably it has seemed to many Southern born men and women that the Southerner of fiction as met with in the North was generally just that—fiction—and nothing else; that in the main he was a figment of the drama and of the story book; a type that had no just claim on existence and yet a type that was currently accepted as a verity.

From well meaning persons who apparently wished to convey an implied compliment for the southern part of this republic I was forever hearing of "southern pride" and "hot southern blood" and "old southern families," these matters being mentioned always with a special emphasis which seemed to betray a profound conviction on the part of the speakers that there was a certain physical, tangible, measurable distinction between, say, the pride of a Southerner and the blood-temperature of a Southerner and the pride and blood heat of a man whose parents had chosen some other part of the United States as a suitable place for him to be born in. Had these persons spoken of things which I knew to be a part and parcel of the Southerner's nature—such things for example as his love for his own state and his honest veneration for the records made by men of southern birth and southern blood in the Civil War—I might have understood them. But seemingly they had never heard of those matters.

I also discovered or thought I discovered that as a rule the Southerner as seen on the stage or found between the covers of a book or a magazine was drawn from a more or less imaginary top stratum of southern life, or else from a bottom-most stratum—either he purported to be an elderly, un-reconstructed, high-tempered gentleman of highly aristocratic tendencies residing in a feudal state of shabby grandeur and proud poverty on a plantation gone to seed; or he purported to be a pure white of the poorest. With a few exceptions the playwright and the story writers were not taking into account sundry millions of southern born people who were neither venerable and fiery colonels with frayed wrist bands and limp collars, nor yet were they snuffdipping, ginseng-digging clay-eaters, but just such folk as allowing for certain temperamental differences—created by climate and soil and tradition and by two other main contributing causes: the ever-present race question and the still living and vivid memories of the great war—might be found as numerously in Iowa or Indiana or any other long-settled, typically American commonwealth as in Tennessee or Georgia or Mississippi, having the same aspirations, the same blood in their veins, the same impulses and being prone under almost any conceivable condition to do the same thing in much the same way.

Viewing my own state and my own people across the perspective of time and distance I had the ambition to set down on paper, as faithfully as I might, a representation of those people as I knew them. By this I do not mean to declare that I sensed any audible and visible demand for such a piece of writing; so far as I know there has been no such demand. It was my own notion solely. I wanted, if I could to describe what I believed to be an average southern community so that others might see it as I had seen it. This book is the result of that desire.

For my material I draw upon the life of that community as I remembered it. Most of the characters that figure in the events hereinafter described were copies, to the best of my ability as a copyist, of real models; and for some of the events themselves there was in the first place a fairly substantial basis of fact.

Having such an aim I wrote what I conceived to be a series of pictures, out of the life of a town in the western part of Kentucky; that part of Kentucky which gave to the nation among others, Abraham Lincoln and Jefferson Davis. These, pictures fell into the form of inter-related stories, and as such were first printed in the *Saturday Evening Post*. They are now offered here as a whole.

New York, November 1912

I. WORDS AND MUSIC

WHEN Breck Tandy killed a man he made a number of mistakes. In the first place, he killed the most popular man in Forked Deer County—the county clerk, a man named Abner J. Rankin. In the second place, he killed him with no witnesses present, so that it stood his word—and he a newcomer and a stranger—against the mute, eloquent accusation of a riddled dead man. And in the third place, he sent north of the Ohio River for a lawyer to defend him.

On the first Monday in June—Court Monday—the town filled up early. Before the field larks were out of the grass the farmers were tying their teams to the gnawed hitch-racks along the square. By nine o'clock the swapping ring below the wagonyard was swimming in red dust and clamorous with the chaffer of the horse-traders. In front of a vacant store the Ladies' Aid Society of Zion Baptist Church had a canvas sign out, announcing that an elegant dinner would be served for twenty-five cents from twelve to one, also ice cream and cake all day for fifteen cents.

The narrow wooden sidewalks began to creak and churn under the tread of many feet. A long-haired medicine doctor emerged from his frock-coat like a locust coming out of its shell, pushed his high hat off his forehead and ranged a guitar, sundry bottles of a potent mixture, his tooth-pulling forceps, and a trick-handkerchief upon the narrow shelf of his stand alongside the Drummers' Home Hotel. In front of the little dingy tent of the Half Man and Half Horse a yellow negro sat on a split-bottom chair limbering up for a hard day. This yellow negro was an artist. He played a common twenty-cent mouth organ, using his left hand to slide it back and forth across his spread lips. The other hand held a pair of polished beef bones, such as end men wield, and about the wrist was buckled a broad leather strap with three big sleigh-bells riveted loosely to the leather, so that he could clap the bones and shake the bells with the same motion. He was a whole orchestra in himself. He could play on his mouth organ almost any tune you wanted, and with his bones and his bells to help out he could creditably imitate a church organ, a fife-and-drum corps, or, indeed, a full brass band. He had his chair tilted back until his woolly head dented a draggled banner depicting in five faded primary colors the physical attractions of the Half Man and Half Horse—Marvel of the Century—and he tested his mouth organ with short, mellow, tentative blasts as he waited until the Marvel and the Marvel's manager finished a belated breakfast within and the first ballyhoo could start. He was practicing the newest of the ragtime airs to get that far South. The name of it was The Georgia Camp-Meeting.

The town marshal in his shirt sleeves, with a big silver shield pinned to the breast of his unbuttoned blue waistcoat and a hickory stick with a crook handle for added emblem of authority, stalked the town drunkard, fair game at all seasons and especially on Court Monday. The town gallant whirled back and forth the short hilly length of Main Street in his new side-bar buggy. A clustering group of negroes made a thick, black blob, like hiving bees, in front of a negro fishhouse, from which came the smell and sounds of perch and channel cat frying on spitting-hot skillets. High up on the squat cupola of the courthouse a red-headed woodpecker clung, barred in crimson, white, and blue-black, like a bit of living bunting, engaged in the hopeless task of trying to drill through the tin sheathing. The rolling rattle of his beak's tattoo came down sharply to the crowds below. Mourning doves called to one another in the trees round the red-brick courthouse, and at ten o'clock, when the sun was high and hot, the sheriff came out and, standing between two hollow white pillars, rapped upon one of them with a stick and called upon all witnesses and talesmen to come into court for the trial of John Breckinridge Tandy, charged with murder in the first degree, against the peace and dignity of the commonwealth of Tennessee and the statutes made and provided.

But this ceremonial by the sheriff was for form rather than effect, since the witnesses and the talesmen all sat in the circuit-court chamber along with as many of the population of Forked Deer County as could squeeze in there. Already the air of the crowded chamber was choky with heat and rancid with smell. Men were perched precariously in' the ledges of the windows. More men were ranged in rows along the plastered walls, dunking their heels against the cracked wooden baseboards. The two front rows of benches were full of women. For this was to be the big case of the June term—a better show by long odds than the Half Man and Half Horse.

Inside the low railing that divided the room and on the side nearer the jury box were the forces of the defense. Under his skin the prisoner showed a sallow paleness born of his three months in the county jail. He was tall and dark and steady eyed, a young man, well under thirty. He gave no heed to those who sat in packed rows behind him, wishing him evil. He kept his head turned front, only bending it sometimes to whisper with one of his lawyers or one of his witnesses. Frequently, though, his hand went out in a protecting, reassuring way to touch his wife's brown hair or to rest a moment on her small shoulder. She was a plain, scared, shrinking little thing. The fingers of her thin hands were plaited desperately together in her lap. Already she was trembling. Once in a while she would raise her face, showing shallow brown eyes dilated with fright, and then sink her head again like a quail trying to hide. She looked pitiable and lonely.

The chief attorney for the defense was half turned from the small counsel table where he might study the faces of the crowd. He was from Middle Indiana, serving his second term in Congress. If his party held control of the state he would go to the Senate after the next election. He was an orator of parts and a pleader of almost a national reputation. He had manly grace and he was a fine, upstanding figure of a man, and before now he had wrung victories out of many difficult cases. But he chilled to his finger-nails with apprehensions of disaster as he glanced searchingly about the close-packed room.

Wherever he looked he saw no friendliness at all. He could feel the hostility of that crowd as though it had substance and body.

It was a tangible thing; it was almost a physical thing. Why, you could almost put your hand out and touch it. It was everywhere there.

And it focussed and was summed up in the person of Aunt Tilly Haslett, rearing on the very front bench with her husband, Uncle Fayette, half hidden behind her vast and over-flowing bulk. Aunt Tilly made public opinion in Hyattsville. Indeed she was public opinion in that town. In her it had its up-comings and its out-flowings. She held herself bolt upright, filling out the front of her black bombazine basque until the buttons down its front strained at their buttonholes. With wide, deliberate strokes she fanned herself with a palm-leaf fan. The fan had an edging of black tape sewed round it—black tape signifying in that community age or mourning, or both. Her jaw was set like a steel latch, and her little gray eyes behind her steel-bowed specs were leveled with a baleful, condemning glare that included the strange lawyer, his client, his client's wife, and all that was his client's.

Congressman Durham looked and knew that his presence was an affront to Aunt Tilly and all those who sat with her; that his somewhat vivid tie, his silken shirt, his low tan shoes, his new suit of gray flannels—a masterpiece of the best tailor in Indianapolis—were as insults, added up and piled on, to this suspendered, gingham-shirted constituency. Better than ever he realized now the stark hopelessness of the task to which his hands were set. And he dreaded what was coming almost as much for himself as for the man he was hired to defend. But he was a trained veteran of courtroom campaigns, and there was a jauntily assumed confidence in his bearing as he swung himself about and made a brisk show of conferring with the local attorney who was to aid him in the choosing of the jurors and the questioning of the witnesses.

But it was real confidence and real jauntiness that radiated from the other wing of the inclosure, where the prosecutor sat with the assembled bar of Forked Deer County on his flanks, volunteers upon the favored side, lending to it the moral support of weight and numbers. Rankin, the dead man, having been a bachelor, State's Attorney Gilliam could bring no lorn widow and children to mourn before the jurors' eyes and win added sympathy for his cause. Lacking these most valued assets of a murder trial he supplied their places with the sisters of the dead man—two sparse-built elderly women in heavy black, with sweltering thick veils down over their faces. When the proper time came he would have them raise these veils and show their woeful faces, but now they sat shrouded all in crepe, fit figures of desolation and sorrow. He fussed about busily, fiddling the quill toothpick that hung perilously in the corner of his mouth and evening up the edges of a pile of law books with freckled calfskin covers. He was a lank, bony garfish of a man, with a white goatee aggressively protruding from his lower lip. He was a poor speaker but mighty as a cross-examiner, and he was serving his first term and was a candidate for another. He wore the official garbing of special and extraordinary occasions—long black coat and limp white waistcoat and gray striped trousers, a trifle short in the legs. He felt the importance of his place here almost visibly—his figure swelled and expanded out his clothes.

"Look yonder at Tom Gilliam," said Mr. Lukins, the grocer, in tones of whispered admiration to his next-elbow neighbor, "jest prunin' and honin' hisse'f to git at that there Tandy and his dude Yankee lawyer. If he don't chaw both of 'em up together I'll be dad-burned."

"You bet," whispered back his neighbor—it was Aunt Tilly's oldest son, Fayette, Junior—"it's like Maw says—time's come to teach them murderin' Kintuckians they can't be a-comin' down here a-killin' up people and not pay for it. I reckon, Mr. Lukins," added Fayette, Junior, with a wriggle of pleased anticipation, "we shore are goin' to see some carryin's-on in this cotehouse today."

Mr. Lukins' reply was lost to history because just then the judge entered—an elderly, kindly-looking man—from his chambers in the rear, with the circuit-court clerk right behind him bearing large leather-clad books and sheaves of foolscap paper. Their coming made a bustle. Aunt Tilly squared herself forward, scrooging Uncle Fayette yet farther into the eclipse of her shapeless figure. The prisoner raised his head and eyed his judge. His wife looked only at the interlaced, weaving fingers in her lap.

The formalities of the opening of a term of court were mighty soon over; there was everywhere manifest a haste to get at the big thing. The clerk called the case of the Commonwealth versus Tandy. Both sides were ready. Through the local lawyer, delegated for these smaller purposes, the accused man pleaded not guilty. The clerk spun the jury wheel, which was a painted wooden drum on a creaking wooden axle, and drew forth a slip of paper with the name of a talesman written upon it and read aloud:

"Isom W. Tolliver."

In an hour the jury was complete: two townsmen, a clerk and a telegraph operator, and ten men from the country—farmers mainly and one blacksmith and one horse-trader. Three of the panel who owned up frankly to a fixed bias had been let go by consent of both sides. Three more were sure they could give the defendant a fair trial, but those three the local lawyer had challenged peremptorily. The others were accepted as they came. The foreman was a brownskinned, sparrowhawk-looking old man, with a smoldering brown eye. He had spare, knotted hands, like talons, and the right one was marred and twisted, with a sprayed bluish scar in the midst of the crippled knuckles like the mark of an old gunshot wound. Juror No. 4 was a stodgy old man, a small planter from the back part of the county, who fanned himself steadily with a brown-varnished straw hat. No. 7 was even older, a white-whiskered patriarch on crutches. The twelfth juryman was the oldest of the twelve—he looked to be almost seventy, but he went into the box after he had sworn that his sight and hearing and general health were good and that he still could do his ten hours a day at his blacksmith shop. This juryman chewed tobacco without pause. Twice after he took his seat at the bade end of the double line he tried for a wooden cuspidor ten feet away. Both were creditable attempts, but he missed each time. Seeing the look of gathering distress in his eyes the sheriff brought the cuspidor nearer, and thereafter No. 12 was content, chewing steadily like some bearded contemplative ruminant and listening attentively to the evidence, meanwhile scratching a very wiry head of whity-red hair with a thumbnail that through some injury had taken on the appearance of a very thick, very black Brazil nut. This scratching made a raspy, filing sound that after a while got on Congressman Durham's nerves.

Back Home

It was late in the afternoon when the prosecution rested its case and court adjourned until the following morning. The state's attorney had not had so very much evidence to offer, really—the testimony of one who heard the single shot and ran in at Rankin's door to find Rankin upon the floor, about dead, with a pistol, unfired, in his hand and Tandy standing against the wall with a pistol, fired, in his; the constable to whom Tandy surrendered; the physician who examined the body; the persons who knew of the quarrel between Tandy and Rankin growing out of a land deal into which they had gone partners—not much, but enough for Gilliam's purposes. Once in the midst of examining a witness the state's attorney, seemingly by accident, let his look fall upon the two black-robed, silent figures at his side, and as though overcome by the sudden realization of a great grief, he faltered and stopped dead and sank down. It was an old trick, but well done, and a little humming murmur like a breeze coming through treetops swept the audience.

Durham was sick in his soul as he came away.

In his mind there stood the picture of a little, scared woman's drawn, drenched face. She had started crying before the last juror was chosen and thereafter all day, at half-minute intervals, the big, hard sobs racked her. As Durham came down the steps he had almost to shove his way through a knot of natives outside the doors. They grudged him the path they made for him, and as he showed them his back he heard a snicker and some one said a thing that cut him where he was already bruised—in his egotism. But he gave no heed to the words. What was the use?

At the Drummers' Home Hotel a darky waiter sustained a profound shock when the imported lawyer declined the fried beefsteak with fried potatoes and also the fried ham and eggs. Mastering his surprise the waiter offered to try to get the Northern gentleman a fried pork chop and some fried June apples, but Durham only wanted a glass of milk for his supper. He drank it and smoked a cigar, and about dusk he went upstairs to his room. There he found assembled the forlorn rank and file of the defense, the local lawyer and three character witnesses—prominent citizens from Tandy's home town who were to testify to his good repute in the place where he was born and reared. These would be the only witnesses, except Tandy himself, that Durham meant to call. One of them was a bustling little man named Felsburg, a clothing merchant, and one was Colonel Quigley, a banker and an ex-mayor, and the third was a Judge Priest, who sat on a circuit-court bench back in Kentucky. In contrast to his size, which was considerable, this Judge Priest had a voice that was high and whiny. He also had the trick, common to many men in politics in his part of the South, of being purposely ungrammatical at times.

This mannerism led a lot of people into thinking that the judge must be an uneducated man—until they heard him charging a jury or reading one of his rulings. The judge had other peculiarities. In conversation he nearly always called men younger than himself, son. He drank a little bit too much sometimes; and nobody had ever beaten him for any office he coveted. Durham didn't know what to make of this old judge—sometimes he seemed simple-minded to the point of childishness almost.

The others were gathered about a table by a lighted kerosene lamp, but the old judge sat at an open window with his low-quarter shoes off and his white-socked feet propped against the ledge. He was industriously stoking at a home-made corncob pipe. He pursed up his mouth, pulling at the long cane stem of his pipe with little audible sucks. From the rocky little street below the clatter of departing farm teams came up to him. The Indian medicine doctor was taking down his big white umbrella and packing up his regalia. The late canvas habitat of the Half Man and Half Horse had been struck and was gone, leaving only the pole-holes in the turf and a trodden space to show where it had stood. Court would go on all week, but Court Monday was over and for another month the town would doze along peacefully.

Back Home

Durham slumped himself into a chair that screeched protestingly in all its infirm joints. The heart was gone clean out of him.

"I don't understand these people at all," he confessed. "We're beating against a stone wall with our bare hands."

"If it should be money now that you're needing, Mister Durham," spoke up Felsburg, "that boy Tandy's father was my very good friend when I first walked into that town with a peddling pack on my back, and if it should be money——?"

"It isn't money, Mr. Felsburg," said Durham. "If I didn't get a cent for my services I'd still fight this case out to the aid for the sake of that game boy and that poor little mite of a wife of his. It isn't money or the lack of it—it's the damned hate they've built up here against the man. Why, you could cut it off in chunks—the prejudice that there was in that courthouse today."

"Son," put in Judge Priest in his high, weedy voice, "I reckon maybe you're right. I've been projectin' around cotehouses a good many years, and I've taken notice that when a jury look at a prisoner all the time and never look at his women folks it's a monstrous bad sign. And that's the way it was all day today."

"The judge will be fair—he always is," said Hightower, the local lawyer, "and of course Gilliam is only doing his duty. Those jurors are as good solid men as you can find in this country anywhere. But they can't help being prejudiced. Human nature's not strong enough to stand out against the feeling that's grown up round here against Tandy since he shot Ab Rankin."

"Son," said Judge Priest, still with his eyes on the darkening square below, "about how many of them jurors would you say are old soldiers?"

"Four or five that I know of," said Hightower—"and maybe more. It's hard to find a man over fifty years old in this section that didn't see active service in the Big War."

"Ah, hah," assented Judge Priest with a squeaky little grunt. "That foreman now—he looked like he might of seen some fightin'?"

"Four years of it," said Hightower. "He came out a captain in the cavalry."

"Ah, hah." Judge Priest sucked at his pipe. "Herman," he J wheezed back over his shoulder to Felsburg, "did you notice a tall sort of a saddle-colored darky playing a juice harp in front of that there sideshow as we came along up? I reckon that nigger could play almost any tune you'd a mind to hear him play?"

At a time like this Durham was distinctly not interested in the versatilities of strange negroes in this corner of the world. He kept silent, shrugging his shoulders petulantly.

"I wonder now is that nigger left town yet?" mused the old judge half to himself.

"I saw him just a while ago going down toward the depot," volunteered Hightower. "There's a train out of here for Memphis at 8:50. It's about twenty minutes of that now."

"Ah, hah, jest about," assented the judge. When the judge said "Ah, hah!" like that it sounded like the striking of a fiddle-bow across a fiddle's tautened E-string.

"Well, boys," he went on, "we've all got to do the best we can for Breck Tandy, ain't we? Say, son'"—this was aimed at Durham—"I'd like mightily for you to put me on the stand the last one tomorrow. You wait until you're through with Herman and Colonel Quigley here, before you call me. And if I should seem to ramble somewhat in giving my testimony—why, son, you just let me ramble, will you? I know these people down here better maybe than you do—and if I should seem inclined to ramble, just let me go ahead and don't stop me, please?"

"Judge Priest," said Durham tartly, "if you think it could possibly do any good, ramble all you like."

9

Back Home

"Much obliged," said the old judge, and he struggled into his low-quarter shoes and stood up, dusting the tobacco fluff off himself.

"Herman have you got any loose change about you?"

Felsburg nodded and reached into his pocket. The judge made a discriminating selection of silver and bills from the handful that the merchant extended to him across the table.

"I'll take about ten dollars," he said. "I didn't come down here with more than enough to jest about buy my railroad ticket and pay my bill at this here tavern, and I might want a sweetenin' dram or somethin'."

He pouched his loan and crossed the room. "Boys," he said, "I think I'll be knockin' round a little before I turn in. Herman, I may stop by your room a minute as I come back in. You boys better turn in early and git yourselves a good night's sleep. We are all liable to be purty tolerable busy tomorrow."

After he was outside he put his head back in the door and said to Durham:

"Remember, son, I may ramble."

Durham nodded shortly, being somewhat put out by the vagaries of a mind that could concern itself with trivial things on the imminent eve of a crisis.

As the judge creaked ponderously along the hall and down the stairs those he had left behind heard him whistling a tune to himself, making false starts at the air and halting often to correct his meter. It was an unknown tune to them all, but to Felsburg, the oldest of the four, it brought a vague, unplaced memory.

The old judge was whistling when he reached the street. He stood there a minute until he had mastered the time to his own satisfaction, and then, still whistling, he shuffled along the uneven board pavement, which, after rippling up and down like a broken-backed snake, dipped downward to a little railroad station at the foot of the street.

In the morning nearly half the town—the white half—came to the trial, and enough of the black half to put a dark hem, like a mourning border, across the back width of the courtroom. Except that Main Street now drowsed in the heat where yesterday it had buzzed, this day might have been the day before. Again the resolute woodpecker drove his bloodied head with unimpaired energy against the tin sheathing up above. It was his third summer for that same cupola and the tin was pocked with little dents for three feet up and down. The mourning doves still pitched their lamenting note back and forth across the courthouse yard; and in the dewberry patch at the bottom of Aunt Tilly Haslett's garden down by the creek the meadow larks strutted in buff and yellow, with crescent-shaped gorgets of black at their throats, like Old Continentals, sending their dear-piped warning of "Laziness g'wine kill you!" in at the open windows of the steamy, smelly courtroom.

The defense lost no time getting under headway. As his main witness Durham called the prisoner to testify in his own behalf. Tandy gave his version of the killing with a frankness and directness that would have carried conviction to auditors more even-minded in their sympathies. He had gone to Rankin's office in the hope of bringing on a peaceful settlement of their quarrel. Rankin had flared up; had cursed him and advanced on him, making threats. Both of them reached for their guns then. Rankin's was the first out, but he fired first—that was all there was to it. Gilliam shone at cross-examination; he went at Tandy savagely, taking hold like a snapping turtle and hanging on like one.

He made Tandy admit over and over again that he carried a pistol habitually. In a community where a third of the male adult population went armed this admission was nevertheless taken as plain evidence of a nature bloody-minded and desperate. It would have been just as bad for Tandy if he said he armed himself especially for his visit to

Back Home

Rankin—to these listeners that could have meant nothing else but a deliberate, murderous intention. Either way Gilliam had him, and he sweated in his eagerness to bring out the significance of the point. A sinister little murmuring sound,4 vibrant with menace, went purring from bench to bench when Tandy told about his pistol-carrying habit.

The cross-examination dragged along for hours. The recess for dinner interrupted it; then it went on again, Gilliam worrying at Tandy, goading at him, catching him up and twisting his words. Tandy would not be shaken, but twice under the manhandling he lost his temper and lashed back at Gilliam, which was precisely what Gilliam most desired. A flary fiery man, prone to violent outbursts—that was the inference he could draw from these blaze-ups.

It was getting on toward five o'clock before Gilliam finally let his bedeviled enemy quit the witness-stand and go back to his place between his wife and his lawyer. As for Durham, he had little more to offer. He called on Mr. Felsburg, and Mr. Felsburg gave Tandy a good name as man and boy in his home town. He called on Banker Quigley, who did the same thing in different words. For these character witnesses State's Attorney Gilliam had few questions. The case was as good as won now, he figured; he could taste already his victory over the famous lawyer from up North, and he was greedy to hurry it forward.

The hot round hub of a sun had wheeled low enough to dart its thin red spokes in through the westerly windows when Durham called his last witness. As Judge Priest settled himself solidly in the witness chair with the deliberation of age and the heft of flesh, the leveled rays caught him full and lit up his round pink face, with the short white-bleached beard below it and the bald white-bleached forehead above. Durham eyed him half doubtfully. He looked the image of a scatter-witted old man, who would potter and philander round a long time before he ever came to the point of anything. So he appeared to the others there, too. But what Durham did not sense was that the homely simplicity of the old man was of a piece with the picture of the courtroom, that he would seem to these watching, hostile people one of their own kind, and that they would give to him in all likelihood a sympathy and understanding that had been denied the clothing merchant and the broadclothed banker.

He wore a black alpaca coat that slanted upon him in deep, longitudinal folds, and the front skirts of it were twisted and pulled downward until they dangled in long, wrinkly black teats. His shapeless gray trousers were short for him and fitted his pudgy legs closely. Below them dangled a pair of stout ankles encased in white cotton socks and ending in low-quarter black shoes. His shirt was clean but wrinkled countlessly over his front. The gnawed and blackened end of a cane pipestem stood out of his breast pocket, rising like a frosted weed stalk.

He settled himself back in the capacious oak chair, balanced upon his knees a white straw hat with a string band round the crown and waited for the question.

"What is your name?" asked Durham. "William Pitman Priest."

Even the voice somehow seemed to fit the setting. Its high nasal note had a sort of whimsical appeal to it.

"When and where were you born?"

"In Calloway County, Kintucky, July 27, 1889."

"What is your profession or business?"

"I am an attorney-at-law."

"What position if any do you hold in your native state?"

"I am presidin' judge of the first judicial district of the state of Kintucky."

"And have you been so long?"

"For the past sixteen years."

"When were you admitted to the bar?"

"In 1860."

"And you have ever since been engaged, I take it, either in the practice of the law before the bar or in its administration from the bench?"

"Exceptin' for the four years from April, 1861, to June, 1866."

Up until now Durham had been sparring, trying to fathom the probable trend of the old judge's expected meanderings. But in the answer to the last question he thought he caught the cue and, though none save those two knew it, thereafter it was the witness who led and the questioner who followed his lead blindly.

"And where were you during those four years?"

"I was engaged, suh, in takin' part in the war."

"The War of the Rebellion?"

"No, suh," the old man corrected him gently but with firmness, "the War for the Southern Confederacy."

There was a least bit of a stir at this. Aunt Tilly's tape-edged palmleaf blade hovered a brief second in the wide regular arc of its sweep and the foreman of the jury involuntarily ducked his head, as if in affiance of an indubitable fact.

"Ahem!" said Durham, still feeling his way, although now he saw the path more clearly. "And on which side were you engaged?"

"I was a private soldier in the Southern army," the old judge answered him, and as he spoke he straightened up. "Yes, suh," he repeated, "for four years I was a private soldier in the late Southern Confederacy. Part of the time I was down here in this very country," he went on as though he had just recalled that part of it. "Why, in the summer of '64 I was right here in this town. And until yistiddy I hadn't been back since."

He turned to the trial judge and spoke to him with a tone and manner half apologetic, half confidential.

"Your Honor," he said, "I am a judge myself, occupyin' in my home state a position very similar to the one which you fill here, and whilst I realize, none better, that this ain't all accordin' to the rules of evidence as laid down in the books, yet when I git to thinkin' about them old soldierin' times I find I am inclined to sort of reminiscence round a little. And I trust your Honor will pardon me if I should seem to ramble slightly?"

His tone was more than apologetic and more than confidential. It was winning. The judge upon the bench was a veteran himself. He looked toward the prosecutor.

"Has the state's attorney any objection to this line of testimony?" he asked, smiling a little.

Certainly Gilliam had no fear that this honest-appearing old man's wanderings could damage a case already as good as won. He smiled back indulgently and waved his arm with a gesture that was compounded of equal parts of toleration and patience, with a top-dressing of contempt. "I fail," said Gilliam, "to see wherein the military history and achievements of this worthy gentleman can possibly affect the issue of the homicide of Abner J. Rankin. But," he added magnanimously, "if the defense chooses to encumber the record with matters so trifling and irrelevant I surely will make no objection now or hereafter."

"The witness may proceed," said the judge. "Well, really, Your Honor, I didn't have so very much to say," confessed Judge Priest, "and I didn't expect there'd be any to-do made over it. What I was trying to git at was that cornin' down here to testify in this case sort of brought back them old days to my mind. As I git along more in years—" he was looking toward the jurors now—"I find that I live more and more in the past."

As though he had put a question to them several of the jurors gravely inclined their heads. The busy cud of Juror No. 12 moved just a trifle slower in its travels from the right side of the jaw to the left and back again. "Yes, suh," he said musingly, "I got up early this mornin' at the tavern where I'm stoppin' and took a walk through your thrivin' little city." This was rambling with a vengeance, thought the puzzled Durham. "I walked down here to a bridge over a little creek and back again. It reminded me mightily of that other time when I passed through this town—in '64—just about this season of the year—and it was hot early today just as it was that other time—and the dew was thick on the grass, the same as 'twas then."

He halted a moment.

"Of course your town didn't look the same this mornin' as it did that other mornin'. It seemed like to me there are twicet as many houses here now as there used to be—it's got to be quite a little city."

Mr. Lukins, the grocer, nodded silent approval of this utterance, Mr. Lukins having but newly completed and moved into a two-story brick store building with a tin cornice and an outside staircase.

"Yes, suh, your town has grown mightily, but"—and the whiny, humorous voice grew apologetic again—"but your roads are purty much the same as they were in '64—hilly in places—and kind of rocky."

Durham found himself sitting still, listening hard. Everybody else was listening too. Suddenly it struck Durham, almost like a blow, that this simple old man had somehow laid a sort of spell upon them all. The flattening sunrays made a kind of pink glow about the old judge's face, touching gently his bald head and his white whiskers. He droned on:

"I remember about those roads particularly well, because that time when I marched through here in '64 my feet was about out ef my shoes and them flints cut 'em up some. Some of the boys, I recollect, left bloody prints in the dust behind 'em. But shucks—it wouldn't a-made no real difference if we'd wore the bottoms plum off our feet! We'd a-kept on goin'. We'd a-gone anywhere—or tried to—behind old Bedford Forrest."

Aunt Tilly's palmleaf halted in air and the twelfth juror's faithful quid froze in his cheek and stuck there like a small wen. Except for a general hunching forward of shoulders and heads there was no movement anywhere and no sound except the voice of the witness:

"Old Bedford Forrest hisself was leadin' us, and so naturally we just went along with him, shoes or no shoes. There was a regiment of Northern troops—Yankees—marchin' on this town that mornin', and it seemed the word had traveled ahead of 'em that they was aimin' to burn it down.

"Probably it wasn't true. When we got to know them Yankees better afterward we found out that there really wasn't no difference, to speak of, between the run of us and the run of them. Probably it wasn't so at all. But in them days the people was prone to believe 'most anything—about Yankees—and the word was that they was comin' across country, a-burnin' and cuttin' and slashin,' and the people here thought they was going to be burned out of house and home. So old Bedford Forrest he marched all night with a battalion of us—four companies—Kintuckians and Tennesseeans mostly, with a sprinklin' of boys from Mississippi and Arkansas—some of us ridin' and some walkin' afoot, like me—we didn't always have horses enough to go round that last year. And somehow we got here before they did. It was a close race though between us—them a-comin' down from the North and us a-comin' up from the other way. We met 'em down there by that little branch just below where your present railroad depot is. There wasn't no depot there then, but the branch looks just the same now as it did then—and the bridge too. I walked acros't it this momin' to see. Yes, suh, right there was where we met 'em. And there was a right smart fight.

"Yes, suh, there was a right smart fight for about twenty minutes—or maybe twenty-five—and then we had breakfast."

He had been smiling gently as he went along. Now he broke into a throaty little chuckle.

"Yes, suh, it all come back to me this mornin'—every little bit of it—the breakfast and all. I didn't have much breakfast, though, as I recall—none of us did—probably just corn pone and branch water to wash it down with."

And he wiped his mouth with the back of his hand as though the taste of the gritty cornmeal cakes was still there.

There was another little pause here; the witness seemed to be through. Durham's crisp question cut the silence like a gash with a knife.

"Judge Priest, do you know the defendant at the bar, and if so, how well do you know him?"

"I was just comin' to that," he answered with simplicity, "and I'm obliged to you for puttin' me back on the track. Oh, I know the defendant at the bar mighty well—as well as anybody on earth ever did know him, I reckin, unless 'twas his own maw and paw. I've known him, in fact, from the time he was born—and a gentler, better-disposed boy never grew up in our town. His nature seemed almost too sweet for a boy—more like a girl's—but as a grown man he was always manly, and honest, and fair—and not quarrelsome. Oh, yes, I know him. I knew his father and his mother before him. It's a funny thing too—comin' up this way—but I remember that his paw was marchin' right alongside of me the day we came through here in '64. He was wounded, his paw was, right at the edge of that little creek down yonder. He was wounded in the shoulder—and he never did entirely git over it."

Again he stopped dead short, and he lifted his hand and tugged at the lobe of his right ear absently. Simultaneously Mr. Felsburg, who was sitting close to a window beyond the jury box, was also seized with nervousness, for he jerked out a handkerchief and with it mopped his brow so vigorously that, to one standing outside, it might have seemed that the handkerchief was actually being waved about as a signal.

Instantly then there broke upon the pause that still endured a sudden burst of music, a rollicking, jingling air. It was only a twenty-cent touth organ, three sleigh bells, and a pair of the rib bones of a beef-cow being played all at once by a saddle-colored negro man but it sounded for all the world like a fife-and-drum corps:

```
If you want to have a good time,
If you want to have a good time,
If you want to have a good time,
If you want to ketch the devil—
Jine the cavalree!
```

To some who heard it now the time was strange; these were the younger ones. But to those older men and those older women the first jubilant bars rolled back the years like a scroll.

```
If you want to have a good time,
If yu want to have a good time,
If you want to have a good time,
If you want to ride with Bedford—
Jine the cavalree!
```

Back Home

The sound swelled and rippled and rose through the windows—the marching song of the Southern trooper—Forrest's men, and Morgan's, and Jeb Stuart's and Joe Wheeler's. It had in it the jingle of saber chains, the creak of sweaty saddle-girths, the nimble clunk of hurrying hoofs. It had in it the clanging memories of a cause and a time that would live with these people as long as they lived and their children lived and their children's children. It had in it the one sure call to the emotions and the sentiments of these people.

And it rose and rose and then as the unseen minstrel went slouching down Main Street, toward the depot and the creek it sank lower and became a thin thread of sound and then a broken thread of sound and then it died out altogether and once more there was silence in the court house of Forked Deer County.

Strangely enough not one listener had come to the windows to look out. The interruption from without had seemed part and parcel of what went on within. None faced to the rear, every one faced to the front.

There was Mr. Lukins now. As Mr. Lukins got upon his feet he said to himself in a tone of feeling that he be dad-fetched. But immediately changing his mind he stated that he would preferably be dad-blamed, and as he moved toward the bar rail one overhearing him might have gathered from remarks let fall that Mr. Lukins was going somewhere with the intention of being extensively dad-burned. But for all these threats Mr. Lukins didn't go anywhere, except as near the railing as he could press.

Nearly everybody else was standing up too. The state's attorney was on his feet with the rest, seemingly for the purpose of making some protest.

Had any one looked they might have seen that the ember in the smoldering eye of the old foreman had blazed up to a brown fire; that Juror No. 4, with utter disregard for expense, was biting segments out of the brim of his new brown-varnished straw hat; that No. 7 had dropped his crutches on the floor, and that no one, not even their owner, had heard them fall; that all the jurors were half out of their chairs. But no one saw these things, for at this moment there rose up Aunt Tilly Haslett, a dominant figure, her huge wide bade blocking the view of three or four immediately behind her.

Uncle Fayette laid a timid detaining hand upon her and seemed to be saying something protestingly.

"Turn loose of me, Fate Haslett!" she commanded. "Ain't you ashamed of yourse'f, to be tryin' to hold me back when you know how my only dear brother died a-followin' after Gineral Nathan Bedford Forrest. Turn loose of me!"

She flirted her great arm and Uncle Fayette spun flutteringly into the mass behind. The sheriff barred her way at the gate of the bar.

"Mizz Haslett," he implored, "please, Mizz Haslett—you must keep order in the cote." Aunt Tilly halted in her onward move, head up high and elbows out, and through her specs, blazing like burning-glasses, she fixed on him a look that instantly charred that, unhappy official into a burning red ruin of his own self-importance.

"Keep it yourse'f, High Sheriff Washington Nash, Esquire," she bade him; "that's whut you git paid good money for doin'. And git out of my way! I'm a-goin' in there to that pore little lonesome thing settin' there all by herself, and there ain't nobody goin' to hinder me neither!"

The sheriff shrunk aside; perhaps it would be better to say he evaporated aside. And public opinion, reorganized and made over but still incarnate in Aunt Tilly Haslett, swept past the rail and settled like a billowing black cloud into a chair that the local attorney for the defense vacated just in time to save himself the inconvenience of having it snatched bodily from under him.

"There, honey," said Aunt Tilly crooningly as she gathered the forlorn little figure of the prisoner's wife in her arms like a child and mothered her up to her ample bombazined bosom, "there now, honey, you jest cry on me."

Then Aunt Tilly looked up and her specs were all blurry and wet. But she waved her palmleaf fan as though it had been the baton of a marshal.

"Now, Jedge," she said, addressing the bench, "and you other gentlemen—you kin go ahead now."

The state's attorney had meant evidently to make some sort of an objection, for he was upon his feet through all this scene. But he looked back before he spoke and what he saw kept him from speaking. I believe I stated earlier that he was a candidate for rejection. So he settled back down in his chair and stretched out his legs and buried his chin in the top of his limp white waistcoat in an attitude that he had once seen in a picture entitled, "Napoleon Bonaparte at St. Helena."

"You may resume, Judge Priest," said the trial judge in a voice that was not entirely free from huskiness, although its owner had been clearing it steadily for some moments.

"Thank you kindly, suh, but I was about through anyhow," answered the witness with a bow, and for all his homeliness there was dignity and stateliness in it. "I merely wanted to say for the sake of completin' the record, so to speak, that on the occasion referred to them Yankees did not cross that bridge." With the air of tendering and receiving congratulations Mr. Lukins turned to his nearest neighbor and shook hands with him warmly.

The witness got up somewhat stiffly, once more becoming a commonplace old man in a wrinkled black alpaca coat, and made his way back to his vacant place, now in the shadow of Aunt Tilly Haslett's form. As he passed along the front of the jury-box the foreman's crippled right hand came up in a sort of a clumsy salute, and the juror at the other end of the rear row—No. 12, the oldest juror—leaned forward as if to speak to him, but remembered in time where his present duty lay. The old judge kept on until he came to Durham's side, and he whispered to him: "Son, they've quit lookin' at him and they're all a-lookin' at her. Son, rest your case." Durham came out of a maze.

"Your Honor," he said as he rose, "the defense rests."

The jury were out only six minutes. Mr. Lukins insisted that it was only five minutes and a half, and added that he'd be dad-rotted if it was a second longer than that.

As the lately accused Tandy came out of the courthouse with his imported lawyer—Aunt Tilly bringing up the rear with his trembling, weeping, happy little wife—friendly hands were outstretched to clasp his and a whiskered old gentleman with a thumbnail like a Brazil nut grabbed at his arm.

"Whichaway did Billy Priest go?" he demanded—"little old Fightin' Billy—whar did he go to? Soon as he started in talkin' I placed him. Whar is he?"

Walking side by side, Tandy and Durham came down the steps into the soft June night, and Tandy took a long, deep breath into his lungs.

"Mr. Durham," he said, "I owe a great deal to you."

"How's that?" said Durham.

Just ahead of them, centered in a shaft of light from the window of the barroom of the Drummers' Home Hotel, stood Judge Priest. The old judge had been drinking. The pink of his face was a trifle more pronounced, the high whine in his voice a trifle weedier, as he counted one by one certain pieces of silver into the wide-open palm of a saddle-colored negro.

"How's that?" said Durham. "I say I owe everything in the world to you," repeated Tandy.

"No," said Durham, "what you owe me is the fee you agreed to pay me for defending you. There's the man you're looking for."

And he pointed to the old judge.

II. THE COUNTY TROT

SATURDAY was the last day of the county fair and the day of the County Trot. It was also Veterans' Day, when the old soldiers were the guests of honor of the management, and likewise Ladies' Day, which meant that all white females of whatever age were admitted free. So naturally, in view of all these things, the biggest day of fair week was Saturday.

The fair grounds lay in a hickory flat a mile out of town, and the tall scaly barks grew so close to the fence that they poked their limbs over its top and shed down nuts upon the track. The fence had been whitewashed once, back in the days of its youth when Hector was a pup; but Hec was an old dog now and the rains of years had washed the fence to a misty gray, so that in the dusk the long, warped panels stood up in rows, palely luminous—like the highshouldered ghosts of a fence. And the rust had run down from the eaten-out nail-holes until each plank had two staring marks in its face—like rheumy, bleared eyes. The ancient grandstand was of wood too, and had lain outdoors in all weathers until its rheumatic rafters groaned and creaked when the wind blew.

Back of the grandstand stood Floral Hall and Agricultural Hall. Except for their names and their flagstaffs you might have taken them for two rather hastily built and long-neglected barns. Up the track to the north were the rows of stables that were empty, odorous little cubicles for fifty-one weeks of the year, but now—for this one week—alive with darky stable hands and horses; and all the good savors of woodfires, clean hay, and turned-up turf were commingled there.

The fair had ideal weather for its windup. No frost had fallen yet, but in the air there were signs and portents of its coming. The long yellow leaves of the hickories had begun to curl up as if to hold the dying warmth of the sap to the last; and once in a while an ash flamed red like a signal fire to give warning for Indian summer, when all the woods would blaze in warpaints before huddling down for the winter under their tufted, ragged tawnies and browns—like buffalo robes on the shoulders of chilled warriors. The first flights of the wild geese were going over, their V's pointed to the Gulf; and that huckstering little bird of the dead treetops, which the negroes call the sweet-potato bird—maybe it's a pewee, with an acquired Southern accent—was calling his mythical wares at the front door of every woodpecker's hole. The woods were perfumy with ripening wild grapes and pawpaws, and from the orchards came rich winy smells where the windfalls lay in heaps and cider mills gushed under the trees; and on the roof of the smokehouse the pared, sliced fruit was drying out yellow and leathery in the sun and looking—a little way off—like countless ears all turned to listen for the same thing.

Saturday, by sunup, the fair grounds were astir. Undershirted concessionaries and privilege people emerged from their canvas sleeping quarters to sniff at a the tantalizing smell that floated across to them from certain narrow trenches dug in the ground. That smell, just by itself, was one square meal and an incentive to another; for these trenches were full of live red hickory coals; and above them, on greenwood stakes that were stretched across, a shoat and a whole sheep, and a rosary of young squirrels impaled in a string, had been all night barbecuing. Uncle Isom Woolfolk was in charge here—mightily and solely in charge—Uncle Isom Woolfolk, no less, official purveyor to the whole county at fish fries or camp breakfasts, secretary of the Republican County Committee, high in his church and his lodges and the best barbecue cook in seven states. He bellowed frequent and contradictory orders to two negro women of his household who were arranging clean white clothes on board trestles; and constantly he went from shoat to sheep and from sheep to squirrels, basting them with a rag wrapped about a stick and dipped into a potent sauce of his own private making. Red pepper and sweet vinegar were two of its main constituents, though, and in turn he painted each carcass as daintily as an artist retouching the miniature of his lady fair, so that under his hand the crackling meatskins sizzled and smoked, and a yellowish glaze like a veneer spread over their surfaces. His white chin-beard waggled with importance and the artistic temperament.

Before Uncle Isom had his barbecue off the fire the crowds were pouring in, coming from the town afoot, and in buggies and hacks, and from the country in farm wagons that held families, from grandsire to baby in arms, all riding in kitchen chairs, with bedquilt lap robes. At noon a thin trickle of martial music came down the pike; and pretty soon then the veterans, forty or fifty of them, marched in, two by two, some in their reunion gray and some in their best Sunday blacks. At the head of the limping line of old men was a fife-and-drum corps—two sons of veterans at the drums and Corporal Harrison Treese, sometime bugler of Terry's Cavalry, with his fife half buried in his whiskers, ripping the high notes out of The Girl I Left Behind Me. Near the tail of the procession was Sergeant Jimmy Bagby, late of King's Hellhounds. Back in war times that organization had borne a more official and a less sanguinary title; but you would never have guessed this, overhearing Sergeant Jimmy Bagby's conversation.

The sergeant wore a little skirtless jacket, absurdly high-collared, faded to all colors and falling to pieces with age. Three tarnished buttons and a rag of rotted braid still clung to its front. Probably it had fitted the sergeant well in the days when he was a slim and limber young partisan ranger; but now the peaked little tail showed halfway up his back where his suspenders forked, and his white-shirted paunch jutted out in front like a big cotton pod bursting out of a gray-brown boll. The sergeant wore his jacket on all occasions of high military and civic state—that, and a gangrened leather cartridge-box bouncing up and down on his plump hip—and over his shoulder the musket he had carried to war and back home again, an ancient Springfield with a stock like a log butt and a hammer like a mule's ear, its barrel merely a streak of rust.

He walked side by side with his closest personal friend and bitterest political foe, Major Ashcroft, late of the Ninth Michigan Volunteers—walking so close to him that the button of the Loyal Legion in the major's left-hand lapel almost touched the bronze Southern Cross pinned high up on the right breast of the sergeant's flaring jacket.

From time to time the sergeant, addressing the comrades ahead of him, would poke the major in the side and call out:

"Boys, I've took the first prisoner—this here pizen Yank is my meat!"

And the imperturbable major would invariably retort:

"Yes, and along about dark the prisoner will have to be loading you into a hack and sending you home—the same as he always does." Thereupon a cackling laugh would run up the double line from its foot to its head.

The local band, up in its coop on the warped gray roof of the grandstand, blared out Dixie, and the crowd cheered louder than ever as the uneven column of old soldiers swung stiffly down the walkway fronting the grandstand and halted at the word—and then, at another word, disbanded and melted away into individuals and groups. Soon the veterans, with their womenfolks, were scattered all over the grounds, elbowing a way through the narrow aisles of Floral Hall to see the oil paintings and the prize cakes and preserves, and the different patterns of home-made rag quilts—Hen-and-Chickens and Lone Star and Log Cabin—or crowding about the showpens where young calves lowed vainly for parental attention and a Berkshire boar, so long of body and so vast of bulk that he only needed to shed his legs to be a captive balloon, was shoving his snout through a crack in his pen and begging for goodies. And in Agricultural Hall were water-melons like green boulders, and stalks of corn fourteen feet long, and saffron blades of prize-winning tobacco, and families of chickens unhappily domiciled in wooden coops. The bray of sideshow barkers, and the squeak of toy balloons, and the barnyard sounds from the tied-up, penned-up farm creatures, went up to the treetops in a medley that drove the birds scurrying over the fence and into the quieter woods. And in every handy spot under a tree basket dinners were spread, and family groups ate cold fried chicken and lemon meringue pie, picnic fashion, upon the grass.

In the middle of this a cracked bugle sounded and there was a rush to the grandstand. Almost instantly its rattling gray boards clamored under the heels of a multitude. About the stall of the one lone bookmaker a small crowd, made up altogether of men, eddied and swirled. There were men in that group, strict church members, who would not touch a playing card or a fiddle—playthings of the devil by the word of their strict orthodoxy; who wouldn't let their children dance any dance except a square dance or go to any parties except play parties, and some of them had never seen the inside of a theater or a circus tent. But they came each year to the county fair; and if they bet on the horses it was their own private affair.

So, at the blare of that leaky bugle, Floral Hall and the cattlepens were on the moment deserted and lonely. The Berkshire boar returned to his wallow, and a young Jersey bullock, with a warm red coat and a temper of the same shade, was left shaking his head and snorting angrily as he tried vainly to dislodge a blue ribbon that was knotted about one of his short, curving black horns. Had he been a second prizewinner instead of a first, that ribbon would have been a red ribbon and there is no telling what might have happened.

The first race was a half-mile dash for running horses. There were four horses entered for it and three of the four jockeys wore regular jockey outfits, with loose blouses and top boots and long-peaked caps; but the fourth jockey was an imp-black stable boy, wearing a cotton shirt and the ruins of an old pair of pants. The brimless wreck of a straw hat was clamped down tight on his wool like a cup. He be-straddled a sweaty little red gelding named Flitterfoot, and Flitterfoot was the only local entry, and was an added starter, and a forlorn hope in the betting.

While these four running horses were dancing a fretful schottische round at the half-mile post, and the starter, old man Thad Jacobson, was bellowing at the riders and slashing a black-snake whip round the shins of their impatient mounts, a slim black figure wormed a way under the arms and past the short ribs of a few belated betters yet lingering about the bookmaker's block. This intruder handled himself so deftly and so nimbly as not to jostle by one hair's breadth the dignity of any white gentleman there present, yet was steadily making progress all the while and in ample time getting down a certain sum of money on Flitterfoot to win at odds.

"Ain't that your nigger boy Jeff?" inquired Doctor Lake of Judge Priest, as the new comer, still boring deftly, emerged from the group and with a last muttered "Scuse me, boss—please, suh—scuse me!" darted away toward the head of the stretch, where others of his race were draping themselves over the top rail of the fence in black festoons.

Back Home

"Yes, I suppose 'tis—probably," said Judge Priest in that high singsong of his. "That black scoundrel of mine is liable to be everywhere—except when you want him, and then he's not anywhere. That must be Jeff, I reckin." And the old judge chuckled indulgently in appreciation of Jeff's manifold talents.

During the parade of the veterans that day Judge Priest, as commandant of the camp, had led the march just behind the fife and drums and just ahead of the color-bearer carrying the silken flag; and all the way out from town Jeff, his manservant, valet, and guardian, had marched a pace to his right. Jeff's own private and personal convictions—convictions which no white man would ever know by word of mouth from Jeff anyhow—

were not with the late cause which those elderly men in gray represented. Jeff's political feelings, if any such he had, would be sure to lean away from them; but it was a chance to march with music—and Jeff had marched, his head up and his feet cutting scallops and double-shuffles in the dust.

Judge Priest's Jeff was a small, jet-black person, swift in his gait and wise in his generation. He kept his wool cropped close and made the part in it with a razor. By some subtle art of his own he could fall heir to somebody else's old clothes and, wearing them, make than look newer and better than when they were new. Overcome by the specious wiles of Jeff some white gentleman of his acquaintance would bestow upon him a garment that seemed shabby to the point of open shame and a public scandal. Jeff would retire for a season with a pressing iron and a bottle of cleansing fluid, and presently that garment would come forth, having undergone a glorious resurrection. Seeing it, then, the former proprietor would repent his generosity and wonder what ever possessed him to part with apparel so splendid.

For this special and gala occasion Jim wore a blue-serge coat that had been given to him in consideration of certain acts of office-tending by Attorney Clay Saunders. Attorney Clay Saunders weighed two hundred and fifty pounds If he weighed an ounce, and Jeff would never see one hundred and twenty-five; but the blue serge was draped upon Jeff's frame with just the fashionable looseness. The sleeves, though a trifle long, hung most beautifully. Jeff's trousers were of a light and pearly gray, and had been the property originally of Mr. Otter-buck, cashier at the bank, who was built long and rangy; whereas Jeff was distinctly short and ducklike. Yet these same trousers, pressed now until you could have peeled peaches with their creases and turned up at the bottoms to a rakish and sporty length, looked as if they might have been specially coopered to Jeff's legs by a skilled tailor.

This was Judge Priest's Jeff, whose feet would fit anybody's shoes and whose head would fit anybody's hat. Having got his money safely down on Flitterfoot to win, Jeff was presently choking a post far up the homestretch. With a final crack of the starter's coiling blacksnake and a mounting scroll of dust, the runners were off on their half-mile dash. While the horses were still spattering through the dust on the far side of the course from him Jeff began encouraging his choice by speech.

"Come on, you little red hoss!" he said in a low, confidential tone. "I asks you lak a gen'leman to come on and win all that money fur me. Come on, you little red hoss—you ain't half runnin'! little red hoss"—his voice sank to a note of passionate pleading—"whut is detainin' you?"

Perhaps even that many years back, when it had just been discovered, there was something to this new theory of thought transference. As if Jeff's tense whispers were reaching to him across two hundred yards of track and open field Flitterfoot opened up a gap between his lathered flanks and the rest of them. The others, in a confused group, scrambled and hinged out with their hoofs; but Flitterfoot turned into a long red elastic rubber band, stretching himself out to twice his honest length and then snapping back again to half. High up on his shoulder the ragged black stable boy hung, with his knees under his chin and his shoulders hunched as though squaring off to do a little flying himself. Twenty long yards ahead of the nearest contender, Flitterfoot scooted over the line a winner. Once across, he expeditiously bucked the crouching small incumbrance off his withers and, with the bridle dangling, bounced riderless back to his stable; while above the roar from the grandstand rose the triumphant remark of Jeff: "Ain't he a regular runnin' and a-jumpin' fool!"

The really important business of the day to most, however, centered about the harness events, which was only natural, this being an end of the state where they raised the standard breds as distinguished from the section whence came the thoroughbreds. A running race might do for an appetizer, like a toddy before dinner; but the big interest would focus in the two-twenty pace and the free-for-all consolation, and finally would culminate in the County Trot—open only to horses bred and owned in the county and carrying with it a purse of two thousand dollars—big money for that country—and a dented and tarnished silver trophy that was nearly fifty years old, and valued accordingly.

After the half-mile dash and before the first heat of the two-twenty pace there was a balloon ascension and parachute drop. Judge Priest's Jeff was everywhere that things were happening. He did two men's part in holding the bulging bag down to earth until the spangled aeronaut yelled out for everybody to let go. When the man dropped, away over by the back fence, Jeff was first on the spot to brush him off and to inquire in a voice of respectful solicitude how he was feeling, now that he'd come down. Up in the grandstand, Mrs. Major Joe Sam Covington, who was stout and wore a cameo breastpin as big as a coffee saucer at her throat, expressed to nobody in particular a desire for a glass of cool water; and almost instantly, it seemed, Judge Priest's Jeff was at her side bowing low and ceremoniously with a brimming dipper in one hand and an itch for the coming tip in the other. When the veterans adjourned back behind Floral Hall for a watermelon cutting, Jeff, grinning and obsequious, arrived at exactly the properly timed moment to receive a whole butt-end of red-hearted, green-rinded lusciousness for his own. Taking the opportunity of a crowded minute about Uncle Isom Woolfolk's barbecued meat stand he bought extensively, and paid for what he bought with a lead half dollar that he had been saving for months against just such a golden chance—a half dollar so palpably leaden that Uncle Isom, discovering it half an hour later, was thrown into a state of intense rage, followed by a period of settled melancholy, coupled with general suspicion of all mankind. Most especially, though, Judge Priest's Jeff concerned himself with the running of the County Trot, being minded to turn his earlier winnings over and over again.

From the outset Jeff, like most of the fair crowd, had favored Van Wallace's black mare, Minnie May, against the only other entry for the race, Jackson Berry's big roan trotting stallion, Blandville Boy. The judgment of the multitude stood up, too, for the first two heats of the County Trot, alternating in between heats of the two-twenty pace and the free-for-all, were won handily by the smooth-gaited mare. Blandville Boy was feeling his oats and his grooming, and he broke badly each time, for all the hobble harness of leather that was buckled over and under him. Nearly everybody was now betting on Minnie May to take the third and the decisive heat.

Waiting for it, the crowd spread over the grounds, leaving wide patches of the grandstand empty. The sideshows and the medicine venders enjoyed heavy patronage, and once more the stalled ox and the fatted pig were surrounded by admiring groups. There was a thick jam about the crowning artistic gem of Floral Hall—a crazy quilt with eight thousand different pieces of silk in it, mainly of acutely jarring shades, so that the whole was a thing calculated to blind the eye and benumb the mind.

The city marshal forcibly calmed down certain exhilarated young bucks from the country—they would be sure to fire off their pistols and yell into every dooryard as they tore home that night, careening in their dusty buggies; but now they were made to restrain themselves. Bananas and cocoanuts advanced steadily in price as the visible supply shrank. There is a type of Southern countryman who, coming to town for a circus day or a fair, first eats extensively of bananas—red bananas preferred; and then, when the raw edge of his hunger is abated, he buys a cocoanut and, after punching out one of its eyes and drinking the sweet milky whey, cracks the shell apart and gorges on the white meat. By now the grass was cumbered with many shattered cocoanut shells, like broken shards; and banana peels, both red and yellow, lay wilted and limp everywhere in the litter underfoot.

The steam Flyin' Jinny—it would be a carousel farther North—ground unendingly, loaded to its gunwales with family groups. Crap games started in remote spots and fights broke out. In a far shadow of the fence behind the stables one darky with brass knuckles felled another, then broke and ran. He scuttled over the fence like a fox squirrel, with a bullet from a constable's big blue-barreled revolver spatting into the paling six indies below him as he scaled the top and lit flying on the other side. Sergeant Jimmy Bagby, dragging his Springfield by the barrel, began a long story touching on what he once heard General Buckner say to General Breckinridge, went to sleep in the middle of it, enjoyed a refreshing nap of twenty minutes, woke up with a start and resumed the anecdote at the exact point where he left off—"An' 'en General Breckinridge he says to General Buckner, he says, 'General—'"

But Judge Priest's Jeff disentangled himself from the center of things, and took a quiet walk up toward the stables to see what might be seen and to hear what might be heard, as befitting one who was speculating heavily and needed all available information to guide him. What he saw was Van Wallace, owner of the mare, and Jackson Berry, owner of the studhorse, slipping furtively into an empty feed-shed. As they vanished within Van Wallace looked about him cautiously, but Jeff had already dived to shelter alongside the shed and was squatting on a pile of stable scrapings, where a swarm of flies flickered above an empty pint flask and watermelon rinds were curling up and drying in the sun like old shoesoles. Jeff had seen something. Now he applied his ear to a crack between the planks of the feedshed and heard something.

For two minutes the supposed rivals confabbed busily in the shelter of a broken hay-'rack. Then, suddenly taking alarm without cause, they both poked their heads out at the door and looked about them searchingly—right and left. There wasn't time for Jeff to get away. He only had a second's or two seconds' warning; but all the conspirators saw as they issued forth from the scene of their intrigue was a small darky in clothes much too large for him lying alongside the shed in a sprawled huddle, with one loose sleeve over his face and one black forefinger shoved like a snake's head down the neck of a flat pocket-flask. Above this figure the flies were buzzing in a greedy cloud.

"Just some nigger full of gin that fell down there to sleep it off," said Van Wallace. And he would have gone on; but Berry, who was a tall red-faced, horsy man—a blusterer on the surface and a born coward inside—booted the sleeper in the ribs with his toe.

"Here, boy!" he commanded. "Wake up here!" And he nudged him again hard.

The negro only flinched from the kicks, then rolled farther over on his side and mumbled through a snore.

"Couldn't hear it thunder," said Berry reassured. "Well, let's get away from here."

"You bet!" said Van Wallace fervently. "No use takin' chances by bein' caught talkin' together. Anyhow, they'll be ringing the startin' bell in a minute or two."

"Don't forget, now!" counseled Berry as Wallace started off, making by a roundabout and devious way for his own stable, where Minnie May, hitched to her sulky and with her legs bandaged, was being walked back and forth by a stable boy.

"Don't you worry; I won't!" said Wallace; and Berry grinned joyously and vanished in the opposite direction, behind the handy feedshed.

On the instant that both of them disappeared Judge Priest's Jeff rose to his feet, magically changing from a drunken darky to an alert and flying black Mercury. His feet hardly hit the high places as he streaked it for the grandstand—looking for Judge Priest as hard as he could look.

Nearly there he ran into Captain Buck Owings. Captain Buck Owings was a quiet, grayish man, who from time to time in the course of a busy life as a steamboat pilot and master had had occasion to shoot at or into divers persons. Captain Buck Owings had a magnificent capacity for attending strictly to his own business and not allowing anybody else to attend to it. He was commonly classified as dangerous when irritated—and tolerably easy to irritate.

"Cap'n Buck! Cap'n Buck!" sputtered

Jeff, so excited that he stuttered. "P-please, suh, is you seen my boss—Jedge Priest? I suttinly must see him right away. This here next heat is goin' to be thro wed."

It was rarely that Captain Buck Owings raised his voice above a low, deliberate drawl. He raised it a trifle now.

"What's that, boy?" he demanded. "Who's goin' to throw this race?"

He caught up with Jeff and hurried along by him, Jeff explaining what he knew in half a dozen panted sentences. As Captain Buck Owings' mind took in the situation, Captain Buck Owings' gray eyes began to flicker a little.

Nowhere in sight was there any one who looked like the judge. Indeed, there were few persons at all to be seen on the scarred green turf across which they sped and those few were hurrying to join the crowds that packed thick upon the seats of the grandstand, and thicker along the infield fence and the homestretch. Somewhere beyond, the stable bell jangled. The little betting ring was empty almost and the lone bookmaker was turning his blackboard down.

His customary luck served Jeff in this crisis, however. From beneath a cuddy under the grandstand that bore a blue board lettered with the word "Refreshments" appeared the large, slow-moving form of the old judge. He was wiping his mouth with an enormous handkerchief as he headed deliberately for the infield fence. His venerable and benevolent pink face shone afar and Jeff literally flung himself at him.

"Oh, Jedge!" he yelled. "Oh, Jedge; please, suh, wait jes' a minute!"

In some respects Judge Priest might be said to resemble Kipling's East Indian elephant. He was large as to bulk and conservative as to his bodily movements; he never seemed to hurry, and yet when he set out to arrive at a given place in a given time he would be there in due season. He faced about and propelled himself toward the queerly matched pair approaching him with such haste.

As they met, Captain Buck Owings began to speak and his voice was back again at its level monotone, except that it had a little steaming sound in it, as though Captain Buck Owings were beginning to seethe and simmer gently somewhere down inside of himself.

"Judge Priest, suh," said Captain Buck, "it looks like there'd be some tall swindlin' done round here soon unless we can stop it. This boy of yours heard something. Jeff tell the judge what you heard just now." And Jeff told, the words bubbling out of him in a stream:

"It's done all fixed up betwixt them w'ite gen'lemen. That there Mr. Jackson Berry he's been tormentin' the stallion ontwell he break and lose the fust two heats. Now, w'en the money is all on the mare, they goin' to turn round and do it the other way. Over on the backstretch that Mr. Van Wallace he's goin' to spite and tease Minnie May ontwell she go all to pieces, so the stallion'll be jest natchelly bound to win; an' 'en they'll split up the money amongst 'em!"

"Ah-hah!" said Judge Priest; "the infernal scoundrels!" Even in this emergency his manner of speaking was almost deliberate; but he glanced toward the bookmaker's block and made as if to go toward it.

"That there Yankee bookmaker gen'leman he's into it too," added Jeff. "I p'intedly heard 'em both mention his name."

"I might speak a few words in a kind of a warnin' way to those two," purred Captain Buck Owings. "I've got a right smart money adventured on this trottin' race myself." And he turned toward the track.

"Too late for that either, son," said the old judge, pointing. "Look yonder!"

A joyful rumble was beginning to thunder from the grandstand. The constables had cleared the track, and from up beyond came the glint of the flashing sulky-spokes as the two conspirators wheeled about to score down and be off.

"Then I think maybe I'll have to attend to 'em personally after the race," said Captain Buck Owings in a resigned tone.

"Son," counseled Judge Priest, "I'd hate mightily to see you brought up for trial before me for shootin' a rascal—especially after the mischief was done. I'd hate that mightily—I would so."

"But, Judge," protested Captain Buck Owings, "I may have to do it! It oughter be done. Nearly everybody here has bet on Minnie May. It's plain robbin' and stealin'!"

"That's so," assented the judge as Jeff danced a dog of excitement just behind him—"that's so. It's bad enough for those two to be robbin' their own fellow-citizens; but it's mainly the shame on our county fair I'm thinkin' of." The old judge had been a director and a stockholder of the County Jockey Club for twenty years or more. Until now its record had been clean. "Tryin' to declare the result off afterward wouldn't do much good. It would be the word of three white men against a nigger—and nobody would believe the nigger," added Captain Buck Owings, finishing the sentence for him.

"And the scandal would remain jest the same," bemoaned the old judge. "Buck, my son, unless we could do something before the race it looks like it's hopeless. Ah!"

The roar from the grandstand above their heads deepened, then broke up into babblings and exclamations. The two trotters had swung past the mark, but Minnie May had slipped a length ahead at the tape and the judges had sent them back again. There would be a minute or two more of grace anyhow. The eyes of all three followed the nodding heads of the horses back up the stretch. Then Judge Priest, still watching, reached out for Jeff and dragged him round in front of him, dangling in his grip like a hooked black eel.

"Jeff, don't I see a gate up yonder in the track fence right at the first turn?" he asked.

"Yas, suh," said Jeff eagerly. "'Tain't locked neither. I come through it myse'f today. It opens on to a little road whut leads out past the stables to the big pike. I kin—"

The old judge dropped his wriggling servitor and had Captain Buck Owings by the shoulder with one hand and was pointing with the other up the track, and was speaking, explaining something or other in a voice unusually brisk for him.

"See yonder, son!" he was saying. "The big oak on the inside—and the gate is jest across from it!"

Comprehension lit up the steamboat captain's face, but the light went out as he slapped his hand back to his hip pocket—and slapped it flat.

"I knew I'd forgot something!" he lamented, despairingly. "Needin' one worse than I ever did in my whole life—and then I leave mine home in my other pants!"

He shot the judge a look. The judge shook his head.

"Son," he said, "the circuit judge of the first judicial district of Kintucky don't tote such things."

Captain Buck Owings raised a clenched fist to the blue sky above and swore impotently. For the third time the grandstand crowd was starting its roar. Judge Priest's head began to waggle with little sidewise motions.

Sergeant Jimmy Bagby, late of King's Hell hounds, rambled with weaving indirectness round the corner of the grandstand not twenty feet from them. His gangrened cartridge-box was trying to climb up over his left shoulder from behind, his eyes were heavy with a warm and comforting drowsiness, and his Springfield's iron butt-plate was scurfing up the dust a yard behind him as he hauled the musket along by the muzzle.

The judge saw him first; but, even as he spoke and pointed, Captain Buck Owings caught the meaning and jumped. There was a swirl of arms and legs as they struck, and Sergeant Jimmy Bagby, sorely shocked, staggered back against the wall with a loud grunt of surprise and indignation.

Half a second later, side by side, Captain Buck Owings and Judge Priest's Jeff sped northward across the earth, and Sergeant Jimmy Bagby staggered toward the only comforter near at hand, with his two empty arms upraised. Filled with a great and sudden sense of loss he fell upon Judge Priest's neck, almost bearing his commander down by the weight of his grief.

"Carried her four years!" he exclaimed piteously; "four endurin' years, Judge, and not a single dam' Yankee ever laid his hand on her! Carried her ever since, and nobody ever dared to touch her! And now to lose her this away!"

His voice, which had risen to a bleat, sank to a sob and he wept unrestrainedly on the old judge's shoulder. It looked as though these two old men were wrestling together, catch-as-catch-can.

The judge tried to shake his distressed friend off, but the sergeant clung fast. Over the bent shoulders of the other the judge saw the wheels flash by, going south, horses and drivers evened up. The "Go!" of the starting judge was instantly caught up by five hundred spectators and swallowed in a crackling yell. Oblivious of all these things the sergeant raised his sorrowing head and a melancholy satisfaction shone through his tears.

"I lost her," he said; "but, by gum, Judge, it took all four of 'em to git her away from me, didn't it?"

None, perhaps, in all that crowd except old Judge Priest saw the two fleeting figures speeding north. All other eyes there were turned to the south, where the county's rival trotters swung round the first turn, traveling together like teammates. None marked Captain Buck Owings as, strangely cumbered, he scuttled across the track from the outer side to the inner and dived like a rabbit under the fence at the head of the homestretch, where a big oak tree with a three-foot bole cast its lengthening shadows across the course. None marked Judge Priest's Jeff coiling down like a black-snake behind an unlatched wooden gate almost opposite where the tree stood.

None marked these things, because at this moment something direful happened. Minnie May, the favorite, was breaking badly on the back length. Almost up on her hindlegs she lunged out ahead of her with her forefeet, like a boxer. That far away it looked to the grandstand crowds as though Van Wallace had lost his head entirely. One instant he was savagely lashing the mare along the flanks, the next he was pulling her until he was stretched out flat on his back, with his head back between the painted sulky wheels. And Blandville Boy, steady as a clock, was drawing ahead and making a long gap between them.

Back Home

Blandville Boy came on grandly—far ahead at the half; still farther ahead nearing the three-quarters. All need for breaking her gait being now over, crafty Van Wallace had steadied the mare and again she trotted perfectly—trotted fast too; but the mischief was done and she was hopelessly out of it, being sure to be beaten and lucky if she saved being distanced.

The whole thing had worked beautifully, without a hitch. This thought was singing high in Jackson Berry's mind as he steered the stud-horse past the three-quarter post and saw just beyond the last turn the straightaway of the homestretch, opening up empty and white ahead of him. And then, seventy-five yards away, he beheld a most horrifying apparition!

Against a big oak at the inner-track fence, sheltered from the view of all behind, but in full sight of the turn, stood Captain Buck Owings, drawing down on him with a huge and hideous firearm. How was Jackson Berry, thus rudely jarred from pleasing prospects, to know that Sergeant Jimmy Bagby's old Springfield musket hadn't been fired since Appomattox—that its lode was a solid mass of corroded metal, its stock worm-eaten walnut and its barrel choked up thick with forty years of rust! All Jackson Berry knew was that the fearsome muzzle of an awful weapon was following him as he moved down toward it and that behind the tall mule's ear of a hammer and the brass guard of the trigger he saw the cold, forbidding gray of Captain Buck Owings' face and the colder, more forbidding, even grayer eye of Captain Buck Owings—a man known to be dangerous when irritated—and tolerably easy to irritate!

Before that menacing aim and posture Jackson Berry's flesh turned to wine jelly and quivered on his bones. His eyes bulged out on his cheeks and his cheeks went white to match his eyes. Had it not been for the stallion's stern between them, his knees would have knocked together. Involuntarily he drew back on the reins, hauling in desperately until Blandville Boy's jaws were pulled apart like the red painted mouth of a hobby-horse and his forelegs sawed the air. The horse was fighting to keep on to the nearing finish, but the man could feel the slugs of lead in his flinching body.

And then—and then—fifty scant feet ahead of him and a scanter twenty above where the armed madman stood—a wide gate flew open; and, as this gap of salvation broke into the line of the encompassing fence, the welcome clarion of Judge Priest's Jeff rose in a shriek: "This way out, boss—this way out!"

It was a time for quick thinking; and to persons as totally, wholly scared as Jackson Berry was, thinking comes wondrous easy. One despairing half-glance he threw upon the goal just ahead of him and the other half on that unwavering rifle-muzzle, now looming so dose that he could catch the glint of its sights. Throwing himself far back in his reeling sulky Jackson Berry gave a desperate yank on the lines that lifted the sorely pestered stallion clear out of his stride, then sawed on the right-hand rein until he swung the horse's head through the opening, grazing one wheel against a gatepost—and was gone past the whooping Jeff, lickety-split, down the dirt road, through the dust and out on the big road toward town.

Jeff slammed the gate shut and vanished instantly. Captain Buck Owings dropped his weapon into the long, rank grass and slid round the treetrunk. And half a minute later Van Wallace, all discomfited and puzzled, with all his fine hopes dished and dashed, sorely against his own will jogged Minnie May a winner past a grandstand that recovered from its dumb astonishment in ample time to rise and yell its approval of the result.

Back Home

Judge Priest being a childless widower of many years' standing, his household was administered for him by Jeff as general manager, and by Aunt Dilsey Turner as kitchen goddess. Between them the old judge fared well and they fared better. Aunt Dilsey was a master hand at a cookstove; but she went home at night, no matter what the state of the weather, wearing one of those long, wide capes—dolmans, I think they used to call them—that hung dear down to the knees, hiding the wearer's hands and whatsoever the hands might be carrying.

It was a fad of Aunt Dilsey's to bring one covered splint basket and one close-mouthed tin bucket with her when she came to work in the morning, and to take both of them away with her—under her dolman cape—at night; and in her cabin on Plunkett's Hill she had a large family of her own and two paying boarders, all of whom had the appearance of being well nourished. If you, reader, are Southern-born, these seemingly trivial details may convey a meaning to your understanding.

So Aunt Dilsey Turner looked after the judge's wants from the big old kitchen that was detached from the rest of the rambling white house, and Jeff had the run of his sideboard, his tobacco caddy, and his wardrobe. The judge was kept comfortable and they were kept happy, each respecting the other's property rights.

It was nine o'clock in the evening of the last day of the county fair. The judge, mellowly comfortable in his shirtsleeves, reclined in a big easy rocking-chair in his sitting room. There was a small fire of hickory wood in the fireplace and the little flames bickered together and the embers popped as they charred a dimmer red. The old judge was smoking his homemade corncob pipe with the long cane stem, and sending smoke wreaths aloft to shred away like cobweb skeins against the dingy ceiling.

"Jeff!" he called to a black shadow fidgeting about in the background.

"Yas, suh, Jedge; right yere!"

"Jeff, if your discernin' taste in handmade sour-mash whisky has permitted any of that last batch of liquor I bought to remain in the demijohn, I wish you'd mix me up a little toddy."

Jeff snickered and mixed the toddy, mixing it more hurriedly then common, because he was anxious to be gone. It was Saturday night—a night dedicated by long usage to his people; and in Jeff's pocket was more ready money than his pocket had ever held before at any one time. Moreover, in the interval between dusk and dark, Jeff's wardrobe had been most grandly garnished. Above Mr. Clay Saunders' former blue serge coat a crimson necktie burned like a beacon, and below the creased legs of Mr. Otterbuck's late pearl-gray trousers now appeared a pair of new patent-leather shoes with pointed toes turned up at the ends like sleigh-runners and cloth uppers in the effective colors of the Douglas plaid and rows of 24-point white pearl buttons.

Assuredly Jeff was anxious to be on his way. He placed the filled toddy glass at the old judge's elbow and sought unostentatiously to withdraw himself.

"Jeff!" said the judge.

"Yas, suh."

"I believe Mr. Jackson Berry did not see fit to return to the fair grounds this evenin' and protest the result of the third heat?"

"No, suh," said Jeff; "frum whut I heared some of the w'ite folks sayin', he driv right straight home and went to bed and had a sort of a chill."

"Ah-hah!" said the judge, sipping reflectively. Jeff fidgeted and drew nearer a halfopen window, listening out into the maple-lined street. Two blocks down the street he could hear the colored brass band playing in front of the Colored Odd Fellows Hall for a "festibul."

"Jeff," said Judge Priest musingly, "violence or a show of violence is always to be deplored." Jeff had only a hazy idea of what the old judge meant by that, but in all his professional life Jeff had never intentionally disagreed in conversation with any white adult—let alone a generous employer. So:

"Yas, suh," assented Jeff promptly; "it suttinly is."

"But there are times and places," went on the old judge, "when it is necessary."

"Yas, suh," said Jeff, catching the drift—"lak at a racetrack!"

"Ah-hah! Quite so," said Judge Priest, nodding. "And, Jeff, did it ever occur to you that there are better ways of killin' a cat than by chokin' him with butter?"

"Indeed yas, suh," said Jeff. "Sometimes you kin do it best with one of these yere ole rusty Confedrit guns!"

At that precise moment, in a little house on the next street, Sergeant Jimmy Bagby's family, having prevailed upon him to remove his shoes and his cartridge-belt before retiring, were severally engaged in an attempt to dissuade him from a firmly expressed purpose of taking his Springfield musket to bed with him.

III. FIVE HUNDRED DOLLARS REWARD

WE had a feud once down in our country, not one of those sanguinary feuds of the mountains involving a whole district and forcing constant enlargements of hillside burying grounds, nor yet a feud handed down as a deadly legacy from one generation to another until its origin is forgotten and its legatees only know how they hate without knowing why, but a shabby, small neighborhood vendetta affecting but two families only, and those in a far corner of the county—the Flemings and the Faxons.

Nevertheless, this feud, such as it was, persisted in a sluggish intermittent kind of a way for twenty years or so. It started in a dispute over a line boundary away back in War Times when a Faxon shot a Fleming and was in turn shot by another Fleming; and it lasted until the Faxons tired of fence-corner, briar-patch warfare and moved down into Tennessee, all but one branch of them, who came into town and settled there, leaving the Flemings dominant in the Gum Spring precinct. So the feud ceased to be an institution after that and became a memory, living only in certain smouldering animosities which manifested themselves at local elections and the like, until it flared up momentarily in the taking-off of old Ranee Fleming at the hands of young Jim Faxon; and then it died, and died for good.

It is the manner of the taking-off of this one of the Flemings that makes material for the story I am telling here. By all accounts it would appear that the Faxons had been rather a weak-spined race who fought mostly on the defensive and were lacking in that malignant persistency that made old Ranee Fleming's name one to scare bad children with in the unsettled days following the Surrender. I remember how we boys used to watch him, half-fearsomely and half-admiringly, when he came to town on a Court Monday or on a Saturday and swaggered about, unkempt and mud-crusted and frequently half drunk. Late in the afternoon he would mount unsteadily to the tilted seat of his spring wagon and go back home to the Gum Spring country lashing at his team until they danced with terror and splitting the big road wide open through the middle. And that night at the places where the older men congregated there would be tales to tell of those troubled mid-sixties when old Ranee had worn the turn-coat of a guerilla, preying first on one side and then on the other.

Now young Jim Faxon, last male survivor of his clan, and direct in the line of the original fighting Faxons, was a different sort of person altogether, a quiet, undersized, decent-spoken young chap who minded well his own business, which was keeping a truck stand on the Market. He lived with his aunt, old Miss Puss Whitley—certain women were still called Miss in our town even though they had been married for twenty years and widowed for as many more, as was the case in this instance—and he was her main support and stand-by. It was common rumor that when young Jim came of age and had a little money laid by on his own account, he meant to marry the little Hardin girl—Emmy Hardin—and this was a romance that nearly everybody in town knew about and favored most heartily. She was his distant cousin and an orphan, and she lived with Miss Puss too. Sometimes in good weather she would come in with him and help out at the truck stand. She was a little quail-like creature, quick in her movements and shy as a bunny, with pretty irregular features and a skin so clear and white that when she blushed, which was a hundred times a day, the color would drench her face to the temples and make her prettier than ever. All of Jim's regular customers approved his choice of a sweetheart and wished him mighty well. He was regarded as about the pick of the thinned-out Faxon breed.

For the years that young Jim was growing up, his tribal enemy left him alone. Perhaps old Ranee regarded the lank sapling of a boy as being not worth even the attention of an insult. Probably in crowds they had rubbed elbows a dozen times with no engendering of friction. But when young Jim had passed his twentieth birthday and was almost a man grown, then all without warning Ranee Fleming set to work, with malice aforethought, to pick a quarrel with him. It was as deliberate and as brutal as anything could be. Of a sudden, it seemed, the torrents of long-submerged hate came spuming up from some deep back eddy in his muddied, fuddled old mind, making an evil whirlpool of passion.

It was on a Saturday afternoon in November that old Ranee came, boiling with his venom, to spew it out on the son of his dead and gone enemy. It happened on the market, and if old Ranee aimed to add brim measure to the humiliation of the boy, not in a year of choosing could he have picked fitter time and place. The green grocer wasn't known then; everybody went to market in person on week day mornings and particularly everybody went of a Saturday afternoon. In the market square, town aristocrat and town commoner met on the same footing, a market basket over every arm, with this distinction only:—that ordinary folk toted their loaded baskets back home and the well-to-do paid to have theirs sent. There were at least twenty darkies who picked up a living by packing market baskets home. They all had their regular patrons and regarded them with jealous, proprietary eyes. You took a customer away from a basket darky and you had him to fight.

There is a new market house now on the site of the old one, a pretentious affair of brick with concrete floors and screened window openings and provision for steam heat in the winter; but then, and for many years before that, the market was a decrepit shed-like thing, closed in the middle and open at the ends, with a shingled roof that sagged in on itself and had hollows in it like the sunken jaws of a toothless old hag; and there were cracks in the side walls that you could throw a dog through, almost. In the middle, under half-way shelter, were the stalls of the butchers, which were handed down from father to son so that one stall would remain in a family for generations; and here one bought the beef steaks of the period—long bib-shaped segments of pale red meat, cut miraculously long and marvelously thin, almost like apron patterns. This thinness facilitated the beating process—the cooks would pound them with tools devised for that purpose—and then they were fried through and through and drenched with a thick flour gravy. Such was the accustomed way of treating a beef steak. Persons with good teeth could eat them so, and for the others the brown flour gravy provided a sustenance. But the spring chickens were marvels for plumpness and freshness and cheapness; and in the early spring the smoked hog jowls hung in rows, fairly begging people to carry them off and boil them with salad greens; and in the fall when the hog killing season was at hand, the country sausage and the chines and backbones and spare ribs made racks of richness upon the worn marble slabs.

Up at the far end of the square beyond the shed eaves stood the public scales, and around it hay growers and cord wood choppers and Old Man Brimm, the official charcoal burner of the county, waited for trade alongside their highpiled wagons. Next to them was the appointed place of the fish hucksters, which was an odorous place, where channel cats and river perch and lake crappies were piled on the benches, some still alive and feebly flapping. The darkies were sure to be thickest here. There was an unsung but none the less authentic affinity existing between a fresh-caught catfish and an old negro man.

Down at the other end was the domain of the gardeners and the truck patch people—an unwritten law as old as the market itself ordained these apportionments of space—and here you might find in their seasons all manner of edibles, wild and tame. The country boys and girls ranged the woods and the fields for sellable things, to go along with the product of orchard and garden and berry patch. In the spring, when herb teas and home-brewed tonics were needed for the thinning of the blood, there would be yellow-red sassafras root tied up in fragrant, pungent bunches, all ready for steeping; and strings of fresh-shot robins for pot-pies were displayed side by side with clumps of turnip-greens and mustard greens. And in summer there would be all manner of wild berries and heaps of the sickish-smelling May apples; and later, after the first light frost, ripe pawpaws and baskets of wild fox grapes, like blue shoe buttons; and then later on, scaly-bark hickory nuts and fresh-brewed persimmon beer in kegs, and piggins and crocks of the real lye hominy, with the big blue grains of the corn all asmoke like slaking lime, and birds—which meant quail always—and rabbits, stretched out stark and stiff, and the native red-skinned yams, and often possums, alive and "suiting" in small wooden cages, or else dead and dressed, with the dark kidney-fat coating their immodestly exposed interiors.

As I was saying, it was on a Saturday in November and getting along toward Thanksgiving when old Ranee Fleming came to the market to shame young Jim Faxon before the crowd. And when he came, you could tell by his look and by the way he shouldered through the press of people between the double rows of stands that all the soured animosities of his nature had swelled to bursting under the yeasty ferment of an unstable, hair-triggered temper.

The liquor he had drunk might have had something to do with it too. He came up with a barely perceptible lurch in his gait and stopped at the Faxon stall, which was the third from the lower end of the shed. With his head down between his shoulders and his legs spraddled he began staring into the face of young Jim.

Deadly offense can be carried just as well in a look as in the spoken word, if you only know how to do it—and Ranee Fleming knew.

There was outright obscenity in his glower.

Instantly it seemed, everybody in that whole end of the market square sensed what was impending. Sellers and buyers ceased trafficking and faced all the same way. Those in the rear were standing on tiptoe the better to see over the heads of those nearer to these two blood enemies. Some climbed upon the wheel hubs of the wagons that were backed up in rows alongside the open shed and balanced themselves there. The silence grew electric and tingled with the feeling of a coming clash.

Young Jim wanted no trouble, that was plain enough to be seen. The first darting realization that his tribal foe had forced a meeting on him seemed to leave him dazed, and at a loss for the proper course to follow. He bent his face away from the blasphemous insistent—glare of the old man and made a poor pretense at straightening up his wares upon the bench in front of him; but his hands trembled so he overturned a little wooden measure that held a nickel's worth of dried lady-peas. The little round peas rolled along a sunken place in the wood and began spattering off in a steady stream, like buck-shot spilling from a canister. A dark red flush came up the back of the boy's neck. He was only twenty, anyhow, and those who looked on were sorry for him and for his youth and helplessness and glad that little Emmy Hardin, his sweetheart, wasn't there.

It was a long half minute that old Ranee, without speaking, stood there, soaking his soul in the sight of a Faxon's discomfiture, and when he spoke he grated the words as though he had grit in his mouth.

"Looky here you," he ordered, and the boy, as though forced to obey by a will stronger than his own, lifted his head and looked at him.

"Mister Fleming," he answered, "what—what is it you want with me—Mister Fleming?"

"Mister Fleming—Mister Fleming," mimicked the older man, catching at his words, "Mister Fleming, huh? Well, you know mighty good and well, I reckin, whut it is I want with you. I want to see if you're as white-livered as the rest of your low-flung, hound-dawg, chicken-hearted breed used to be. And I reckin you are.

"Mister Fleming, huh? Well, from now on that's whut it better be and don't you fail to call me by them entitlements either. The next time I come by I reckin you better take off your hat to me too. Do you hear me, plain, whut I'm a-sayin'? You—"

He called him the unforgivable, unatonable name—the fighting word, than which, by the standards of that community and those people, no blow with a clenched fist could be in one twentieth part so grievous an injury; yes, it was worse than a hundred blows of a fist. So at that, the onlookers gave back a little, making way for the expected rush and grapple. But there was no forward rush by the younger man, no grapple with the older.

Young Jim Faxon took it—he just stood and took it without a word or a step. Old Ranee looked at him and laughed out his contempt in a derisive chuckle and then he turned and slouched off, without looking back, as though he disdained to watch for a rear attack from so puny and spineless an enemy. It all started and happened and was over with in a minute or less. The last of the spilt lady peas were still spattering down upon the rough bricks of the market and running away and hiding themselves in cracks. Young Jim, his head on his breast and his shamed eyes looking down at nothing, was fumbling again with his wares and Ranee Fleming's hunching shoulders were vanishing at the end of the shed.

People talked about it that night and for days after. It was not a thing to forget—a man near grown who lacked the sand to resent that insult. A fist fight might have been forgotten, even a fist fight between these two heritors of a feud instinct, but not this. Some of the younger fellows didn't see, they said, how Jim Faxon could hold his head up again and look people in the eye. And Jim didn't hold his head up—not as high as he had held it before this happened. Broody-eyed and glum and tight-lipped, he tended Miss Puss Whitley's truck patch and brought his products to market every morning. He had always been quiet and sparing of speech; now he was quiet to the point almost of dumbness.

Back Home

A month and more went by, and old Ranee didn't ride in from Gum Spring, and then the Christmas came. Christmas Day fell on a Monday so that the Christmas itself properly started on the Saturday before. It was a warm and a green Christmas as most of them are in that climate, mild enough at midday for folks to sit on their front porches and just cold enough at night to beard the grass with a silver-gray frost rime. Languid looking house flies crawled out in the afternoons and cleaned their gummy wings while they sunned themselves on the southern sides of stables. The Christmas feeling was in the air. At the wharfboat lay the Clyde, deep laden for her annual jug-trip, with thousands of bottles and jugs and demi-johns consigned to the dry towns up the river. There was a big sidewalk trade going on in fire crackers and rockets, the Christinas and not the Fourth being the time for squibbing of crackers in the South, the market, though, was the busiest place of all. It fairly milled with people. Every huckster needed four hands, and still he wouldn't have had enough.

Jimmy Faxon had little Emmy Hardin helping him through the hours when the pressure was greatest and the customers came fastest. She kept close to him, with little nestling motions, and yet there was something protecting in her attitude, as though she would stand between him and any danger, or any criticism. The looks she darted at him were fairly caressing. Through the jam appeared Ranee Fleming, elbowing his way roughly. His face above his straggly whiskers was red with temper and with liquor. His cotton shirt was open at the throat so that his hairy chest showed. His shapeless gray jeans trousers—gray originally but now faded and stained to a mud color—were both beltless and suspenderless, and were girthed tightly about his middle by the strap at the back. From much ramming of his hands into the pockets, they were now crowded down far upon his hips, showing an unwontedly long expanse of shirt; and this gave to him an abnormally short-legged, long-waisted look.

A lot of those little fuzzy parasitic pods called beggar-lice were stuck thick upon his bagged knees—so thick they formed irregular patterns in grayish green. He wore no coat nor waistcoat, but an old mud-stiffened overcoat was swung over his shoulders with the arms tied loosely around his neck and the skirts dangling in folds behind him; and cuckleburrs clung to a tear in the lining. He was a fit model of unclean and unwholesome ferocity.

Before young Jim or little Emmy Hardin saw him, he was right up on them; only the width of the bench separated him from them. He leaned across it and called Jim that name again and slapped him in the face with a wide-armed sweeping stroke of his open hand. The boy flinched back from the coming blow so that only the ends of old Ranee's flailing fingers touched his cheek, but the intent was there. Before the eyes of his sweetheart, he had been slapped in the face. The girl gave a startled choking gasp and tried to put her arms about young Jim. He shook her off.

Well content with his work, old Ranee fell back, all the time watching young Jim. People gave way for him involuntarily. When he was clear of the shed he turned and made for one of the saloons that lined the square on its western side. He had a choice of several such places; the whole row was given over to saloons, barring only a couple of cheap john clothing stores and a harness store, and two or three small dingy pawn shops. Pistol stores these last were, in the vernacular of the darkies, being so called because the owners always kept revolvers and spring-back knives on display in the show windows, along with battered musical instruments and cheap watches.

The spectators followed old Ranee's figure with their eyes until the swinging doors of the nearest bar room closed behind him. When they looked back again toward Stall No. 3 young Jim was gone too. He had vanished silently; and Emmy Hardin was alone, with her face buried in her arms and her arms stretched across the counter, weeping as though she would never leave off.

From the next stall there came to her, comfortingly, a middle aged market woman, a motherly figure in a gray shawl with puckered and broad red hands. She lifted Emmy up and led her away, calling out to her nearest neighbor to watch her stall and the Faxon stall until she got back.

"There's liable to be trouble," she added, speaking in a side whisper so the sobbing girl wouldn't hear what she said.

"I reckin not," said the man. "It looks to me like Jimmy Faxon is plumb cowed down and 'feared of that there old bush whacker—it looks like he ain't got the spirit of a rabbit left in him. But you take her on away somewheres, Mizz Futrell—me and my boys will 'tend stand for both of you, and you needn't worry."

Under such merciful guardianship little Emmy Hardin was taken away and so she was spared the sight of what was to follow.

Old Ranee stayed in the nearest saloon about long enough to take one drink and then he came out and headed for the next saloon along the row. To reach it he must pass one of the pawn-brokers' shops. He had just passed it when a sort of smothered warning outcry went up from behind him somewhere, and he swung round to look his finish square in the face.

Young Jim Faxon was stepping out of the pawn-broker's door. He was crying so the tears streamed down his face. His right arm was down at his side stiffly and the hand held clenched a weapon which the Daily Evening News subsequently described as "a Brown & Rogers thirty-eight calibre, nickle plated, single-action, with a black rubber handle, and slightly rusted upon the barrel."

Old Ranee made no move toward his own hip pocket. It came out at the inquest that he was not carrying so much as a pen-knife. He half crouched and began stumbling backward toward the front of the building with his arms out and his hands making empty pawing clutches behind him as though he were reaching for some solid support to hold him up in his peril. But before he had gone three steps, young Jim brought the pistol up and fired—just once.

Once was enough. If you had never before this seen a man shot, you would have known instinctively that this one was mortally stricken. Some who were near and looking right at him told afterward how the loose end of one overcoat sleeve, dangling down on his breast, flipped up a little at the shot. A slightly pained, querulous look came into his face and he brought his arms round and folded them tightly across his stomach as though taken with a sudden cramp. Then he walked, steadily enough, to the edge of the sidewalk and half-squatted as though he meant to sit on the curbing with his feet in the gutter. He was half way down when death took him in his vitals. He pitched forward and outward upon his face with his whiskers flattening in the street. Two men ran to him and turned him over on his back. His face had faded already from its angry red to a yellowish white, like old tallow. He breathed hard once or twice and some thought they saw his eyelids bat once; then his chest fell inward and stayed so, and he seemed to shrink up to less than his proper length and bulk.

Young Jim stood still ten feet away looking at his handiwork. He had stopped crying and he had dropped the pistol and was wiping both hands flatly against the breast of his wool sweater as though to cleanse them of something. Allard Jones, the market-master, who had police powers and wore a blue coat and a German silver star to prove it, came plowing through the ring of on-lookers, head tilt, and laid hands upon him. Allard Jones fumbled in his pocket and produced a pair of steel nippers and made as if to twine the chain round the boy's right wrist.

"You don't need to be putting those things on me, Mr. Jones," said his prisoner. "I'll go all right—I'll go with you. It's all over now—everything's over!"

Back Home

Part of the crowd stayed behind, forming a scrooging, shoving ring around the spot in front of Benny Michelson's pawn shop where the body of old Ranee lay face upward across the gutter with the stiffening legs on the sidewalk, and the oddly foreshortened body out in the dust of the road; and the rest followed Allard Jones and young Jim as they walked side by side up Market Square to Court Street and along Court Street a short block to the lock-up.

The sympathy of the community was with young Jim—and the law of the land was dead against him on all counts. He had not fired in sudden heat and passion; there had been time, as the statutes measured time, for due deliberation. However great the provocation and by local standards the provocation had been great enough and pressing hard to the breaking point, he could not claim self-defense. Even though Fleming's purpose had been, ultimately, to bring things to a violent issue, he was retreating, actually, at the moment itself. As a bar to punishment for homicide, the plea of temporary insanity had never yet been set up in our courts. Jim Faxon was fast in the snarls of the law.

From the lock-up he went to the county jail, the charge, wilful and premeditated murder. Dr. Lake and Mr. Herman Felsburg and Major Covington, all customers of the accused, and all persons of property, stood ready to go bail for him in any sum namable, but murder was not bailable. In time a grand jury buttressed the warrant with an indictment—murder in the first degree, the indictment read—and young Jim stayed in jail awaiting his trial when circuit court should open in the spring.

Nobody, of course, believed that his jury would vote the extreme penalty. The dead man's probable intentions and his past reputation, taken with the prisoner's youth and good repute, would stand as bars to that, no matter how the letter of the law might read; but it was generally accepted that young Jim would be found guilty of manslaughter. He might get four years for killing old Ranee, or six years or even ten—this was a subject for frequent discussion. There was no way out of it. People were sorrier than ever for Jim and for his aunt and for the tacky, pretty little Hardin girl.

All through the short changeable winter, with its alternate days of snow flurrying and sunshine, Emmy Hardin and Miss Puss Whitley, a crushed forlorn pair, together minded the stall on the market, accepting gratefully the silent sympathy that some offered them, and the awkward words of good cheer from others. Miss Puss put a mortgage of five hundred dollars on her little place out in the edge of town. With the money she hired Dabney Prentiss, the most silvery tongued orator of all the silver tongues at the county bar, to defend her nephew. And every day, when market hours were over, in rain or snow or shine, the two women would drive in their truck wagon up to the county jail to sit with young Jim and to stay with him in his cell until dark.

Spring came earlier than common that year. The robins came back from the Gulf in February on the tail of a wet warm thaw. The fruit trees bloomed in March and by the beginning of April everything was a vivid green and all the trees were clumped with new leaves. Court opened on the first Monday.

On the Sunday night before the first Monday, Judge Priest sat on his porch as the dusk came on, laving his spirits in the balm of the young spring night. In the grass below the steps the bull-cricket that wintered under Judge Priest's front steps was tuning his fairy-fiddle at regular, half-minute intervals. Bull bats on the quest for incautious gnats and midges were flickering overhead, showing white patches on the tinder sides of their long wings. A flying squirrel, the only night-rider of the whole squirrel tribe, flipped out of his hole in a honey locust tree, and cocked his head high, and then he spread the furry gray membranes along his sides and sailed in a graceful, downward swoop to the butt of a silver leaf poplar, fifty feet away, where he clung against the smooth bark so closely and so flatly he looked like a little pelt stretched and nailed up there to dry.

Back Home

The front gate clicked and creaked. The flying squirrel flipped around to the safe side of his tree and fled upward to the shelter of the branches, like a little gray shadow, and Judge Priest, looking down the aisle of shady trees, saw two women coming up the walk toward him, their feet crunching slowly on the gravel. He laid his pipe aside and pulled chairs forward for his callers, whoever they might be. They were right up to the steps before he made them out—Miss Puss Whitley and little Emmy Hardin.

"Howdy do, ladies," said the old Judge with his homely courtesy. "Howdy, Miss Puss? Emmy, child, how are you? Come in and set down and rest yourselves."

But for these two, this was no time for the small civilities. The weight of trouble at their hearts knocked for utterance at their lips. Or, at least, it was so with the old aunt.

"Jedge Priest," she began, with a desperate, driven eagerness, "we've come here tonight to speak in private with you about my boy—about Jimmy."

In the darkness they could not see that the old Judge's plump figure was stiffening.

"Did Mister Dabney Prentiss—did anyone, send you here to see me on this business?" he asked, quickly.

"No, suh, nobody a'tall," answered the old woman. "We jest came on our own accord—we felt like as if we jest had to come and see you. Court opens in the mornin' and Jimmy's case, as you know, comes up the first thing. And oh, Jedge Priest, we air in so much trouble, Emmy and me—and you've got the name of bein' kind hearted to them that's borne down and in distress—and so we come to you."

He raised his hand, as though to break in on her, but the old woman was not to be stopped. She was pouring out the grievous burden of her lament:

"Jedge Priest, you knowed my husband when he was alive, and you've knowed me these many years. And you know how it was in them old days that's gone that the Flemings was forever and a day fightin' with my people and forcin' trouble on 'em 'till finally they hunted 'em plum' out of the county and out of the State, away from the places where they was born and raised. And you know Jimmy too, and know what a hard time he had growin' up, and how he's always stood by me and helped me out, jest the same as if he was my own son. And I reckin you know about him—and Emmy here."

She broke off to wipe her eyes. Had it been a man who came on such an errand the Judge would have sent him packing—he would have been at no loss to put his exact meaning into exact language; for the Judge held his place on the bench in a high and scriptural regard. But here, in the presence of these two woeful figures, their faces drenched and steeped with sorrow, he hesitated, trying to choose words that would not bruise their wounds.

"Miss Puss," he said very softly, almost as though he were speaking to a child, "whatever my private feelin's may be towards you and yours, it is not proper for me as the Judge upon the bench, to express them in advance of the trial. It is my sworn duty to enforce the law, as it is written and laid down in the books. And the law is merciful, and is just to all."

The old woman's angular, slatty figure straightened. In the falling light her pinched and withered face showed, a white patch with deep grayish creases in it, the color of snow in a quick thaw.

"The law!" she flared out, "the law, you say, Jedge. Well, you kin talk mighty big about the law, but what kind of a law is that that lets a fightin', swearin', drunken bully like Ranee Fleming plague a poor boy and call him out of his name with vile words and shame him before this child here, and yit not do nothin' to him for it? And what kind of a law is it that'll send my boy up yonder to that there penitentiary and wreck his life and

Emmy's life and leave me here alone in my old age, ashamed to lift my head amongst my neighbors ever again?"

"Madame," said the Judge with all kindliness in his tone, "it's not for me to discuss these matters with you, now. It's not even proper that I should let you say these things to me."

"Oh, but Jedge," she said, "you must listen to me, please. You oughter know the truth and there ain't no way for you to know it without I tell it to you. Jimmy didn't want no quarrel with that man—it wasn't never none of his choosin'. He tried not to bear no grudge for what had gone before—he jest craved to be let alone and not be pestered. Why, when Ranee Fleming cussed him that first time, last Fall, he come home to me cryin' like his heart would break. He said he'd been insulted and that he'd have to take it up and fight it out with Ranee Fleming; he felt like he just had to. But we begged him on our bended knees mighty nigh, me and Emmy did, not to do nothin' for our sakes—and for our sakes he promised to let it go, and say nothin'. Even after that, if Ranee Fleming had just let him be, all this turrible trouble wouldn't a-come on us. But Ranee Fleming he come back again and slapped Jimmy's face, and Jimmy knowed then that sooner or later he'd have to kill Ranee Fleming or be killed his-self—there wasn't no other way out of it for him.

"Jedge Priest, he's been the best prop a lone woman ever had to lean on—he's been like a son to me. My own son couldn't a-been more faithful or more lovin. I jest ask you to bear all these things in mind tomorrow."

"I will, Madame," said the old Judge, rather huskily. "I promise you I will. Your nephew shall have a fair trial and all his rights shall be safe-guarded. But that is all I can say to you now."

Emmy Hardin, who hadn't spoken at all, plucked her by the arm and sought to lead her away. Shaking her head, the old woman turned away from the steps.

"Jest one minute, please, Miss Puss," said Judge Priest, "I'd like to ask you a question, and I don't want you to think I'm pryin' into your private and personal affairs; but is it true what I hear—that you've mortgaged your home place to raise the money for this boy's defense?"

"I ain't begredgin' the money," she protested. "It ain't the thought of that, that brought me here tonight. I'd work my fingers to the bone if 'twould help Jimmy any, and so would Emmy here. We'd both of us be willin' and ready to go to the porehouse and live and die there if it would do him any good."

"I feel sure of that," repeated the old Judge patiently, "but is it true about this mortgage?"

"Yes, suh," she answered, and then she began to cry again, "it's true, but please don't even let Jimmy know. He thinks I had the money saved up from the marketin' to hire Mr. Prentiss with, and I don't never want him to know the truth. No matter how his case goes I don't never want him to know." They had moved off down the gravel walk perhaps twenty feet, when suddenly the smouldering feud-hate stirred in the old woman's blood; and it spread through her and made her meager frame quiver as if with an ague. And now the words came from her with a hiss of feeling:

"Jedge Priest, that plague-taken scoundrel deserved killin'! He was black hearted from the day he came into the world and black hearted he went out of it. You don't remember, maybe—you was off soldierin' at the time—when he was jayhawkin' back and forth along the State line here, burnin' folks' houses down over their heads and mistreatin' the wimmin and children of them that was away in the army. I tell you, durin' that last year before you all got back home, there was soldiers out after him—out with guns in their

Back Home

hands and orders to shoot him down on sight, like a sheep-killin' dog. He didn't have no right to live!"

The girl got her quieted somehow; she was sobbing brokenly as they went away. For a long five minutes after the gate clicked behind the forlorn pair, Judge Priest stood on his porch in the attitude of one who had been pulled up short by the stirring of a memory of a long forgotten thing. After a bit he reached for his hat and closed the front door. He waddled heavily down the steps and disappeared in the aisle of the maples and silver leaf trees.

Half an hour later, clear over on the other side of town, two windows of the old court house flashed up as rectangles of light, set into a block of opaque blackness. Passers by idling homeward under the shade trees of the Square, wondered why the lights should be burning in the Judge's chambers. Had any one of them been moved to investigate the whys and wherefores of this phenomenon he would have discovered the Judge at his desk, with his steel bowed spectacles balanced precariously on the tip of his pudgy nose and his round old face pulled into a pucker of intenseness as he dug through one sheaf after another of musty, snuffy-smelling documents. The broad top of the desk in front of him was piled with windrows of these ancient papers, that were gray along their creases with the pigeonhole dust of years, and seamy and buffed with age. Set in the wall behind him was a vault and the door of the vault was open, and within was a gap of emptiness on an upper shelf, which showed where all these papers had come from; and for further proof that they were matters of court record there was a litter of many crumbly manila envelopes bearing inscriptions of faded ink, scattered about over the desk top, and on the floor where they had fallen.

For a good long time the old Judge rummaged briskly, pawing into the heaps in front of him and snorting briskly as the dust rose and tickled his nostrils. Eventually he restored most of the papers to their proper wrappers and replaced them in the vault, and then he began consulting divers books out of his law library—ponderous volumes, bound in faded calf skin with splotches of brown, like liverspots, on their covers. It was nearly midnight before he finished. He got up creakily, and reaching on tiptoe—an exertion which created a distinct hiatus of inches between the bottom of his wrinkled vest and the waistband of his trousers—he turned out the gas jets. Instantly the old courthouse, sitting among the trees, became a solid black mass. He felt his way out into the hallway, barking his shins on a chair, and grunting softly to himself.

When young Jim Faxon's case was called the next morning and the jailor brought him in, Jim wore hand-cuffs. At the term of court before this, a negro cow thief had got away coming across the court house yard and the Judge had issued orders to the jailor to use all due precautions in future. So the jailor, showing no favoritism, had seen fit to handcuff young Jim. Moreover, he forgot to bring along the key to the irons and while he was hurrying back to the jail to find it, young Jim had to wait between his women folk, with his bonds still fast upon him. Emmy Hardin bent forward and put her small hands over the steel, as though to hide the shameful sight of it from the eyes of the crowd and she kept her hands there until Jailor Watts came back and freed Jim. The little group of three sitting in a row inside the rail, just back of Lawyer Dabney Prentiss' erect and frock-coated back, were all silent and all pale-faced, young Jim with the pallor of the jail and Emmy Hardin with the whiteness of her grief and her terror, but the old aunt's face was a streaky, grayish white, and the wrinkles in her face and in her thin, corded neck looked inches deep.

Right away the case was called and both sides—defense and commonwealth—announced as ready to proceed to trial. The audience squared forward to watch the picking of the jurors, but there were never to be any jurors picked for the trial of this particular case.

37

For Judge Priest had readied the point where he couldn't hold in any longer. He cleared his throat and then he spoke, using the careful English he always used on the bench—and never anywhere else.

"Before we proceed," he began, and his tone told plainly enough that what he meant to say now would be well worth the hearing, "before we proceed, the court has something to say, which will have a direct bearing upon the present issue." He glanced about him silently, commanding quiet. "The defendant at the bar stands charged with the death of one Ransom Fleming and he is produced here to answer that charge."

From the desk he lifted a time-yellowed, legal-looking paper, folded flat; he shucked it open with his thumb. "It appears, from the records, that in the month of February and of the year 1865, the said Ransom Fleming, now deceased, was a fugitive from justice, going at large and charged with divers and sundry felonious acts, to wit, the crime of arson and the crime of felonious assault with intent to kill, and the crime of confederating with others not named, to destroy the property of persons resident in the State of Kentucky. It appears further that a disorganized condition of the civil government existed, the State being overrun with stragglers and deserters from both armies then engaged in civil war, and therefore, because of the inability or the failure of the duly constituted authorities to bring to justice the person charged with these lawless and criminal acts, the Governor of this State did offer a reward of $500 for the apprehension of Ransom Fleming, dead or alive."

Now, for sure, the crowd knew something pregnant with meaning for the prisoner at the bar was coming—knew it without knowing yet what shape it would assume. Heads came forward row by row and necks were craned eagerly.

"I hold here in my hand an official copy of the proclamation issued by the Governor of the State," continued Judge Priest. "Under its terms this reward was open to citizens and to officers of the law alike. All law-abiding persons were in fact urged to join in ridding the commonwealth of this man. He stood outside the pale of the law, without claim upon or right to its protection.

"It would appear further,"—the old Judge's whiny voice was rising now—"that this proclamation was never withdrawn, although with the passage of years it may have been forgotten. Under a strict construction of the law of the land and of the commonwealth, it may be held to have remained in force up to and including the date of the death of the said Ransom Fleming. It accordingly devolves upon this court, of its own motion, to set aside the indictment against the defendant at the bar and to declare him free—"

For the time being His Honor got no further than that. Even the stupidest listener there knew now what had come to pass—knew that Judge Priest had found the way to liberty for young Jim Faxon. Cheering broke out—loud, exultant cheering and the stamping of many feet. Persons outside, on the square and in the street, might have been excused for thinking that a dignified and orderly session of court had suddenly turned into a public rally—a ratification meeting. Most of those actually present were too busy venting their own personal satisfaction to notice that young Jim was holding his sweetheart and his aunt in his arms; and there was too much noise going on round about them for any one to hear the panted hallelujahs of joy and relief that poured from the lips of the young woman and the old one.

The Judge pounded for order with his gavel, pounding long and hard, before the uproar simmered down into a seething and boiling of confused, excited murmurings.

"Mister Sheriff," he ordered, with a seeming sternness which by no means matched the look on his face, "keep order in this court! If any further disorder occurs here you will arrest the offenders and arraign them for contempt."

The sheriff's bushy eyebrows expressed bewilderment. When it came to arresting a whole court house full of people, even so vigilant and earnest-minded an official as Sheriff Giles Bindsong hardly knew where to start in. Nevertheless he made answer promptly.

"Yes, suh, Your Honor," he promised, "I will."

"As I was saying when this interruption occurred," went on the Judge, "it now devolves upon the court to discharge the defendant at the bar from custody and to declare him entitled to the reward of $500 placed upon the head of the late Ransom Fleming by the Governor of Kentucky in the year 1865—" Young Jim Faxon with his arms still around the heaving shoulders of the women, threw his head up:

"No Judge, please, sir, I couldn't touch that money—not that"—he began, but Judge Priest halted him:

"The late defendant not being of legal age, the court rules that this reward when collected may be turned over to his legal guardian. It may be that she will find a good and proper use to which this sum of money may be put." This time, the cheering, if anything, was louder even than it had been before; but when the puzzled sheriff looked around for instructions regarding the proper course of procedure in such an emergency, the judge on the bench was otherwise engaged. The judge on the bench was exchanging handshakes of an openly congratulatory nature with the members of the county bar headed by Attorney for the Defense, Dabney Prentiss.

IV. A JUDGMENT COME TO DANIEL

THE sidewheel packet Belle of Memphis landed at the wharf, and the personal manager of Daniel the Mystic came up the gravel levee with a darky behind him toting his valises. That afternoon all of the regular town hacks were in use for a Masonic funeral, or he could have ridden up in solitary pomp. You felt on first seeing him that he was the kind of person who would naturally prefer to ride.

He was a large man and, to look at, very impressive. On either lapel of his coat he wore a splendid glittering golden emblem. One was a design of a gold ax and the other was an Indian's head. His watch-charm was made of two animal claws—a tiger's claws I know now they must have been—jointed together at their butts by a broad gold band to form a downward-dropping crescent. On the middle finger of his right hand was a large solitaire ring, the stone being supported by golden eagles with their wings interwoven. His vest was the most magnificent as to colors and pattern that I ever saw. The only other vest that to my mind would in any way compare with it I saw years later, worn by the advance agent of a trained dog and pony show.

From our perch on the whittled railings of the boat-store porch we viewed his advent into our town. Steamboats always brought us to the river front if there was no business more pressing on hand, and particularly the Belle of Memphis brought us, because she was a regular sidewheeler with a double texas, and rising suns painted on her paddle boxes, and a pair of enormous gilded buckhorns nailed over her pilot house to show she held the speed record of the White Collar Line. A big, red, sheet-iron spread-eagle was swung between her stacks, and the tops of the stacks were painted red and cut into sharp points like spearheads. She had a string band aboard that came out on the guards and played Suwannee River when she was landing and Goodby, My Lover, Goodby when she pulled out, and her head mate had the loudest swearing voice on the river and, as everybody knew, would as soon kill you as look at you, and maybe sooner.

The Belle was not to be compared with any of our little stem wheel local packets. Even her two mud clerks, let alone her captain and her pilots, wore uniforms; and she came all the way from Cincinnati and ran clean through to New Orleans, clearing our wharf of the cotton and tobacco and the sacked ginseng and peanuts and such commonplace things, and leaving behind in their stead all manner of interesting objects in crates and barrels. Once she brought a whole gipsy caravan—the Stanley family it was called—men, women and children, dogs, horses, wagons and all, a regular circus procession of them.

She was due Tuesdays, but generally didn't get in until Wednesdays, and old Captain Rawlings would be the first to see her smoke coiling in a hazy smudge over Livingston Point and say the Belle was coming. Captain Rawlings had an uncanny knack of knowing all the boats by their smokes. The news would spread, and by the time she passed the Lower Towhead and was quartering across and running down past town, so she could turn and land upstream, there would be a lot of pleasurable excitement on the wharf. The black draymen standing erect on their two-wheeled craft, like Roman chariot racers, would whirl their mules down the levee at a perilous gallop, scattering the gravel every which way, and our leisure class—boys and darkies—and a good many of the business men, would come down to the foot of Main Street to see her land and watch the rousters swarm off ahead of the bellowing mates and eat up the freight piles. One trip she even had white rousters, which was an event to be remembered and talked about afterward. They were grimy foreigners, who chattered in an outlandish tongue instead of chanting at their work as regular rousters did.

This time when the Belle of Memphis came and the personal manager of Daniel the Mystic came up the levee, half a dozen of us were there and saw him coming. We ran down the porch steps and trailed him at a respectful distance, opinion being acutely divided among us as to what he might be. He was associated with the great outer world of amusement and entertainment; we knew that by the circumstances of his apparel and his jewels and high hat and all, even if his whole bearing had not advertised his calling as with banners. Therefore, we speculated freely as we trailed him. He couldn't be the man who owned the Eugene Robinson Floating Palace, because the Floating Palace had paid its annual visit months before and by now must be away down past the Lower Bends in the bayou country. Likewise, the man who came in advance of the circus always arrived by rail with a yellow car full of circus bills and many talented artists in white overalls. I remember I decided that he must have something to do with a minstrel show—Beach & Bowers' maybe, or Thatcher, Primrose & West's.

He turned into the Richland House, with the darky following him with his valises and us following the darky; and after he had registered, old Mr. Dudley Dunn, the clerk, let us look at the register. But two or three grown men looked first; the coming of one who was so plainly a personage had made some stir among the adult population. None there present, though, could read the name the stranger had left upon the book. Old Mr. Dunn, who was an expert at that sort of thing, couldn't decide himself whether it was O. O. Driscoll or A. A. Davent. The man must have spent years practicing to be able to produce a signature that would bother any hotel clerk. I have subsequently ascertained that there are many abroad gifted as he was—mainly traveling salesmen. But if you couldn't read his name, all who ran might read the nature of his calling, for 'twas there set forth in two colors—he had borrowed the red-ink bottle from Mr. Dunn to help out the customary violet—and done in heavy shaded letters—"Representing Daniel the Mystic"—with an ornamental flourish of scrolls and feathery beaded lines following after. The whole took up a good fourth of one of Mr. Dudley Dunn's blue-ruled pages.

Inside of an hour we were to know, too, who Daniel the Mystic might be, for in the hotel office and in sundry store windows were big bills showing a likeness of a man of magnificent mien, with long hair and his face in his hand, or rather in the thumb and forefinger of his hand, with the thumb under the chin and the finger running up alongside the cheek. Underneath were lines to the effect that Daniel the Mystic, Prince of Mesmerism and Seer of the Unseen, was Coming, Coming! Also that night the Daily Evening News had a piece about him. He had rented St. Clair Hall for two nights hand-running and would give a mysterious, edifying and educational entertainment dealing with the wonders of science and baffling human description. The preliminaries, one learned, had been arranged by his affable and courteous personal representative now in our midst, Mr. D. C. Davello—so old Mr. Dudley Dunn was wrong in both of his guesses.

Next morning Daniel the Mystic was on hand, looking enough like his pictured likeness to be recognized almost immediately. True, his features were not quite so massive and majestic as we had been led to expect, and he rather disappointed us by not carrying his face in his hand, but he was tall and slim enough for all purposes and wore his hair long and was dressed all in black. He had long, slender hands, and eyes that, we agreed, could seem to look right through you and tell what you were thinking about.

For one versed in the mysteries of the unseen he was fairly democratic in his minglings with the people; and as for D. C. Davello, no one, not even a candidate, could excel him in cordiality. Together they visited the office of the Daily Evening News and also the office of our other paper, the Weekly Argua-Eye, which was upstairs over Leaken's job-printing shop. They walked through the market house and went to the city hall to call on the mayor and the city marshal and invite them to come to St. Clair Hall that night and bring their families with them, free of charge. Skinny Collins, who was of their tagging juvenile escort, at once began to put on airs before the rest. The city marshal was his father.

About the middle of the afternoon they went into Felsburg Brothers Oak Hall Clothing Emporium, steered by Van Wallace, who seemed to be showing them round. We followed in behind, half a dozen or more of us, scuffling our dusty bare feet on the splintery floor between the aisles of racked-up coats. In the rear was Willie Richey, limping along on one toe and one heel. Willie Richey always had at least one stone bruise in the stone-bruise season, and sometimes two.

They went clear back to the end of the store where the office was and the stove, but we, holding our distance, halted by the counter where they kept the gift suspenders and neckties—Felsburg Brothers gave a pair of suspenders or a necktie with every suit, the choice being left to the customer and depending on whether in his nature the utilitarian or the decorative instinct was in the ascendency. We halted there, all eyes and ears and wriggling young bodies. The proprietors advanced and some of the clerks, and Van Wallace introduced the visitors to Mr. Herman Felsburg and to Mr. Ike Felsburg, his brother. Mr. Herman said, "Pleased to meetcher," with professional warmth, while Mr. Ike murmured, "Didn't catch the name?" inquiringly, such being the invariable formula of these two on greeting strangers. Cigars were passed round freely by D. C. Davello. He must have carried a pocketful of cigars, for he had more of them for some of the business men who came dropping in as if by chance. All of a sudden Van Wallace, noting how the group had grown, said it would be nice if the professor would show us what he could do. D. C. Davello said it wasn't customary for Daniel the Mystic to vulgarize his art by giving impromptu demonstrations, but perhaps he would make an exception just for this once. He spoke to Daniel the Mystic who was sitting silently in the Messrs. Felsburg's swivel office-chair with his face in his hands—the poster likeness was vindicated at last—and after a little arguing he got up and looked all about him slowly and in silence. His eye fell on the little huddle of small boys by the necktie counter and he said sharp and quick to Jack Irons: "Come here, boy!"

I don't know yet how Jack Irons came to be of our company on that day; mostly Jack didn't run with us. He was sickly. He had spells and was laid up at home a good deal.

He couldn't even go barefooted in summer, because if he did his legs would be broken out all over with dew poison in no time.

Jack Irons didn't belong to one of the prominent families either. He lived in a little brown house on the street that went down by the old Enders place. His mother was dead, and his sister worked in the county clerk's office and always wore black alpaca sleeves buttoned up on her forearms. His father was old Mr. Gid Irons that stayed in Scotter's hardware store. He didn't own the store, he just clerked there. Winter and summer he passed by our house four times a day, going to work in the morning and coming back at night, coming to dinner at twelve o'clock and going back at one. He was so regular that people used to say if the whistle on Langstock's planing mill ever broke down they could still set the clocks by old Mr. Gid Irons. Perhaps you have known men who were universally called old while they were yet on the up-side of middle life? Mr. Gid Irons was such a one as that.

I used to like to slip into Scotter's just to see him scooping tenpenny nails and iron bolts out of open bins and kegs with his bare hands. Digging his hands down into those rusty, scratchy things never seemed to bother him, and it was fascinating to watch him and gave you little flesh-crawling sensations. He was a silent, small man, short but very erect, and when he walked he brought his heels down very hard first. The skin of his face and of his hands and his hair and mustache were all a sort of faded pinkish red, and he nearly always had iron rust on his fingers, as though to advertise that his name was Irons.

By some boy intuition of my own I knew that he cut no wide swath in the lazy field of town life. When the veterans met at the city hall and organized their veterans' camp and named it the Gideon K. Irons Camp, it never occurred to me that they could be offering that honor to our old Mr. Gid Irons. I took it as a thing granted that there were some other Gideon Irons somewhere, one with a K in his name, a general probably, and no doubt a grand looking man on a white horse with a plume in his hat and a sword dangling, like the steel engraving of Robert E. Lee in our parlor. Whereas our Mr. Irons was shabby and poor; he didn't even own the house he lived in.

This Jack Irons who was with us that day was his only son, and when Daniel the Mystic looked at him and called him, Jack stepped out from our midst and went toward him, his feet dragging a little and moving as if some one had him by the shoulders leading him forward. His thin arms dangled at his sides. He went on until he was close up to Daniel the Mystic. The man threw up one hand and snapped out "Stop," as though he were teaching tricks to a dog, and Jack flinched and dodged. He stopped though, with red spots coming and going in the cheeks as though under the stoking of a blowpipe, and he breathed in sharp puffs that pulled his nostrils almost shut. Standing so, he looked as poor and weak and futile as a sprig of bleached celery, as a tow string, as a limp rag, as anything helpless and spineless that you had a mind to think of. The picture of him has hung in my mind ever since. Even now I recall how his meager frame quivered as Daniel the Mystic stooped until his eyes were on a level with Jack's eyes, and said something to Jack over and over again in a half-whisper.

Suddenly his hands shot out and he began making slow stroking motions downward before Jack's face, with his fingers outstretched as though he were combing apart banks of invisible yam. Next with a quick motion he rubbed Jack's eyelids closed, and massaged his temples with his thumbs, and then stepped back.

There stood Jack Irons with his eyes shut, fast asleep. He was still on his feet, bolt upright, but fast asleep—that was the marvel of it—with his hands at his side and the flushed color all gone from his cheeks. It scared us pretty badly, we boys. I think some of the grown men were a little bit scared too. We were glad that none of us had been singled out for this, and yet envious of Jack and his sudden elevation to prominence and the center of things.

Daniel the Mystic seemed satisfied. He mopped drops of sweat off his face. He forked two fingers and darted them like a snake's tongue at Jack, and Jack, still asleep, obeyed them, as if he had been steel and they the two horns of a magnetic horseshoe. He swayed back and forth, and then Daniel the Mystic gave a sharp shove at the air with the palms of both hands—and Jack fell backward as though he had been hit.

But he didn't fall as a boy would, doubling up and giving in. He fell stiff, like a board, without a bend in him anywhere. Daniel the Mystic leaped forward and caught him before he struck, and eased him down flat on his back and folded his arms up across his breast, and that made him look like dead.

More wonders were coming. Daniel the Mystic and D. C. Davello hauled two wooden chairs up close together and placed them facing each other; then lifting Jack, still rigid and frozen, they put his head on the seat of one chair and his heels on the seat of the other and stepped back and left him suspended there in a bridge. We voiced our astonishment in an anthem of gasps and overlapping exclamations. Not one of us in that town, boy or man, had ever seen a person in hypnotic catalepsy.

Before we had had time enough to take this marvel all in, Daniel the Mystic put his foot on Jack and stepped right up on his stomach, balancing himself and teetering gently above all our heads. He was tall and must have been heavy; for Jack's body bent and swayed under the weight, yet held it up in the fashion of a hickory springboard. Some of the men jumped up then and seemed about to interfere. Old Mr. Herman Felsburg's face was red and he sputtered, but before he could get the words out Daniel the Mystic was saying soothingly:

"Be not alarmed, friends. The subject is in no danger. The subject feels no pain and will suffer no injury."

"Just the same, Mister, you get down off that little boy," ordered Mr. Felsburg. "And you please wake him up right away. I don't care much to see things done like that in my store."

"As you say," said Daniel the Mystic easily, smiling all round him at the ring of our startled faces. "I merely wished to give you a small demonstration of my powers. And, believe me, the subject feels no pain whatsoever."

He stepped off of him, though, and Jack's body came up straight and flat again. They lifted him off the chairs and straightened him up, and Daniel the Mystic made one or two rapid passes in front of his face. Jack opened his eyes and began to cry weakly. One of the clerks brought him a drink, but he couldn't swallow it for sobbing, and only blubbered up the water when Mr. Felsburg held the glass to his lips. Van Wallace, who looked a little frightened and uneasy himself, gave two of the boys a nickel apiece and told us we had better get Jack home.

Jack could walk all right, with one of us upon either side of him, but he was crying too hard to answer the questions we put to him, we desiring exceedingly to know how he felt and if he knew anything while he was asleep. Just as we got him to his own gate he gasped out, "Oh, fellows, I'm sick!" and collapsed bodily at our feet, hiccoughing and moaning. His sister met us at the door as we lugged Jade in by his arms and legs. Even at

Back Home

home she had her black alpaca sleeves buttoned up to her elbows. I think she must have slept in them. We told her what had happened, or tried to tell her, all of us talking at once, and she made us lay Jack on a little rickety sofa in their parlor—there was a sewing machine in there, too, I noticed—and as we were coming away we saw a negro girl who worked for them running across the street to Tillman & Son's grocery where there was a telephone that the whole neighborhood used.

When I got home it was suppertime and the family were at the table. My sister said somebody must be sick down past the old Enders place, because she had seen Doctor Lake driving out that way as fast as his horse would take him. But I listened with only half an ear, being mentally engaged elsewhere. I was wondering how I was going to get my berry-picking money out of a nailed-up cigar-box savings bank without attracting too much attention on the part of other members of the family. I had been saving up that money hoping to amass seventy-five cents, which was the lowest cash price for Tom Birch's tame flying squirrel, a pet thing that would stay in your pocket all day and not bite you unless you tried to drag him out; but now I had a better purpose in view for my accumulated funds. If it took the last cent I meant to be in St. Clair Hall that night.

There was no balcony in St. Clair Hall, but only a sort of little hanging coop up above where the darkies sat, and the fifteen-cent seats were the two back rows of seats on the main floor. These were very handy to the door but likely to be overly warm on cold nights, when the two big, pearshaped stoves would be red hot, with the live coals showing through the cracks in their bases like broad grins on the faces of apoplectic twins. The cracked varnish upon the back of the seats would boil and bubble visibly then and the scorching wood grow so hot you couldn't touch your bare hand to it, and a fine, rich, turpentiny smell would savor up the air.

Being the first of the boys to arrive I secured the coveted corner seat from which you had a splendid view of the stage, only slightly obscured by one large wooden post painted a pale sick blue. D. C. Davello was at the door taking tickets, along with Sid Farrell, who ran

St. Clair Hall. It kept both of them pretty busy, because there were men paying their way in whom I had never seen there at all except when the Democrats had their rally just before election, or when the ladies were holding memorial services on President Jefferson Davis' birthday—men like old Judge Priest, and Major Joe Sam Covington, who owned the big tan yard, and Captain Howell, the bookdealer, and Mr. Herman Felsburg, and Doctor Lake, and a lot of others. Most of them took seats well down in front, I supposing that the educational and scientific features of the promised entertainment had drawn them together.

The curtain was cracked through in places and had a peephole in the middle, with black smudges round it like a bruised eye. It had a painting on it showing a street full of backwater clean up to the houses, and some elegant ladies and gentlemen in fancy-dress costumes coming down the stone steps of a large building like a county courthouse and getting into a couple of funny-looking skiffs. I seem to have heard somewhere that this represented a street scene in Venice, but up until the time St. Clair Hall burned down I know that I considered it to be a picture of some other, larger town than ours during a spring rise in the river, the same as we had every March. All round the inundated district were dirty white squares containing the lettered cards of business houses—Doctor Cupps, the dentist, and Anspach, the Old-Established Hatter—which never varied from year to year, even when an advertiser died or went out of business. We boys knew these signs by heart.

But to pass the time of waiting we read them over and over again, until the curtain rolled up disclosing the palace scene, with a double row of chairs across the stage in half-moon formation, and down in front, where the villains died at regular shows, a table with a water pitcher on it. Daniel the Mystic came out of the wings and bowed, and there was a thin splashing of hand-clapping, mostly from the rear seats, with Sid Farrell and D. C. Davello furnishing lustier sounds of applause. First off Daniel the Mystic made a short speech full of large, difficult words. We boys wriggled during it, being anxious for action. We had it soon. D. C. Davello mounted the stage and he and Daniel the Mystic brought into view a thing they called a cabinet, but which looked to us like a box frame with black calico curtains nailed on it. When they got this placed to their satisfaction, Daniel the Mystic, smiling in a friendly way, asked that a committee of local citizens kindly step up and see that no fraud or deception was practiced in what was about to follow. I was surprised to see Doctor Lake and Mr. Herman Felsburg rise promptly at the invitation and go up on the stage, where they watched closely while D. C. Davello tied Daniel the Mystic's hands behind him with white ropes, and then meshed him to a chair inside the cabinet with so many knottings and snarlings of the twisted bonds that he looked like some long, black creature helplessly caught in a net. This done, the two watchers slipped into chairs at opposite ends of the half-moon formation. D. C. Davello laid a tambourine, a banjo and a dinner bell on the bound man's knees and whipped the calico draperies to. Instantly the bell rang, the banjo was thrummed and the tambourine rattled giddily, and white hands flashed above the shielding draperies. But when the manager cried out and jerked the curtains back, there sat the Mystic one still a prisoner, tied up all hard and fast. We applauded then like everything.

The manager unroped him and went back to his place by the door, and after Daniel the Mystic had chafed his wrists where the red marks of the cords showed he came down a sort of little wooden runway into the audience, and standing in the aisle said something about now giving a demonstration of something. I caught the words occultism and spiritualism, both strangers to my understanding up to that time. He put his hands across his eyes for a moment, with his head thrown bade, and then he walked up the aisle four or five steps hesitating and faltering, and finally halted right alongside of Mr. Morton Harrison, the wharf master.

"I seem," he said slowly, in a deep, solemn voice, "to see a dim shape of a young man hovering here. I get the name of Claude—no, no, it is Clyde. Clyde would tell you," his voice sank lower and quavered effectively—"Clyde says to tell you that he is very happy over there—he says you must not worry about a certain matter that is now worrying you for it will all turn out for the best—and you will be happy. And now Clyde seems to be fading away. Clyde is gone!"

We didn't clap our hands at that—it would have been too much like clapping hands at a funeral—because we knew it must be Clyde Harrison, who had got drowned not two months before trying to save a little girl that fell overboard off the wharfboat. Just a day or two before there had been a piece in the paper telling about the public fund that was being raised to put a monument over Clyde's grave.

So we couldn't applaud that, wonderful as it was, and we shivered in a fearsome, wholly delightful anticipation and sat back and waited for more spirits to come. But seemingly there weren't any more spirits about just then, and after a little Daniel the Mystic returned to the stage and announced that we would now have the crowning achievement of the evening's entertainment—a scientific exhibition of the new and awe-inspiring art of mesmerism in all its various branches.

"For this," he stated impressively, "I desire the aid of volunteers from the audience, promising them that I will do them no harm, but on the contrary will do them much good. I want fellow townspeople of yours for this—gentlemen in whom you all have confidence and respect. I insist only upon one thing—that they shall be one and all total strangers to me."

Back Home

He advanced to the tin trough of the flickering gas footlights and smiled out over it at us.

"Who among you will come forward now? Come!"

Before any one else could move, two young fellows got up from seats in different parts of the hall and went up the little runway. We had never seen either of them before, which seemed a strange thing, for we boys kept a sharp eye upon those who came and went. They were both of them tall and terribly thin, with lank hair and listless eyes, and they moved as though their hip joints were rusty and hurt them. But I have seen the likes of them often since then—lying in a trance in a show window, with the covers puckered close up under the drawn face. I have peered down a wooden chute to see such a one slumbering in his coffin underground for a twenty-four or forty-eight-hour test. But these were the first of the tribe our town had encountered.

On their lagging heels followed two that I did know. One was the lumpish youth who helped Riley Putnam put up showbills and the other was Buddy Grogan, who worked in Sid Farrell's livery stable. Both of them were grinning sheepishly and falling over their own feet. And following right behind them in turn came a shabby little man who had iron rust on his clothes, and walked all reared back, bringing his heels down hard with thumps at every step. It was old Mr. Gid Irons. We gaped at him.

I had never seen Mr. Gid Irons at St. Clair Hall before, none of us had; and in our limited capacities we were by way of being consistent patrons of the drama. In a flash it came over me that Jack must have told his father what a wonderful sensation it was to be put to sleep standing up on your feet, and that his father had come to see for himself how it felt. I judged that others besides us were surprised. There was a burring little stir, and some of the audience got up and edged down closer to the front.

Mr. Gid Irons went on up the little runway and took a seat near one end of the half-moon of chairs. Where he sat the blowy glare of one of the gas footlights flickered up in his face and we could see that it seemed redder than common, and his eyes were drawn together so close that only little slits of them showed under his red-gray, bushy eyebrows. But that might have been the effect of the gaslight at his feet. You could tell though that Daniel the Mystic was puzzled and perplexed, startled almost, by the appearance of this middle-aged person among his volunteers. He kept eyeing him furtively with a worried line between his eyes as he made a round of the other four, shaking hands elaborately with each and bending to find out the names. He came to Mr. Irons last.

"And what is the name of this friend?" he asked in his grand, deep voice.

Mr. Irons didn't answer a word. He stood up, just so, and hauled off and hit Daniel the Mystic in the face. Daniel the Mystic said "Ouch!" in a loud, pained tone of voice, and fell backward over a chair and sat down hard right in the middle of the stage. George Muller, the town wit, declared afterward that he was looking right at Daniel the Mystic, and that Daniel the Mystic sat down so hard it parted his hair in the middle.

I heard somebody behind me make a choking outcry and turned to see D. C. Davello just bursting in upon us, with shock and surprise spreading all over his face. But just at that precise moment Fatty McManus, who was the biggest man in town, jumped up with an awkward clatter of his feet and stumbled and fell right into D. C. Davello, throwing his mighty arms about him as he did so. Locked together they rolled backward out of the door, and with a subconscious sense located somewhere in the back part of my skull I heard them go bumping down the steep stairs. I think there were ten distinct bumps.

David Pryor, one of our policemen, was sitting almost directly in front of me. He had been a policeman only two or three months and was the youngest of the three who policed the town at nights. When old Mr. Gid Irons knocked Daniel the Mystic down

David Pryor bounced out of his seat and called out something and started to run toward them.

Old Judge Priest blocked his way on the instant, filling the whole of the narrow aisle. "Son," he said, "where you aimin' to go to?"

"Lemme by, Judge," sputtered David Pryor; "there's a fight startin' up yonder!"

Judge Priest didn't budge a visible inch, except to glance quickly backward over his shoulder toward the stage.

"Son," he asked, "it takes two, don't it, to make a fight?"

"Yes," panted David Pryor, trying to get past him, "yes, but—"

"Well, son, if you'd take another look up there you'd see there's only one person engaged in fightin' at this time. That's no fight—only a merited chastisement."

"A chesty which?" asked David Pryor, puzzled. He was young and new to his job and full of the zeal of duty. But Judge Priest stood for law and order embodied, and David Pryor wavered.

"David, my son," said Judge Priest, "if you, a sworn officer of the law, don't know what chastisement means you ought to. Set down by me here and I'll try to explain its meanin's." He took him by the arm and pulled the bewildered young policeman down into a seat alongside his own and held him there, though David was still protesting and struggling feebly to be loose.

This I heard and saw out of a corner of my mind, the rest of me being concentrated on what was going on up on the stage among the overturning chairs and those scattering recruits in the cause of mesmerism. I saw Daniel the Mystic scramble to his feet and skitter about. He was wildly, furiously pained and bewildered. It must be painful in the extreme, and bewildering too, to any man to be suddenly and emphatically smitten in his good right eye by one who seemed all peace and elderly sedateness, and to behold an audience, which though cold, perhaps, had been friendly enough, arise in its entirety and most vociferously cheer the smiting. How much more so, then, in the case of a Seer of the Unseen, who is supposed to be able to discern such things ahead of their happening?

Daniel the Mystic looked this way and that, seeking a handy way of escape, but both ways were barred to him. At one side of the stage was Doctor Lake, aiming a walking stick at him like a spear; and at the other side was Mr. Felsburg, with an umbrella for a weapon.

Old Mr. Gid Irons was frightfully quick. His hands shot out with hard, fast dabbing motions like a cat striking at a rolling ball, and he planted his fists wheresoever he aimed.

Daniel the Mystic's long arms flew and flailed wildly in air and his mane of hair tossed. He threw his crossed hands across his face to save it and Mr. Irons hit him in the stomach. He lowered his hands to his vitals in an agonized clutch and Mr. Irons hit him in the jaw.

I know now in the light of a riper experience of such things that it was most wonderfully fast work, and all of it happening much faster than the time I have taken here to tell it, Mr. Gid Irons wading steadily in and Daniel the Mystic flopping about and threshing and yelling—he was beginning to yell—and the chairs flipping over on their backs and every-, body standing up and whooping. All of a sudden Daniel the Mystic went down flat on his back, calling for help on some one whose name I will take oath was not D. C. Davello. It sounded more like Thompson.

Doctor Lake dropped his walking stick and ran out from the wings.

"It would be highly improper to strike a man when he's down," he counseled Mr. Irons as he grabbed Daniel the Mystic by the armpits and heaved him up flappingly. "Allow me to help the gentleman to his feet."

Mr. Irons hit him just once more, a straight jabbing center blow, and knocked him clear into and under his black calico cabinet, so far in it and under it that its curtains covered all but his legs, which continued to flutter and waggle feebly.

"Get a couple-a chairs, Gideon." This advice came from Mr. Herman Felsburg who jumped up and down and directed an imaginary orchestra of bass drummers with his umbrella for a baton—"Get a couple-a chairs and stand on the son-of-a-gun's stomach. It does the subcheck no harm and the subcheck feels no pain. As a favor to me, Gideon, I ask you, stand on his stomach."

But Mr. Irons was through. He turned about and came down the runway and passed out, rearing back and jarring his heels down hard. If he had spoken a single word the whole time I hadn't heard it. As I remarked several times before he was a small man and so I am not trying to explain the optical delusion of the moment. I am only trying to tell how Mr. Gid Irons looked as he passed me. He looked seven feet tall.

It must have been just about this time that D. C. Davello worked his way out from underneath the hippopotamously vast bulk of Fatty McManus and started running back up the stairs. But before he reached the door the city marshal, who had been standing downstairs all the time and strange to say, hadn't, it would appear, heard any of the clamor, ran up behind him and arrested him for loud talking and disorderly conduct. The city marshal obtusely didn't look inside the door for visual evidences of any trouble within; he would listen to no reason. He grabbed D. C. Davello by the coat collar and pulled him back to the sidewalk and had him halfway across Market Square to the lock-up before the captive could make him understand what had really happened. Even then the official displayed a dense and gummy stupidity, for he kept demanding further details and made the other tell everything over to him at least twice. This also took time, because D. C. Davello was excited and stammering and the city marshal was constantly interrupting him. So that, by the time he finally got the straight of things into his head and they got back to St. Clair Hall, the lights were out and the stairs were dark and the last of the audience was tailing away. The city marshal stopped, as if taken with a clever idea, and looked at his watch and remarked to D. C. Davello that he and his friend the Professor would just about have time to catch the 10:50 accommodation for Louisville if they hurried; which seemed strange advice to be giving, seeing that D. C. Davello hadn't asked about trains at all.

Nevertheless he took it—the advice—which also necessitated taking the train.

Even in so short a time the news seemed to have spread with most mysterious speed, that Daniel the Mystic had canceled his second night's engagement and would be leaving us on the 10:50. Quite a crowd went to the depot to see him off. We boys tagged along, too, keeping pace with Judge Priest and Doctor Lake and Major Joe Sam Covington and certain other elderly residents, who, as they tramped along, maintained a sort of irregular formation, walking two by two just as they did when the Veterans' Camp turned out for a funeral or a reunion.

There must have been something wrong down the road that night with the 10:50. Usually she was anywhere from one to three hours late, but this night she strangely came in on time. She was already whistling for the crossing above Kattersmith's brickyard when we arrived, moving in force. D. C. Davello saw us from afar and remembered some business that took him briskly back behind the freight shed. But Daniel the Mystic sat on a baggage truck with a handkerchief to his face, and seemed not to see any of us coming until our advance guard filed up and flanked him.

"Well, suh," said Judge Priest, "you had a signal honor paid you in this community tonight."

Daniel the Mystic raised his head. The light from a tin reflector lamp. shone on his face and showed its abundant damages. You would hardly have known Daniel the Mystic for the same person. His gorgeousness and grandeur of person had fallen from him like a discarded garment, and his nose dripped redly.

"I—had—what?" he answered, speaking somewhat thickly because of his swollen lip.

"A mighty signal honor," said Judge Priest, in his thin whine. "In the presence of a representative gatherin' of our best people you were licked by the most efficient and the quickest-actin' scout that ever served in General John Morgan's entire cavalry command."

But the reply of Daniel the Mystic, if he made one, was never heard of living man, because at that moment the 10:50 accommodation came in and her locomotive began exhausting.

V. UP CLAY STREET

ONE behind the other, three short sections of a special came sliding into the yard sidings below the depot.

The cars clanked their drawheads together like manacles, as they were chivied and bullied and shoved about by a regular chain-gang boss of a switch engine. Some of the cars were ordinary box cars, just the plain galley slaves of commerce, but painted a uniform blue and provided with barred gratings; some were flat cars laden with huge wheeled burdens hooded under tarpaulins; and a few were sleeping cars that had been a bright yellow at the beginning of the season, with flaring red lettering down the sides, but now were faded to a shabby saffron.

It was just getting good broad day. The sleazy dun clouds that had been racked up along the east—like mill-ends left over from night's remnant counter, as a poet might have said had there been a poet there to say it—were now torn asunder, and through the tear the sun showed out, blushing red at his own nakedness and pushing ahead of him long shadows that stretched on the earth the wrong way. There was a taste of earliness in the air, a sort of compounded taste of dew and dust and maybe a little malaria.

Early as it was, there was a whopping big delegation of small boys, white and black, on hand for a volunteer reception committee. The eyes of these boys were bright and expectant in contrast to the eyes of the yard hands, who looked half dead for sleep and yawned and shivered. The boys welcomed the show train at the depot and ran alongside its various sections. They were mainly barefooted, but they avoided splinters in the butts of the crossties and sharp clinkers in the cinder ballast of the roadbed with the instinctive agility of a race of primitives.

Almost before the first string of cars halted and while the clanking of the iron links still ran down its length like a code signal being repeated, a lot of mop-headed men in overalls appeared, crawling out from all sorts of unsuspected sleeping places aboard. Magically a six-team of big white Norman horses materialized, dragging empty traces behind them. They must have been harnessed up together beforehand in a stock car somewhere. A corrugated wooden runway appeared to sprout downward and outward from an open car door, and down it bumped a high, open wagon with a big sheet-iron cooking range

Back Home

mounted on it and one short length of stovepipe rising above like a stumpy fighting-top on an armored cruiser. As the wheels thumped against the solid earth a man in a dirty apron, who had been balancing himself in the wagon, touched a match to some fuel in his firebox. Instantly black smoke came out of the top of the stack and a stinging smell of burning wood trailed behind him, as the six-horse team hooked on and he and his moving kitchen went lurching and rolling across shallow gulleys and over a rutted common, right into the red eye of the upcoming sun.

Other wagons followed, loaded with blue stakes, with coils of ropes, with great rolls of earth-stained canvas, and each took the same route, with four or six horses to drag it and a born charioteer in a flannel shirt to drive it. The common destination was a stretch of flat land a quarter of a mile away from the track. Truck patches backed up against this site on one side and the outlying cottages of the town flanked it on the other, and it was bordered with frayed fringes of ragweed and niggerheads, and was dotted over with the dried-mud chimneys of crawfish. In the thin turf here a geometric pattern of iron laying-out pins now appeared to spring up simultaneously, with rag pennons of red and blue fluttering in the tops, and at once a crew of men set to work with an orderly confusion, only stopping now and then to bellow back the growing swarms of boys who hung eagerly on the flank of each new operation. True to the promise of its lithographed glories the circus was in our midst, rain or shine, for this day and date only.

If there is any of the boy spirit left in us circus day may be esteemed to bring it out. And considering his age and bulk and his calling, there was a good deal of the boy left in our circuit judge—so much boy, in fact, that he, an early riser of note in a town much given to early rising, was up and dressing this morning a good hour ahead of his usual time. As he dressed he kept going to the side window of his bedroom and looking out. Eventually he had his reward. Through a break in the silver-leaf poplars he saw a great circus wagon crossing his line of vision an eighth of a mile away. Its top and sides were masked in canvas, but he caught a flicker of red and gold as the sun glinted on its wheels, and he saw the four horses tugging it along, and the dipping figure of the driver up above. The sight gave the old judge a little thrill down inside of him.

"I reckin that fellow was right when he said a man is only as old as he feels," said Judge Priest to himself. "And I'm glad court ain't in session—I honestly am." He opened his door and called down into the body of the silent house below: "Jeff! Oh, Jeff!"

"Yas, suh," came up the prompt answer.

"Jeff, you go out yonder to the kitchen and tell Aunt Dilsey to hurry along my breakfast. I'll be down right away."

"Yas, suh," said Jeff; "I'll bring it right in, suh."

Jeff was as anxious as the judge that the ceremony of breakfast might be speedily over; and, to tell the truth, so was Aunt Dilsey, who fluttered with impatience as she fried the judge's matinal ham and dished up the hominy. Aunt Dilsey regularly patronized all circuses, but she specialized in sideshows. The sideshow got a dime of hers before the big show started and again after it ended. She could remember from year to year just how the sideshow banners looked and how many there were of them, and on the mantelpiece in her cabin was ranged a fly-blown row of freaks' photographs purchased at the exceedingly reasonable rate of ten cents for cabinet sizes and twenty-five for the full length.

So there was no delay about serving the judge's breakfast or about clearing the table afterward. For that one morning, anyhow, the breakfast dishes went unwashed. Even as the judge put on his straw hat and came out on the front porch, the back door was already discharging Jeff and Aunt Dilsey. By the time the judge had traversed the shady yard and unlatched the front gate, Jeff was halfway to the showground and mending his gait all the time. Less than five minutes later Jeff was being ordered, somewhat rudely, off the side of a boarded-up cage, upon which he had climbed with a view to ascertaining, by a peep through the barred air-vent under the driver's seat, whether the mysterious creature inside looked as strange as it smelled; and less than five minutes after that, Jeff, having reached a working understanding with the custodian of the cage, who likewise happened to be in charge of certain ring stock, was conveying a string of trick ponies to the water-trough over by the planing mill. Aunt Dilsey, moving more slowly—yet guided, nevertheless, by a sure instinct—presently anchored herself at the precise spot where the sideshow tent would stand. Here several lodge sisters soon joined her. They formed a comfortable brown clump, stationary in the midst of many brisk; activities.

The judge stood at his gate a minute, lighting his corncob pipe. As he stood there a farm wagon clattered by, coming in from the country. Its bed was full of kitchen chairs and the kitchen chairs contained a family, including two pretty country girls in their teens, who were dressed in fluttering white with a plenitude of red and blue ribbons. The head of the family, driving, returned the judge's waved greeting somewhat stiffly. It was plain that his person was chafed and his whole being put under restraint by the fell influences of a Sunday coat and the hard collar that was buttoned on to the neckband of his blue shirt.

His pipe being lighted, the judge headed leisurely in the same direction that the laden farm wagon had taken. Along Clay Street from the judge's house to the main part of town, where the business houses and the stores centered, was a mile walk nearly, up a fairly steepish hill and down again, but shaded well all the way by water maples and silver-leaf trees. There weren't more than eight houses or ten along Clay Street, and these, with the exception of the judge's roomy, white-porched house standing aloof in its two acres of poorly kept lawn, were all little two-room frame houses, each in a small, bare inclosure of its own, with wide, weed-grown spaces between it and its next-door neighbors. These were the homes of those who in a city would have been tenement dwellers. In front of them stretched narrow wooden sidewalks, dappled now with patches of shadow and of soft, warm sunshine.

Perhaps halfway along was a particularly shabby little brown house that pushed dose up to the street line. A straggly catalpa tree shaded its narrow porch. This was the home of Lemuel Hammersmith; and Hammersmith seems such a name as should by right belong to a masterful, upstanding man with something of Thor or Vulcan or Judas Maccabaeus in him—it appears to have that sound. But Lemuel Hammersmith was no such man. In a city he would have been lost altogether—swallowed up among a mass of more important, pushing folk. But in a town as small as ours he had distinction. He belonged to more secret orders than any man in town—he belonged to all there were. Their small mummeries and mysteries, conducted behind closed doors, had for him a lure that there was no resisting; he just had to join. As I now recall, he never rose to high rank in any one of them, never wore the impressive regalia and the weighty title of a supreme officer; but when a lodge brother died he nearly always served on the committee that drew up the resolutions of respect. In moments of half-timid expanding he had been known to boast mildly that his signature, appended to resolutions of respect, suitably engrossed and properly framed, hung on the parlor walls of more than a hundred homes. He was a small and inconsequential man and he led a small and inconsequential life, giving his days to clerking in Noble & Barry's coal office for fifty dollars a month, and his nights to his lodge meetings and to drawing up resolutions of respect. In the latter direction he certainly had a gift; the underlying sympathy of his nature found its outlet there. And he had a pale, sickly wife and a paler, sicklier child.

On this circus day he had been stationed in front of his house for a good half hour, watching up the street for some one. This some one, as it turned out, was Judge Priest. At sight of the old judge coming along, Mr. Hammersmith went forward to meet him and fell in alongside, keeping pace with him.

"Good momin', son," said the old judge, who knew everybody that lived in town. "How's the little feller this mornin'?"

"Judge, I'm sorry to say that Lemuel Junior ain't no better this momin'," answered the little coal clerk with a hitching of his voice. "We're afraid—his mother and me—that he ain't never goin' to be no better. I've had Doctor Lake in again and he says there really ain't anything we can do—he says it's just a matter of a little time now. Old Aunt Hannah Holmes says he's got bone erysipelas, and that if we could 'a' got him away from here in time we might have saved him. But I don't know—we done the best we could. I try to be reconciled. Lemuel Junior he suffers so at times that it'll be a mercy, I reckin—but it's hard on you, judge—it's tumble hard on you when it's your only child."

"My son," said the old judge, speaking slowly, "it's so hard that I know nothin' I could say or do would be any comfort to you. But I'm sorry—I'm mighty sorry for you all. I know what it is. I buried mine, both of 'em, in one week's time, and that's thirty years and more ago; but it still hurts mightily sometimes. I wish't there was something I could do."

"Well, there is," said Hammersmith—"there is, judge, maybe. That's why I've been standin' down here waitin' for you. You see, Lemmy he was tumble sharp set on goin' to the circus today. He's been readin' the circus bills that I'd bring home to him until he knew 'em off by heart. He always did have a mighty bright mind for rememberin' things. We was aimin' to take him to the show this evenin', bundled up in a bedquilt, you know, and settin' off with him in a kind of a quiet place somewhere. But he had a bad night and we just can't make out to do it—he's too weak to stand it—and it was most breakin' his heart for a while; but then he said if he could just see the parade he'd be satisfied.

"And, judge, that's the point—he's took it into his head that you can fix it some way so he can see it. We tried to argue him out of it, but you know how it is, tryin' to argue with a child as sick as Lemuel Junior's been. He—he won't listen to nothin' we say."

A great compassion shadowed the judge's face. His hand went out and found the sloping shoulder of the father and patted it clumsily. He didn't say anything. There didn't seem to be anything to say.

"So we just had to humor him along. His maw has had him at the front window for an hour now, propped up on a pillow, waitin' for you to come by. He wouldn't listen to nothin' else. And, judge—if you can humor him at all—any way at all—do it, please—"

He broke off because they were almost in the shadow of the catalpa tree, and now the judge's name was called out by a voice that was as thin and elfin as though the throat that spoke it were strung with fine silver wires.

"Oh, judge—oh, Mister Judge Priest!"

The judge stopped, and, putting his hands on the palings, looked across them at the little sick boy. He saw a face that seemed to be all eyes and mouth and bulging, blue-veined forehead—he was shockingly reminded of a new-hatched sparrow—and the big eyes were feverishly alight with the look that is seen only in the eyes of those who already have begun to glimpse the great secret that lies beyond the ken of the rest of us.

"Why, hello, little feller," said the judge, with a false heartiness. "I'm sorry to see you laid up again."

"Judge Priest, sir," said the sick boy, panting with weak eagerness, "I want to see the grand free street parade. I've been sick a right smart while, and I can't go to the circus; but I do want mightily to see the grand free street parade. And I want you, please, sir, to have 'em come up by this house."

Back Home

There was a world of confidence in the plea. Unnoticed by the boy, his mother, who had been fanning him, dropped the fan and put her apron over her face and leaned against the window-jamb, sobbing silently. The father, silent too, leaned against the fence, looking fixedly at nothing and wiping his eyes with the butt of his hand. Yes, it is possible for a man to wipe his eyes on his bare hand without seeming either grotesque or vulgar—even when the man who does it is a little inconsequential man—if his child is dying and his sight is blurred and his heart is fit to burst inside of him. The judge bent across the fence, and his face muscles were working but his voice held steady.

"Well, now, Lemmy," he said, "I'd like to do it for you the best in the world; but, you see, boy, I don't own this here circus—I don't even know the gentleman that does own it."

"His name is Silver," supplied the sick child—"Daniel P. Silver, owner of Silver's Mammoth United Railroad Shows, Roman Hippodrome and Noah's Ark Menagerie—that's the man! I kin show you his picture on one of the showbills my paw brought home to me, and then you kin go right and find him."

"I'm afraid it wouldn't do much good if I did know him, Lemmy," said the old judge very gently. "You see—"

"But ain't you the judge at the big cote-house?" demanded the child; "and can't you put people in jail if they don't do what you tell 'em? That's what my grandpop says. He's always tellin' me stories about how you and him fought the Yankees, and he always votes for you too—my grandpop talks like he thought you could do anything. And, judge, please, sir, if you went to Mister Daniel P. Silver and told him that you was the big judge—and told him there was a little sick boy livin' right up the road a piece in a little brown house—don't you reckin he'd do it? It ain't so very far out of the way if they go down Jefferson Street—it's only a little ways Judge, you'll make 'em do it, won't you—for me?"

"I'll try, boy, I'll shorely try to do what I can," said the old judge; "but if I can't make 'em do it you won't be disappointed, will you, Lemmy?" He fumbled in his pocket. "Here's four bits for you—you tell your daddy to buy you something with it. I know your maw and daddy wouldn't want you to take money from strangers, but of course it's different with old friends like you and me. Here, you take it. And there's something else," he went on. "I'll bet you there's one of those dagoes or somebody like that downtown with a lot of these here big toy rubber balloons—red and green and blue. You tell me which color you like the best and I'll see that it's sent right up here to you—the biggest balloon the man's got—"

"I don't want any balloon," said the little voice fretfully, "and I don't want any four bits. I want to see the grand free street parade, and the herd of elephants, and the down, and the man-eatin' tigers, and everything. I want that parade to come by this house."

The judge looked hopelessly from the child to the mother and then to the father—they both had their faces averted still—and back into the sick child's face again. The four-bit piece lay shining on the porch floor where it had fallen. The judge backed away, searching his mind for the right words to say.

"Well, I'll do what I can, Lemmy," he repeated, as though he could find no other phrase—"I'll do what I can."

The child rolled his head back against the pillow, satisfied. "Then it'll be all right, sir," he said with a joyful confidence. "My grand-pop he said you could do 'most anything. You tell 'em, Mister Judge Priest, that I'll be a-waitin' right here in this very window for 'em when they pass."

Walking with his head down and his steps lagging, the old judge, turning into the main thoroughfare, was almost run over by a mare that came briskly along, drawing a light buggy with a tall man in it. The tall man pulled up the mare just in time. His name was Settle.

"By gum, judge," he said apologetically, "I came mighty near gettin' you that time!"

"Hello, son," said the judge absently; "which way are you headed?"

"Downtown, same as everybody else," said Settle. "Jump in and I'll take you right down, sir."

"Much obliged," assented the old judge, as he heaved himself heavily up between the skewed wheels and settled himself so solidly at Settle's left that the seat springs whined; "but I wish't, if you're not in too big a hurry, that you'd drive me up by the showgrounds first."

"Glad to," said Settle, as he swung the mare round. "I just come from there myself—been up lookin' at the stock. 'Tain't much. Goin' up to look their stock over yourself, judge?" he asked, taking it for granted that any man would naturally be interested in horseflesh, as indeed would be a true guess so far as any man in that community was concerned.

"Stock?" said the judge. "No, I want to see the proprietor of this here show. I won't keep you waitin' but a minute or two."

"The proprietor!" echoed Settle, surprised. "What's a circuit judge goin' to see a circus man for—is it something about their license?"

"No," said the judge—"no, just some business—a little private business matter I want to see him on."

He offered no further explanation and Settle asked for none. At the grounds the smaller tents were all up—there was quite a little dirty-white encampment of them—and just as they drove up the roof of the main tent rose to the tops of its center poles, bellying and billowing like a stage sea in the second act of Monte Cristo. Along the near edge of the common, negro men were rigging booths with planks for counters and sheets for awnings, and negro women were unpacking the wares that would presently be spread forth temptingly against the coming of the show crowds—fried chicken and slabs of fried fish, and ham and pies and fried apple turnovers. Leaving Settle checking the restive mare, the old judge made his way across the sod, already scuffed and dented by countless feet. A collarless, redfaced man, plainly a functionary of some sort, hurried toward him, and the judge put himself in this man's path.

"Are you connected with this institution, suh?" he asked.

"Yes," said the man shortly, but slowing his gait.

"So I judged from your manner and deportment, suh," said the judge. "I'm lookin'," he went on, "for your proprietor."

"Silver? He's over yonder by the cookhouse."

"The which?" asked the judge.

"The cookhouse—the dining tent," explained the other, pointing. "Right round yonder beyond that second stake wagon—where you see smoke rising. But he's likely to be pretty busy."

Behind the second stake wagon the judge found a blocky, authoritative man, with a brown derby hat tilted back on his head and heavy-lidded eyes like a frog's, and knew him at once for the owner; but one look at the face made the judge hesitate. He felt that his was a lost cause already; and then the other opened his mouth and spoke, and Judge Priest turned on his heel and came away. The judge was reasonably well seasoned to sounds of ordinary profanity, but not to blasphemy that seemed to loose an evil black smudge upon the clean air. He came back to the buggy and climbed in.

Back Home

"See your man?" asked Settle.

"Yes," said the judge slowly, "I saw him."

Especially downtown things had a holidaying look to them. Wall-eyed teams of country horses were tethered to hitching-racks in the short by-streets, flinching their flanks and setting themselves for abortive stampedes later on. Pedlers of toy balloons circulated; a vender with a fascinating line of patter sold to the same customers, in rapid succession, odorous hamburger and flat slabs of a heat-resisting variety of striped ice cream. At a main crossing, catercornered across from each other, the highpitch man and his brother of the flat joint were at work, one selling electric belts from the back of a buggy, the other down in the dust manipulating a spindle game. The same group of shillabers were constantly circulating from one faker to the other, and as constantly investing. Even the clerks couldn't stay inside the stores—they kept darting out and darting back in again. A group of darkies would find a desirable point of observation along the sidewalk and hold it for a minute or two, and then on a sudden unaccountable impulse would desert it and go streaking off down the middle of the street to find another that was in no way better. In front of the wagon yard country rigs were parked three deep. Every small boy who wasn't at the showground was swarming round underfoot somewhere, filled with a most delicious nervousness that kept him moving. But Judge Priest, who would have joyed in these things ordinarily, had an absent eye for it all. There was another picture persisting in his mind, a picture with a little brown house and a ragged catalpa tree for a background.

In front of Soule's drug store his weekday cronies sat—the elder statesmen of the town—tilted back in hard-bottomed chairs, with their legs drawn up under them out of the tides of foot travel. But he passed them by, only nodding an answer to their choraled greeting, and went inside back behind the prescription case and sat down there alone, smoking his pipe soberly.

"Wonder what ails Judge Priest?" said Sergeant Jimmy Bagby. "He looks sort of dauncy and low in his mind, don't he?"

"He certainly does," some one agreed.

Half an hour later, when the sheriff came in looking for him, Judge Priest was still sitting alone behind the prescription case. With the sheriff was a middle-aged man, a stranger, in a wrinkled check suit and a somewhat soiled fancy vest. An upper pocket of this vest was bulged outward by such frank articles of personal use as a red celluloid toothbrush, carried bristle-end up, a rubber mustache-comb and a carpenter's flat pencil. The stranger had a longish mustache, iron-gray at the roots and of a greenish, blue-black color elsewhere, and he walked with a perceptible limp. He had a way, it at once developed, of taking his comb out and running it through his mustache while in conversation, doing so without seeming to affect the flow or the volume of his language.

"Mornin', Judge Priest," said the sheriff. "This here gentleman wants to see you a minute about gittin' out an attachment. I taken him first to the county judge's office, but it seems like Judge Landis went up to Louisville last night, and the magistrates' offices air closed—both of them, in fact; and so seein' as this gentleman is in a kind of a hurry, I taken the liberty of bringin' him round to you."

Before the judge could open his mouth, he of the dyed mustache was breaking in.

"Yes, sirree," he began briskly. "If you're the judge here I want an attachment. I've got a good claim against Dan Silver, and blame me if I don't push it. I'll fix him—red-lighting me off my own privilege car!" He puffed up with rage and injury.

"What appears to be the main trouble?" asked the judge, studying this belligerent one from under his hatbrim.

Back Home

"Well, it's simple enough," explained the man. "Stanton is my name—here's my card—and I'm the fixer for this show—the legal adjuster, see? Or, anyhow, I was until last night. And I likewise am—or was—half partner with Dan Silver in the privilege car and in the speculative interests of this show—the flat joints and the rackets and all. You make me now, I guess? Well, last night, coming up here from the last stand, me and Silver fell out over the split-up, over dividing the day's profits—you understand, the money is cut up two ways every night—and I ketched him trying to trim me. I called him down good and hard then, and blame if he didn't have the nerve to call in that big boss razor-back of his, named Saginaw, and a couple more rousters, and red-light me right off my own privilege car! Now what do you know about that?"

"Only what you tell me," replied Judge Priest calmly. "Might I ask you what is the process of red-lightin' a person of your callin' in life?"

"Chucking you off of a train without waiting for the train to stop, that's what," expounded the aggrieved Mr. Stanton. "It was pretty soft for me that I lit on the side of a dirt bank and we wasn't moving very fast, else I'd a been killed. As 'twas I about ruined a suit of clothes and scraped most of the meat off of one leg." He indicated the denuded limb by raising it stiffly a couple of times and then felt for his comb. Use of it appeared to have a somewhat soothing effect upon his feelings, and he continued: "So I limped up to the next station, two of the longest miles in the world, and caught a freight coming through, and here I am. And now I want to file against him—the dirty, red-lighting dog!

"Why, he owes me money—plenty of it. Just like I told you, I'm the half owner of that privilege car, and besides he borrowed money off of me at the beginning of the season and never offered to pay it back. I've got his personal notes right here to prove it." He felt for the documents and spread them, soiled and thumbed, upon the prescription shelf under the judge's nose. "He's sure got to settle with me before he gets out of this town. Don't worry about me—I'll put up cash bond to prove I'm on the level," fishing out from his trousers pocket a bundle of bills with a rubber band on it. "Pretty lucky for me they didn't know I had my bankroll with me last night!"

"I suppose the attachment may issue," said the judge preparing to get up.

"Fine," said Stanton, with deep gratification in his bearing. "But here, wait a minute," he warned. "Don't make no mistake and try to attach the whole works, because if you do you'll sure fall down on your face, judge. That's all been provided for. The wagons and horses are all in Silver's name and the cage animals are all in his wife's name. And so when a hick constable or somebody comes round with an attachment, Dan says to him, 'All right,' he says, 'go on and attach, but you can't touch them animals,' he says; and then friend wife flashes a bill of sale to show they are hers. The rube says 'What'll I do?' and Silver says, 'Why, let the animals out and take the wagons; but of course,' he says, 'you're responsible for the lions and that pair of ferocious man-eating tigers and the rest of 'em. Go right ahead,' he says, 'and help yourself.' 'Yes,' his wife says, 'go ahead; but if you let any of my wild animals get away I'll hold you liable, and also if you let any of 'em chew up anybody you'll pay the damages and not me,' she says. 'You'll have to be specially careful about Wallace the Ontamable,' she says; 'he's et up two trainers already this season and crippled two-three more of the hands.'

"Well, if that don't bluff the rube they take him round and give him a flash at Wallace. Wallace is old and feeble and he ain't really much more dangerous than a kitten, but he looks rough; and Dan sidles up 'longside the wagon and touches a button that's there to use during the ballyhoo, and then Wallace jumps up and down and roars a mile. D'ye make me there? Well, the floor of the cage is all iron strips, and when Dan touches that button it shoots about fifty volts of the real juice—electricity, you know—into Wallace's feet and he acts ontamable. So of course that stumps the rube, and Dan like as not gets away with it without ever settling. Oh, it's a foxy trick! And to think it was me myself that first put Silver on to it!" he added lamentingly, with a sidelong look at the sheriff to see how that official was taking the disclosure of these professional secrets. As well as one might judge by a glance the sheriff was taking it unmoved. He was cutting off a chew of tobacco from a black plug. Stowing the morsel in his jaw, he advanced an idea of his own:

"How about attachin' the receipts in the ticket wagon?"

"I don't know about that either," said the sophisticated Stanton. "Dan Silver is one of the wisest guys in this business. He had to be a wise guy to slip one over on an old big-leaguer like yours truly, and that's no sidewalk banter either. You might attach the wagon and put a constable or somebody inside of it, and then like as not Dan'd find some way to flimflam him and make his getaway with the kale intact. You gotter give it to Dan Silver there. I guess he's a stupid guy—yes, stupid like a bear cat!" His tone of reluctant admiration indicated that this last was spoken satirically and that seriously he regarded a bear cat as probably the astutest hybrid of all species.

"Are all circuses conducted in this general fashion, suh?" inquired the old judge softly.

"No," admitted Stanton, "they ain't—the big ones ain't anyway; but a lot of the small ones is. They gotter do it because a circus is always fair game for a sore rube. Once the tents come down a circus has got no friends.

"I tell you what," he went on, struck amidships with a happy notion—"I tell you what you do. Lemme swear out an attachment against the band wagon and the band-wagon team, and you go serve it right away, sheriff. That'll fix him, I guess."

"How so?" put in the judge, still seeking information for his own enlightenment.

"Why, you see, if you tie up that band wagon Dan Silver can't use it for parading. He ain't got but just the one, and a circus parade without a band wagon will look pretty sick, I should say. It'll look more like something else, a funeral, for example." The pleased grafter grinned maliciously.

"It's like this—the band wagon is the key to the whole works," he went on. "It's the first thing off the lot when the parade starts—the band-wagon driver is the only one that has the route. You cut the band wagon out and you've just naturally got that parade snarled up to hell and gone."

Judge Priest got upon his feet and advanced upon the exultant stranger. He seemed more interested than at any time.

"Suh," he asked, "let me see if I understand you properly. The band wagon is the guidin' motive, as it were, of the entire parade—is that right?"

"You've got it," Stanton assured him. "Even the stock is trained to follow the band wagon. They steer by the music up ahead. Cop the band wagon out and the rest of 'em won't know which way to go—that's the rule where-ever there's a road show traveling."

"Ah hah," said the judge reflectively, "I see."

"But say, look here, judge," said Stanton. "Begging your pardon and not trying to rush you nor nothing, but if you're going to attach that band wagon of Dan Silver's for me you gotter hurry. That parade is due to leave the lot in less'n half an hour from now."

He was gratified to note that his warning appeared to grease the joints in the old judge's legs. They all three went straightway to the sheriff's office, which chanced to be only two doors away, and there the preliminaries necessary to legal seizures touching on a certain described and specified parade chariot, tableau car or band wagon were speedily completed. Stanton made oath to divers allegations and departed, assiduously combing himself and gloating openly over the anticipated discomfiture of his late partner. The sheriff lingered behind only a minute or two longer while Judge Priest in the privacy of a back room impressed upon him his instructions. Then he, too, departed, moving at his top walking gait westward out Jefferson Street. There was this that could be said for Sheriff Giles Birdsong—he was not gifted in conversation nor was he of a quick order of intellect, but he knew his duty and he obeyed orders literally when conveyed to him by a superior official. On occasion he had obeyed them so literally—where the warrant had said dead or alive, for example—that he brought in, feet first, a prisoner or so who manifested a spirited reluctance against being brought in any other way. And the instructions he had now were highly explicit on a certain head.

Close on Sheriff Birdsong's hurrying heels the judge himself issued forth from the sheriff's office. Hailing a slowly ambling public vehicle driven by a languid darky, he deposited his person therein and was driven away. Observing this from his place in front of the drug store, Sergeant Jimmy Bagby was moved to remark generally to the company: "You can't tell me I wasn't right a while ago about Judge Billy Priest. Look at him yonder now, puttin' out for home in a hack, without waitin' for the parade. There certainly is something wrong with the judge and you can't tell me there ain't."

If the judge didn't wait nearly everybody else did—waited with what patience and impatience they might through a period that was punctuated by a dozen false alarms, each marked with much craning of elderly necks and abortive rushes by younger enthusiasts to the middle of the street. After a while, though, from away up at the head of Jefferson Street there came down, borne along on the summer air, a faint anticipatory blare of brazen horns, heard at first only in broken snatches. Then, in a minute or two, the blaring resolved itself into a connected effort at melody, with drums throbbing away in it. Farmers grabbed at the bits of restive horses, that had their ears set sharply in one direction, and began uttering soothing and admonitory "whoas." The stores erupted clerks and customers together. The awning poles on both sides of the street assumed the appearance of burdened grape trellises, bearing ripe black and white clusters of small boys. At last she was coming!

She was, for a fact. She came on until the thin runlet of ostensible music became a fanfaring, crashing cataract of pleasing and exhilarating sound, until through the dancing dust could be made out the arching, upcurved front of a splendid red-and-gold chariot. In front of it, like wallowing waves before the prow of a Viking ship, were the weaving broad backs of many white horses, and stretching behind it was a sinuous, colorful mass crowned with dancing, distant banner-things, and suggesting in glintings of gold and splashings of flame an oncoming argosy of glitter and gorgeousness.

She was coming all right! But was she? A sort of disappointed, surprised gasp passed along the crowded sidewalks, and boys began sliding down the awning poles and running like mad up the street. For instead of continuing straight on down Jefferson, as all circus parades had always done, the head of this one was seen now, after a momentary halt as of indecision, to turn short off and head into Clay. But why Clay Street—that was the question? Clay Street didn't have ten houses on it, all told, and it ran up a steep hill and ended in an abandoned orchard just beyond the old Priest place. Indeed the only way to get out of Clay Street, once you got into it, was by a distant lane that cut through to the paralleling street on the right. What would any circus parade in possession of its sane senses be doing going up Clay Street?

But that indeed was exactly what this parade was doing—with the added phenomena of Sheriff Giles Birdsong sitting vigilantly erect on the front seat of the band wagon, and a band-wagon driver taking orders for once from somebody besides his rightful boss—taking them protestingly and profanely, but nevertheless taking them.

Yes, sir, that's what she was doing. The band wagon, behind the oblique arc of its ten-horse team, was swinging into Clay Street, and the rest of the procession was following its leader and disappearing, wormlike, into a tunnel of overarching maples and silver-leaf poplars.

Back Home

And so it moved, slowly and deliberately, after the fashion of circus parades, past some sparsely scattered cottages that were mainly closed and empty, seeing that their customary dwellers were even now downtown, until the head of it came to a particularly shabby little brown house that was not closed and was not empty. From a window here looked out a worn little woman and a little sick boy, he as pale as the pillow against which he was propped, and from here they saw it all—she through tears and he with eyes that burned with a dumb joy unutterable—from here these two beheld the unbelievable marvel of it. It was almost as though the whole unspeakable grandeur of it had been devised for those eyes alone—first the great grand frigate of a band wagon pitching and rolling as if in heavy seas, with *artistes* of a world-wide repute discoursing sweet strains from its decks, and drawn not by four or six, but by ten snow-white Arabian stallions with red pompons nodding above their proud heads—that is to say, they were snow-white except perhaps for a slight grayish dappling. And on behind this, tailing away and away, were knights and ladies on mettled, gayly caparisoned steeds, and golden pageant dens filled with ferocious rare beasts of the jungle, hungrily surveying the surging crowds—only, of course, there weren't any crowds—and sun-bright tableau cars, with crystal mirrors cunningly inset in the scrolled carved work, so that the dancing surfaces caught the sunlight and threw it back into eyes already joyously dazzled; and sundry closed cages with beautiful historical paintings on their sides, suggesting by their very secrecy the presence of marvelous prisoned creatures; and yet another golden chariot with the Queen of Sheba and her whole glittering court traveling in imperial pomp atop of it.

That wasn't all—by no means was it all. There succeeded an open den containing the man-eating Bengal tigers, striped and lank, with the intrepid spangled shoulders of the trainer showing as he sat with his back against the bars, holding his terrible charges in dominion by the power of the human eye, so that for the time being they dared not eat anybody. And then followed a whole drove of trick ponies drawing the happy family in its wheeled home, and behind that in turn more cages, closed, and a fife-and-drum corps of old regimentals in blue and buff, playing Yankee Doodle with martial spirit, and next the Asiatic camel to be known by his one hump, and the genuine Bactrian dromedary to be known by his two, slouching by as though they didn't care whether school kept or not, flirting their under lips up and down and showing profiles like Old Testament characters. And then came more knights and ladies and more horses and more heroes of history and romance, and a veritable herd of vast and pondrous pachyderm performers, or elephants—for while one pachyderm, however vast and pachydermic, might not make a herd, perhaps, or even two yet surely three would, and here were no less than three, holding one another's tails with their trunks, which was a droll conceit thought up by these intelligent creatures on the spur of the moment, no doubt, with the sole idea of giving added pleasure to a little sick boy.

That wasn't all either. There was more of this unapproachable pageant yet winding by—including such wonders as the glass-walled apartment of the lady snake-charmer, with the lady snake-charmer sitting right there in imminent peril of her life amidst her loathsome, coiling and venomous pets; and also there was Judge Priest's Jeff, hardly to be recognized in a red-and-yellow livery as he led the far-famed sacred ox of India; and then the funny old clown in his little blue wagon, shouting out "Whoa, January" to his mule and dodging back as January kicked up right in his face, and last of all—a crowning glory to all these other glories—the steam calliope, whistling and blasting and shrilling and steaming, fit to split itself wide open!

You and I, reader, looking on at this with gaze unglamoured by the eternal, fleeting spirit of youth, might have noted in the carping light of higher criticism that the oriental trappings had been but poor shoddy stuffs to begin with, and were now all torn and dingy and shedding their tarnished spangles; might have noted that the man-eating tigers seemed strangely bored with life, and that the venomous serpents draped upon the form of the lady snake-charmer were languid, not to say torpid, to a degree that gave the lady snake-charmer the appearance rather of a female suspender pedler, carrying her wares hung over her shoulders. We might have observed further had we been so minded—as probably we should—that the Queen of Sheba bore somewhat a weatherbeaten look and held a quite common-appearing cotton umbrella with a bone handle over her regal head; that the East-Indian mahout of the elephant herd needed a shave, and that there were mud-stained overalls and brogan shoes showing plainly beneath the flowing robes of the Arabian camel-driver. We might even have guessed that the biggest tableau car was no more than a ticket wagon in thin disguise, and that the yapping which proceeded from the largest closed cage indicated the presence merely of a troupe of uneasy performing poodles.

But to the transported vision of the little sick boy in the little brown house there were no flaws in it anywhere—it was all too splendid for words, and so he spoke no words at all as it wound on by. The lurching shoulders of the elephants had gone over the hill beyond and on down, the sacred ox of India had passed ambling from sight, the glass establishment of the snake-charmer was passing, and January and the down wagon and the steam calliope were right in front of the Hammersmith house, when something happened on ahead, and for a half minute or so there was a slowing-up and a closing-up and a halting of everything.

Although, of course, the rear guard didn't know it for the time being, the halt was occasioned by the fact that when the band wagon reached the far end of Clay Street, with the orchard trees looming dead ahead, the sheriff, riding on the front seat of the band wagon, gave an order. The band-wagon driver instantly took up the slack of the reins that flowed through his fingers in layers, so that they stopped right in front of Judge Priest's house, where Judge Priest stood leaning on his gate. The sheriff made a sort of saluting motion of his fingers against the brim of his black slouch hat.

"Accordin' to orders, Your Honor," he stated from his lofty perch.

At this there spoke up another man, the third and furthermost upon the wide seat of the band wagon, and this third man was no less a personage than Daniel P. Silver himself, and he was as near to bursting with bottled rage as any man could well be and still remain whole, and he was as hoarse as a frog from futile swearing.

"What in thunder does this mean—" he began, and then stopped short, being daunted by the face which Sheriff Giles Birdsong turned upon him.

"Look here, mister," counseled the sheriff, "you art now in the presence of the presidin' judge of the first judicial district of Kintucky, settin' in chambers, or what amounts to the same thing, and you air liable to git yourself into contempt of cote any minute."

Baffled, Silver started to swear again, but in a lower key.

"You better shut up your mouth," said the sheriff with a shifting forward of his body to free his limbs for action, "and listen to whut His Honor has to say. You act like you was actually anxious to git yourself lamed up."

"Sheriff," said the judge, "obeyin' your orders you have, I observe, attached certain properties—to wit, a band wagon and team of horses—and still obeyin' orders, have produced said articles before me for my inspection. You will continue in personal possession of same until said attachment is adjudicated, not allowin' any person whatsoever to remove them from your custody. Do I make myself sufficiently plain?"

"Yes, suh, Your Honor," said the sheriff. "You do."

"In the meanwhile, pendin' the termination of the litigation, if the recent possessor of this property desires to use it for exhibition or paradin' purposes, you will permit him to do so, always within proper bounds," went on the judge. "I would suggest that you could cut through that lane yonder in order to reach the business section of our city, if such should be the desire of the recent possessor."

The heavy wheels of the band wagon began turning; the parade started moving on again. But in that precious half-minute's halt something else had happened, only this happened in front of the little brown house halfway down Clay Street. The clown's gaze was roving this way and that, as if looking for the crowd that should have been there and that was only just beginning to appear, breathless and panting, and his eyes fell upon a wasted, wizened little face looking straight out at him from a nest of bedclothes in a window not thirty feet away; and—be it remembered among that clown's good deeds in the hereafter—he stood up and bowed, and stretched his painted, powdered face in a wide and gorgeous grin, just as another and a greater Grimaldi once did for just such another audience of a grieving mother and a dying child. Then he yelled "Whoa, January," three separate times, and each time he poked January in his long-suffering flanks and each time January kicked up his small quick hoofs right alongside the clown's floury ears.

The steam calliope man had an inspiration too. He was a person of no great refinement, the calliope man, and he worked a shell game for his main source of income and lived rough and lived hard, so it may not have been an inspiration after all, but merely the happy accident of chance. But whether it was or it wasn't, he suddenly and without seeming reason switched from the tune he was playing and made his calliope sound out the first bars of the music which somebody once set to the sweetest childhood verses that Eugene Field ever wrote—the verses that begin:

```
The little toy dog is covered with dust,
But sturdy and stanch he stands;
And the little toy soldier is red with rust,
And his musket molds in his hands.
```

The parade resumed its march then and went on, tailing away through the dappled sunshine under the trees, and up over the hill and down the other side of it, but the clown looked back as he scalped the crest and waved one arm, in a baggy calico sleeve, with a sort of friendly goodby motion to somebody behind him; and as for the steam calliope man, he kept on playing the little Boy Blue verses until he disappeared.

As a matter of fact, he was still playing them when he passed a wide-porched old white house almost at the end of the empty street, where a stout old man in a wrinkly white linen suit leaned across a gate and regarded the steam calliope man with a satisfied almost a proprietorial air.

VI. WHEN THE FIGHTING WAS GOOD

MISTER SHERIFF," ordered the judge, "bring Pressley G. Harper to the bar."

Judge Priest, as I may have set forth before, had two habits of speech—one purposely ungrammatical and thickly larded with the vernacular of the country crossroads—that was for his private walks and conversations, and for his campaignings; but the other was of good and proper and dignified English, and it he reserved for official acts and utterances. Whether upon the bench or off it, though, his voice had that high-pitched, fiddle-string note which carried far and clearly; and on this day, when he spoke, the sheriff roused up instantly from where he had been enjoying forty winks between the bewhittled arms of a tilted chair and bestirred himself. He hurried out of a side door. A little, whispering, hunching stir went through the courtroom. Spectators reclining upon the benches, partly on their spines and partly on their shoulderblades, straightened and bent forward. Inside the rail, which set apart the legal goats from the civic sheep, a score of eyes were fixed speculatively upon the judge's face, rising above the top of the tall, scarred desk where he sat; but his face gave no dew to his thoughts; and if the mind back of the beneficent, mild blue eyes was troubled, the eyes themselves looked out unvexed through the steel-bowed spectacles that rode low on the old judge's nose.

There was a minute's wait. The clerk handed up to the judge a sheaf of papers in blue wrappers. The judge shuffled through them until he found the one he wanted. It was the middle of the afternoon of a luscious spring day—the last day of the spring term of court. In at the open windows came spicy, moist smells of things sprouting and growing, and down across the courthouse square the big star-shaped flowers of the dogwood trees showed white and misty, like a new Milky Way against a billowy green firmament.

A minute only and then the sheriff reëntered. At his side came a man. This newcomer must have been dose to seventy years—or sixty-five, anyway. He was long and lean, and he bore his height with a sort of alert and supple erectness, stepping high, with the seemingly awkward gait of the man trained at crossing furrows, yet bringing his feet down noiselessly, like a house-cat treading on dead leaves. The way he moved made you think of a deerstalker. Strength, tremendous strength, was shown in the outward swing of the long arms and the huge, knotty hands, and there was temper in the hot, brown eyes and in the thick, stiff crop of reddish-gray hair, rising like buckwheat stubble upon his scalp. He had high cheekbones and a long, shaven face, and his skin was tanned to a leathery red, like a well-smoked ham. Except for the colors of his hair and eyes, he might have passed for half Indian. Indeed, there was a tale in the county that his great-grandmother was a Shawnee squaw. He was more than six feet tall—he must have been six feet two.

With the sheriff alongside him he came to the bar—a sagged oaken railing—and stood there with his big hands cupped over it. He was newly shaved and dressed in what was evidently his best.

"Pressley G. Harper at the bar," sang out the clerk methodically. Everybody was listening.

"Pressley G. Harper," said the judge, "waiving the benefit of counsel and the right of trial by jury, you have this day pleaded guilty to an indictment charging you with felonious assault in that you did, on the twenty-first day of January last, shoot and wound with a firearm one Virgil Settle, a citizen of this county. Have you anything to say why the sentence of the law should not be pronounced upon you?"

Only eying him steadfastly, the confessed offender shook his head.

"It is the judgment of this court, then, that you be confined in the state penitentiary for the period of two years at hard labor."

A babbling murmur ran over the room—for his sins old Press Harper was catching it at last. The prisoner's hands gripped the oaken rail until his knuckles nails showed white, and it seemed that the tough wood fibers would be dented in; other than that he gave no sign, but took the blow braced and steady, like a game man facing a firing squad. The sheriff inched toward him; but the judge raised the hand that held the blue-wrapped paper as a sign that he had more to say.

"Pressley G. Harper," said the judge, "probably this is not the time or the place for the court to say how deeply it regrets the necessity of inflicting this punishment upon you. This court has known you for many years—for a great many years. You might have been a worthy citizen. You have been of good repute for truthfulness and fair dealing among your neighbors; but you have been beset, all your life, with a temper that was your abiding curse, and when excited with liquor you have been a menace to the safety of your fellowman. Time and time again, within the recollection of this court, you have been involved in unseemly brawls, largely of your own making. That you were generally inflamed with drink, and that you afterward seemed genuinely penitent and made what amends you could, does not serve to excuse you in the eyes of the law. That you have never taken a human life outright is a happy accident of chance.

"Through the leniency of those appointed to administer the law you have until now escaped the proper and fitting consequences of your behavior; but, by this last wanton attack upon an inoffensive citizen, you have forfeited all claim upon the consideration of the designated authorities."

He paused for a little, fumbling at the bow of his spectacles.

"In the natural course of human events you have probably but a few more years to live. It is to be regretted by all right-thinking men that you cannot go to your grave free from the stigma of a prison. And it is a blessing that you have no one closely related to you by ties of blood or marriage to share in your disgrace." The old judge's high voice grew husked and roughened here, he being himself both widowed and childless. "The judgment of the court stands—two years at hard labor."

He made a sign that he was done. The sheriff edged up again and touched the sentenced man upon the arm. Without turning his head, Harper shook off the hand of authority with so violent a shrug that the sheriff dodged back, startled. Then for the first time the prisoner spoke.

"Judge, Your Honor," he said quietly, "jest a minute ago you asked me if I had anything to say and I told you that I had not. I've changed my mind; I want to ask you something—I want to ask you a mighty big favor. No, I ain't askin' you to let me off—it ain't that," he went on more quickly, reading the look on the judge's face. "I didn't expect to come clear in this here case. I pleaded guilty because I was guilty and didn't have no defense. My bein' sorry for shootin' Virge Settle the way I did don't excuse me, as I know; but, Judge Priest, I'll say jest this to you—I don't want to be dragged off to that there penitentiary like a savage dumb beast. I don't want to be took there by no sheriff. And what I want to ask you is this: Can't I go there a free man, with free limbs? I promise you to go and to serve my time faithful—but I want to go by myself and give myself up like a man."

Instantly visualized before the eyes of all who sat there was the picture which they knew must be in the prisoner's mind—the same picture which all or nearly all of them had seen more than once, since it came to pass, spring and fall, after each term of court—a little procession filing through the street to the depot; at its head, puffed out with responsibility, the sheriff and one of his deputies—at its tail more deputies, and in between them the string of newly convicted felons, handcuffed in twos, with a long trace-chain looping back from one pair to the next pair, and so on, binding all fast together in a clanking double file—the whites in front and the negroes back of them, maintaining even in that shameful formation the division of race; the whites mainly marching with downcast heads and hurrying feet, clutching pitiably small bundles with their free hands—the negroes singing doggerel in chorus and defiantly jingling the links of their tether; some, the friendless ones, hatless and half naked, and barefooted after months of lying in jail—and all with the smell of the frowsy cells upon them. And, seeing this familiar picture spring up before them, it seemed all of a sudden a wrong thing and a very shameful thing that Press Harper, an old man and a member of a decent family, should march thus, with his wrists chained and the offscourings and scum of the county jail for company. All there knew him for a man of his word. If old Press Harper said he would go to the penitentiary and surrender himself they knew he would go and do it if he had to crawl there on his knees. And so now, having made his plea, he waited silently for the answer.

The old judge had half swung himself about in his chair and with his hand at his beard was looking out of the window.

"Mister Sheriff," he said, without turning his head, "you may consider yourself relieved of the custody of the defendant at the bar. Mister Clerk, you may make out the commitment papers." The clerk busied himself with certain ruled forms, filling in dotted lines with writing. The judge went on: "Despite the irregularity of the proceeding, this court is disposed to grant the request which the defendant has just made. Grievous though his shortcomings in other directions may have been, this court has never known the defendant to break his word. Does the defendant desire any time in which to arrange his personal affairs? If so how much time?"

"I would like to have until the day after tomorrow," said Harper. "If I kin I want to find a tenant for my farm."

"Has the commonwealth's attorney any objection to the granting of this delay?" inquired the judge, still with his head turned away.

"None, Your Honor," said the prosecutor, half rising. And now the judge was facing the prisoner, looking him full in the eye.

"You will go free on your own recognizance, without bond, until the day after tomorrow," he bade him. "You will then report yourself to the warden of the state penitentiary at Frankfort. The clerk of this court will hand you certain documents which you will surrender to the warden at the same time that you surrender yourself."

The tall old man at the rail bowed his head to show he understood, but he gave no thanks for the favor vouchsafed him, nor did the other old man on the bench seem to expect any thanks. The clerk's pen, racing across the ruled sheets, squeaked audibly.

"This consideration is granted, though, upon one condition," said the judge, as though a new thought had just come to him. "And that is, that between this time and the time you begin serving your sentence you do not allow a drop of liquor to cross your lips. You promise that?"

"I promise that," said Harper slowly and soberly, like a man taking a solemn oath.

No more was said. The clerk filled out the blanks—two of them—and Judge Priest signed them. The clerk took them back from him, folded them inside a long envelope; backed the envelope with certain writings, and handed it over the bar rail to Harper. There wasn't a sound as he stowed it carefully into an inner pocket of his ill-fitting black coat; nor, except for the curiously light tread of his own steps, was there a sound as he, without a look side-wise, passed down the courtroom and out at the doorway.

"Mister Clerk," bade Judge Priest, "adjourn the present term of this court."

As the crowd filed noisily out, old Doctor Lake, who had been a spectator of all that happened, lingered behind and, with a nod and a gesture to the clerk, went round behind the jury-box and entered the door of the judge's private chamber, without knocking. The lone occupant of the room stood by the low, open window, looking out over the green square. He was stuffing the fire-blackened bowl of his corncob pipe with its customary fuel; but his eyes were not on the task, or his fingers trembled—or something; for, though the pipe was already packed to overflowing, he still tamped more tobacco in, wasting the shreddy brown weed upon the floor.

"Come in, Lew, and take a chair and set down," he said. Doctor Lake, however, instead of taking a chair and sitting down, crossed to the window and stood beside him, putting one hand on the judge's arm.

"That was pretty hard on old Press, Billy," said Doctor Lake.

Judge Priest was deeply sensitive of all outside criticism pertaining to his official conduct; his life off the bench was another matter. He stiffened under the touch.

"Lewis Lake," he said—sharply for him—"I don't permit even my best friends to discuss my judicial acts."

"Oh, I didn't mean that, Billy," Doctor Lake made haste to explain. "I wasn't thinking so much of what happened just now in the court yonder. I reckon old Press deserved it—he's been running hog-wild round this town and this county too long already. Let him get that temper of his roused and a few drinks in him and he is a regular mad dog. Nobody can deny that. Of course I hate it—and I know you do too—to see one of the old company—one of the boys who marched out of here with us in '61—going to the pen. That's only natural; but I'm not finding fault with your sending him there. What I was thinking of is that you're sending him over the road day after tomorrow."

"What of that?" asked the judge.

"Why, day after tomorrow is the day we're starting for the annual reunion," said Doctor Lake; "and, Billy, if Press goes on the noon train—which he probably will—he'll be traveling right along with the rest of us—for a part of the way. Only he'll get off at the Junction, and we—well, we'll be going on through, the rest of us will, to the reunion That's what I meant."

"That's so!" said the judge regretfully—"that's so! I did forget all about the reunion startin' then—I plum' forgot it. I reckin it will be sort of awkward for all of us—and for Press in particular." He paused, holding the unlighted and overflowing pipe in his hands absently, and then went on:

"Lewis, when a man holds an office such as mine is he has to do a lot of things he hates mightily to do. Now you take old Press Harper's case. I reckin there never was a braver soldier anywhere than Press was. Do you remember Brice's Crossroads?"

"Yes," said the old doctor, his eyes suddenly afire. "Yes, Billy—and Vicksburg too."

"Ah-hah!" went on the old judge—"and the second day's fight at Chickamauga, when we lost so many out of the regiment, and Press came back out of the last charge, draggin' little Gil Nicholas by the arms, and both of them purty nigh shot to pieces? Yes, suh; Press always was a fighter when there was any fightin' to do—and the fightin' was specially good in them days. The trouble with Press was he didn't quit fightin' when the rest of us did. Maybe it sort of got into his blood. It does do jest that sometimes, I judge."

"Yes," said Doctor Lake, "I suppose you're right; but old Press is in a fair way to be cured now. A man with his temper ought never to touch whisky anyhow."

"You're right," agreed the judge. "It's a dangerous thing, licker is—and a curse to some people. I'd like to have a dram right this minute. Lew, I wish mightily you'd come on and go home with me tonight and take supper. I'll send my nigger boy Jeff up to your house to tell your folks you won't be there until late, and you walk on out to my place with me. I feel sort of played out and lonesome—I do so. Come on now. We'll have a young chicken and a bait of hot waffles—I reckin that old nigger cook of mine does make the best waffles in the created world. After supper we'll set a spell together and talk over them old times when we were in the army—and maybe we can kind of forget some of the things that've come up later."

The noon accommodation would carry the delegation from Gideon K. Irons Camp over the branch line to the Junction, where it would connect with a special headed through for the reunion city. For the private use of the Camp the railroad company provided a car which the ladies of the town decorated on the night before with draped strips of red and white bunting down the sides, and little battle-flags nailed up over the two doors. The rush of the wind would soon whip away the little crossed flags from their tack fastenings end roll the bunting streamers up into the semblance of peppermint sticks; but the car, hitched to the tail end of the accommodation and surrounded by admiring groups of barelegged small boys, made a brave enough show when its intended passengers came marching down a good half hour ahead of leaving-time.

Considering the wide swath which death and the infirmities of age had been cutting in the ranks all these years, the Camp was sending a good representation—Judge Priest, the commandant; and Doctor Lake; and Major Joe Sam Covington; and Sergeant Jimmy Bagby, who never missed a reunion; and Corporal Jake Smedley, the color-bearer, with the Camp's flag furled on its staff and borne under his arm; and Captain Shelby Woodward—and four or five more. There was even one avowed private. Also, and not to be overlooked on any account, there was Uncle Zach Matthews, an ink-black, wrinkled person, with a shiny bald head polished like old rosewood, and a pair of warped legs bent outward like saddlebows. Personally Uncle Zach was of an open mind regarding the merits and the outcome of the Big War. As he himself often put it:

"Yas, suh—I ain't got no set prejudices ary way. In de spring of '61 I went out wid my own w'ite folks, as body-sarvant to my young marster, Cap'n Harry Matthews—and we suttinly did fight dem bluebellies up hill and down dale fer three endurin' years or more; but in de campaignin' round Nashville somewhars I got kind of disorganized and turn't round someway; and, when I sorter comes to myself, lo and behole, ef I ain't been captured by de Fed'rul army! So, rather'n have any fussin' 'bout it, I j'ined in wid dem; and frum den on till de surrender I served on de other side—cookin' fer one of their gin'els and doin' odd jobs round de camp; but when 'twas all over I come on back home and settled down ag'in 'mongst my own folks, where I properly belonged. Den, yere a few years back, some of 'em tum't in and done some testifyin' fer me so's I could git my pension. Doctor Lake, he says to me hisse'f, he says; 'Zach, bein' as de Yankee Gover'mint is a passin' out dis yere money so free you might jess as well have a little chunk of it too!' And he—him and Mistah Charley Reed and some others, they helped me wid my papers; and, of course, I been mighty grateful to all dem gen'l'men ever since."

So Uncle Zach drew his pension check quarterly, and regularly once a year went to the reunion as general factotum of the Camp, coming home laden with badges and heavy with small change. He and Judge Priest's Jeff, who was of the second generation of freedom, now furnished a touch of intense color relief, sitting together in one of the rearmost seats, guarding the piled-up personal baggage of the veterans.

Shortly before train-time carriages came, bringing young Mrs. McLaurin, little Rita Covington and Miss Minnie Lyon—the matron of honor, the sponsor and the maid of honor respectively of the delegation. Other towns no larger would be sure to send a dozen or more sponsors and maids and matrons of honor; but the home Camp was proverbially moderate in this regard. As Captain Woodward had once said: "We are charmed and honored by the smiles of our womanhood, and we worship every lovely daughter of the South; but, at a reunion of veterans, somehow I do love to see a veteran interspersed here and there in among the fair sex."

So now, as their special guests for this most auspicious occasion, they were taking along just these three—Rita Covington, a little eighteen-year-old beauty, and Minnie Lyon, a tall, fair, slender, pretty girl, and Mrs. Mc-Laurin. The two girls were in white linen, with touches of red at throat and waist; but young Mrs. McLaurin, who was a bride of two years' standing and plump and handsome, looked doubly handsome and perhaps a wee mite plumper than common in a tailor-made suit of mouse-gray, that was all tricked out with brass buttons and gold-braided cuffs, and a wide black belt, with a cavalry buckle. That the inspired tailor who built this costume had put the stars of a major-general on the collar and the stripes of a corporal on the sleeve was a matter of no consequence whatsoever. The color was right, the fit of the coat was unflawed by a single wrinkle fore or aft, and the brass buttons poured like molten gold down the front. Originally young Mrs. McLaurin had intended to reserve her military suit for a crowning sartorial stroke on the day of the big parade; but at the last moment pride of possession triumphed over the whisperings of discretion, and so here she was now, trig and triumphant—though, if it must be confessed, a trifle closely laced in. Yet she found an immediate reward in the florid compliments of the old men. She radiated her satisfaction visibly as Doctor Lake and Captain Woodward ushered her and her two charges aboard the car with a ceremonious, Ivanhoeish deference, which had come down with them from their day to this, like the scent of old lavender lingering in ancient cedar chests.

A further martial touch was given by the gray coats of the old men, by the big Camp badges and bronze crosses proudly displayed by all, and finally by Sergeant Jimmy Bagby, who, true to a habit of forty years' standing, was wearing the rent and faded jacket that he brought home from the war, and carrying on his shoulder the ancient rusted musket that had served him from Sumter to the fall of Richmond.

The last of the party was on the decorated coach, the last ordinary traveler had boarded the single day-coach and the conductor was signaling for the start, when an erect old man, who all during the flurry of departure had been standing silent and alone behind the protecting shadow of the far side of the station, came swiftly across the platform, stepping with a high, noiseless, deerstalker's tread, and, just as the engine bleated its farewell and the wheels began to turn, swung himself on the forward car. At sight of two little crossed flags fluttering almost above his head he lifted his slouch hat in a sort of shamed salute; but he kept his face turned resolutely away from those other old men to the rear of him. He cramped his great length down into a vacant seat in the daycoach, and there he sat, gazing straight ahead at nothing, as the train drew out of the station, bearing him to his two years at hard labor and these one-time comrades of his to their jubilating at the annual reunion.

As for the train, it went winding its leisurely and devious way down the branch line toward the Junction, stopping now and then at small country stations. The air that poured in through the open windows was sweet and heavy with Maytime odors of blossoming and blooming. In the tobacco patches the adolescent plants stood up, fresh and velvet-green. Mating red birds darted through every track-side tangle of underbrush and wove threads of living flame back and forth over every sluggish, yellow creek; and sparrowhawks teetered above the clearings, hunting early grasshoppers. Once in a while there was a small cotton-patch.

It was warm—almost as warm as a summer day. The two girls fanned themselves with their handkerchiefs and constantly brushed cinders off their starched blouses. Mrs. McLaurin, buttoned in to her rounded throat, sat bolt-upright, the better to keep wrinkles from marring the flawless fit of her regimentals. She suffered like a Christian martyr of old, smiling with a sweet content—as those same Christian martyrs are said to have suffered and smiled. Judge Priest, sitting one seat to the rear of her, with Major Covington alongside him, napped lightly with his head against the hot red plush of the seat-back. Sergeant Jimmy Bagby found the time fitting and the audience receptive to his celebrated and more than familiar story of what on a certain history-making occasion he heard General Breckinridge say to General Buckner, and what General Buckner said to General Breckinridge in reply.

In an hour or so they began to draw out of the lowlands fructifying in the sunlight, and in among the craggy foothills. Here the knobs stood up, like the knuckle-bones of a great rough hand laid across the peaceful countryside. "Deadenings" flashed by, with the girdled, bleached tree-trunks rising, deformed and gaunt, above the young corn. The purplish pink of the redbud trees was thick in clumps on the hillsides. The train entered a cut with a steep fill running down on one side and a seamed cliff standing close up on the other. Small saplings grew out of the crannies in the rocks and swung their boughs downward so that the leaves almost brushed the dusty tops of the coaches sliding by beneath them.

Suddenly, midway of this cut, there came a grinding and sliding of the wheels—the cars began creaking in all their joints as though they would rack apart; and, with a jerk which wakened Judge Priest and shook the others in their seats, the train halted. From up ahead somewhere, heard dimly through the escape of the freed steam, came a confusion of shouted cries. Could they be nearing the Junction so soon? Mrs. McLaurin felt in a new handbag—of gray broadcloth with a gold clasp, to match her uniform—for a powder-rag. Then she shrank cowering back in her place, for leaping briskly up the car steps there appeared, framed in the open doorway just beyond her, an armed man—a short, broad man in a flannel shirt and ragged overalls, with a dirty white handkerchief bound closely over the bridge of his nose and shielding the lower part of his face. A long-barreled pistol was in his right hand and a pair of darting, evilly disposed eyes looked into her startled ones from under the brim of a broken hat.

"Hands up, everybody!" he called out, and swung his gun right and left from his hip, so that its muzzle seemed to point all ways at once. "Hands up, everybody—and keep 'em up!"

Behind this man, back to back with him, was the figure of another man, somewhat taller, holding similar armed dominion over the astounded occupants of the day-coach. This much, and this much only, in a flash of time was seen by Uncle Zach Matthews and Judge Priest's Jeff, as, animated by a joint instantaneous impulse, they slid off their seat at the other end of the car and lay embraced on the floor, occupying a space you would not have believed could have contained one darky—let alone two. And it was seen more fully and at greater length by the gray veterans as their arms with one accord rose stiffly above the level of their heads; and also it was seen by the young matron, the sponsor and the maid of honor, as they huddled together, clinging to one another desperately for the poor comfort of close contact. Little Rita Covington, white and still, looked up with blazing gray eyes into the face of the short man with the pistol. She had the palms of both her hands pressed tightly against her ears. Rita was brave enough—but she hated the sound of firearms. Where she half knelt, half crouched, she was almost under the elbow of the intruder.

The whole thing was incredible—it was impossible! Train robberies had passed out of fashion years and years before. Here was this drowsing, quiet country lying just outside the windows, and the populous Junction only a handful of miles away; but, incredible or not, there stood the armed trampish menace in the doorway, shoulder to shoulder with an accomplice. And from outside and beyond there came added evidence to the unbelievable truth of it in the shape of hoarse, unintelligible commands rising above a mingling of pointless outcries and screams.

"Is this a joke, sir, or what?" demanded Major Covington, choking with an anger born of his own helplessness and the undignifiedness of his attitude.

"Old gent, if you think it's a joke jest let me ketch you lowerin' them arms of yourn," answered back the yeggman. His words sounded husky, coming muffled through the handkerchief; but there was a grim threat in them, and for just a breathless instant the pistol-barrel stopped wavering and centered dead upon the major's white-vested breast.

"Set right still, major," counseled Judge Priest at his side, not firing his eyes off the muffled face. "He's got the drop on us."

"But to surrender without a blow—and we all old soldiers too!" lamented Major Covington, yet making no move to lower his arms.

"I know—but set still," warned Judge Priest, his puckered glance taking toll sideways of his fellow travelers—all of them with chagrin, amazement and indignation writ large upon their faces, and all with arms up and palms opened outward like a calisthenic class of elderly gray beards frozen stiff and solid in the midst of some lung-expanding exercise. Any other time the picture would have been funny; but now it wasn't. And the hold-up man was giving his further orders.

"This ain't no joke and it ain't no time for foolin'. I gotter work fast and you all gotter keep still, or somebody'll git crippled up bad!"

With his free hand he pulled off his broken derby, revealing matted red hair, with a dirty bald spot in the front. He held the hat in front of him, crown down.

"I'm goin' to pass through this car," he announced, "and I want everybody to contribute freely. You gents will lower one hand at a time and git yore pokes and kettles—watches and wallets—out of yore clothes. And remember, no monkey business—no goin' back to yore hip pockets—unless you wanter git bored with this!" he warned; and he followed up the warning with a nasty word which borrowed an added nastiness coming through his rag mask.

His glance flashed to the right, taking in the quivering figures of the two girls and the young woman. "Loidies will contribute too," he added.

"Oh!" gasped Mrs. McLaurin miserably; and mechanically her right hand went across to protect the slender diamond bracelet on her left wrist; while tall Miss Lyon, crumpled and trembling, pressed herself still farther against the side of the car, and Rita Covington involuntarily clutched the front of her blouse, her fingers closing over the little chamois-skin bag that hung hidden there, suspended by a ribbon about her throat. Rita was an only daughter and a pampered one; her father was the wealthiest man in town and she owned handsomer jewels than an eighteen-year-old girl commonly possesses. The thief caught the meaning of those gestures and his red-rimmed eyes were greedy.

"You dog, you!" snorted old Doctor Lake; and he, like the major, sputtered in the impotence of his rage. "You're not going to rob these ladies too?"

"I'm a-goin' to rob these loidies too," mimicked the thief. "And you, old gent, you'd better cut out the rough talk." Without turning his head, and with his pistol making shifting fast plays to hold the car in subjection, he called back: "Slim, there's richer pickin' here than we expected. If you can leave them rubes come help me clean up."

"Just a second," was the answer from behind him, "till I git this bunch hypnotized good."

"Now then," called the red-haired man, swearing vilely to emphasize his meaning, "as I said before, cough up! Loidies first—you!" And he motioned with his pistol toward Mrs. McLaurin and poked his hat out at her. Her trembling fingers fumbled at the clasp of her bracelet a moment and the slim band fell flashing into the hat.

"You are no gentleman—so there!" quavered the unhappy lady, as a small, gemmed watch with a clasp, and a silver purse, followed the bracelet. Bessie Lyon shrank farther and farther away from him, with sobbing intakes of her breath. She was stricken mute and helpless with fear.

"Now then," the red-haired man was addressing Rita, "you next. Them purties you've got hid there inside yore shirt—I'll trouble you for them! Quick now!" he snarled, seeing that she hesitated. "Git 'em out!"

"I ca-n't," she faltered, and her cheeks reddened through their dead pallor; "my waist—buttons—behind. I can't and I won't."

The thief shifted his derby hat from his left hand to his right, holding it fast with his little finger hooked under the brim, while the other fingers kept the cocked revolver poised and ready.

"I'll help you," he said; and as the girl tried to dodge away from him he shoved a stubby finger under the collar of her blouse and with a hard jerk ripped the lace away, leaving her white neck half bare. At her cry and the sound of the tearing lace her father forgot the threat of the gunbarrel—forgot everything.

"You vile hound!" he panted. "Keep your filthy hand off of my daughter!" And up he came out of his seat. And old Judge Priest came with him, and both of them lunged forward over the seatback at the ruffian, three feet away.

So many things began to happen then, practically all simultaneously, that never were any of the active participants able to recall exactly just what did happen and the order of the happening. It stood out afterward, though, from a jumble of confused recollections, that young Mrs. McLaurin screamed and fainted; that Bessie Lyon fainted quietly without screaming; and that little Rita Covington neither fainted nor screamed, but snatched outward with a lightning quick slap of her hand at the fist of the thief which held the pistol, so that the bullet, exploding out of it with a jet of smoke, struck in the aisle instead of striking her father or Judge Priest. It was this bullet, the first and only one fired in the whole mix-up, that went slithering diagonally along the car floor, guttering out a hole like a worm-track in the wood and kicking up splinters right in the face of Unde Zach Matthews and Judge Priest's Jeff as they lay lapped in tight embrace, so that they instantly separated and rose, like a brace of flushed blackbirds, to the top of the seat in front. From that point of vantage, with eyes popped and showing white all the way round, they witnessed what followed in the attitude of quiveringly interested onlookers.

All in an instant they saw Major Covington and Judge Priest struggling awkwardly with the thief over the intervening seatback, pawing at him, trying to wrest his hot weapon away from him; saw Mrs. McLaurin's head roll back inertly; saw the other hold-up man pivot about to come to his bleaguered partner's aid; and saw, filling the doorway behind this second ruffian, the long shape of old man Press Harper, as he threw himself across the joined platforms upon their rear, noiseless as a snake and deadly as one, his lean old face set in a square shape of rage, his hot red hair erect on his head like a Shawnee's scalplock, his gaunt, long arms upraised and arched over and his big hands spread like grapples. And in that same second the whole aisle seemed filled with gray-coated, gray-haired old men, falling over each other and impeding each other's movements in their scrambling forward surge to take a hand in the fight.

To the end of their born days those two watching darkies had a story to tell that never lost its savor for teller or for audience—a story of how a lank, masked thief was taken by surprise from behind; was choked, crushed, beaten into instant helplessness before he had a chance to aim and fire; then was plucked backward, lifted high in the arms of a man twice his age and flung sidelong, his limbs flying like a whirligig as he rolled twenty feet down the steep slope to the foot of the fill. But this much was only the start of what Uncle Zach and Judge Priest's Jeff had to tell afterward.

For now, then, realizing that an attack was being made on his rear, the stockier thief broke Judge Priest's fumbling grip upon his gun-hand and half swung himself about to shoot the unseen foe, whoever it might be; but, as he jammed its muzzle into the stomach of the newcomer and pressed the trigger, the left hand of old Harper closed down fast upon the lock of the revolver, so that the hammer, coming down, only pinched viciously into his horny thumb. Breast to breast they wrestled in that narrow space at the head of the aisle for possession of the weapon. The handkerchief mask had fallen away, showing brutal jaws covered with a red stubble, and loose lips snarled away from the short stained teeth. The beleaguered robber, young, stocky and stout, cursed and mouthed blasphemies; but the old man was silent except for his snorted breathing and his frame was distended and swollen with a terrible Berserker lust of battle.

While Major Covington and Judge Priest and the foremost of the others got in one another's way and packed in a solid, heaving mass behind the pair, all shouting and all trying to help, but really not helping at all, the red ruffian, grunting with the fervor of the blow, drove his clenched fist into old Harper's face, ripping the skin on the high Indian cheekbone. The old man dealt no blows in return, but his right hand found a grip in the folds of flesh at the tramp's throat and the fingers closed down like iron clamps on his wind.

There is no telling how long a man of Harper's age and past habits might have maintained the crushing strength of that hold, even though rage had given him the vigor of bygone youth; but the red-stubbled man, gurgling and wriggling to be free, began to die of suffocation before the grip weakened. To save himself he let go of the gunbutt, and the gun fell and bounced out of sight under a seat. Bearing down with both hands and all his might and weight upon Harper's right wrist, he tore the other's clasp off his throat and staggered back, drawing the breath with sobbing sounds back into his bursting lungs. He would have got away then if he could, and he turned as though to flee the length of the car and escape by the rear door.

The way was barred, by whooping, panting old men, hornet-hot. Everybody took a hand or tried to. The color-bearer shoved the staff of the flag between his legs and half tripped him, and as he regained his feet Sergeant Jimmy Bagby, jumping on a seat to get at him over the bobbing heads of his comrades, dealt him a glancing, clumsy blow on the shoulder with the muzzle of his old musket. Major Covington and Judge Priest were still right on him, bearing their not inconsiderable bulk down upon his shoulders.

He could have fought a path through these hampering forces. Wrestling and striking out, he half shoved, half threw them aside; but there was no evading the gaunt old man who bore down on him from the other direction. The look on the face of the old warlock daunted him. He yelled just once, a wordless howl of fear and desperation, and the yell was smothered back into his throat as Harper coiled down on him like a python, fettering with his long arms the shorter, thicker arms of the thief, crushing his ribs in, smothering him, killing him with a frightful tightening pressure. Locked fast in Harper's embrace, he went down on his back underneath; and now—all this taking place much faster than it has taken me to write it or you to read it—the old man reared himself up. He put his booted foot squarely on the contorted face of the yeggman and twisted the heel brutally, like a man crushing a worm, and mashed the thief's face to pulp. Then he seized him by the collar of his shirt, dragged him like so much carrion back the length of the car, the others making a way for him, and, with a last mighty heave, tossed him off the rear platform and stood watching him as he flopped and rolled slackly down the steep grade of the right-of-way to the gully at the bottom.

All this young Jeff and Uncle Zach witnessed, and at the last they began cheering. As they cheered there was a whistle of the air and the cars began to move—slowly at first, with hard jerks on the couplings; and then smoother and faster as the wheels took hold on the rails', and the track-joints began to click-clack in regular rhythm. And, as the train slid away, those forward who mustered up the hardihood to peer out of the windows saw one man—a red-haired, half-bald one—wriggling feebly at the foot of the cut, and another one struggling to his feet uncertainly, meanwhile holding his hands to his stunned head; and, still farther along, a third, who fled nimbly up the bank and into the undergrowth beyond, without a backward glance. Seemingly, all told, there had been only three men concerned in the abortive holdup.

Throughout its short length the train sizzled with excitement and rang with the cries of some to go on and of others to go back and make prisoners of the two crippled yeggs; but the conductor, like a wise conductor, signaled the engineer to make all speed ahead, being glad enough to have saved his train and his passengers whole. On his way through to take an inventory of possible damage and to ascertain the cause of things, he was delayed in the day-coach by the necessity of calming a hysterical country woman, so he missed the best part of what was beginning to start in the decorated rear coach.

There Mrs. McLaurin and tall Miss Lyon were emerging from their fainting fits, and little Rita Covington, now that the danger was over and past, wept in a protecting crook of her father's arm. Judge Priest's Jeff was salvaging a big revolver, with one chamber fired, from under a seat. Eight or nine old men were surrounding old Press Harper, all talking at once, and all striving to pat him on the bade with clumsy, caressing slaps. And out on the rear platform, side by side, stood Sergeant Jimmy Bagby and Corporal Jake Smedley; the corporal was wildly waving his silk flag, now unfurled to show the blue St. Andrew's cross, white-starred on a red background, waving it first up and down and then back and forth with all the strength of his arms, until the silk square popped and whistled in the air of the rushing train; the sergeant was going through the motions of loading and aiming and firing his ancient rusted musket. And at each imaginary discharge both of them, in a cracked duet, cheered for Jefferson Davis and the Southern Confederacy!

Just about then the locomotive started whistling for the Junction; outlying sheds and shanties, a section house and a water-tank or so began to flitter by. At the first blast of the whistle all the lingering fire of battle and victory faded out of Harper's face and he sat down heavily in a seat, fumbling at the inner breast pocket of his coat. There was a bloody smear high up on his cheek and blood dripped from the ball of his split thumb.

"Boys, there's some fight left in us yet," exulted Captain Shelby Woodward, "and nobody knows it better than those two scoundrels back yonder! We all took a hand—we all did what we could; but it was you, Press—it was you that licked 'em both—single-handed! Boys," he roared, glancing about him, "won't this make a story for the reunion—and won't everybody there be making a fuss over old Press!" He stopped then—remembering.

"I don't go through with you," said old Press, steadily enough. "I git off here. You fellers are goin' on through—but I git off here to wait for the other train."

"You don't do no such of a thing!" broke in Judge Priest, his voice whanging like a bowstring. "Press Harper, you don't do no such of a thing. You give me them papers!" he demanded almost roughly. "You're goin' right on through to the reunion with the rest of us—that's where you're goin'. You set right where you are in this car, and let little Rita Covington wipe that there blood off your face and tie up that thumb of yours. Why, Press, we jest naturally couldn't get along without you at the reunion. Some of us are liable to celebrate a little too much and maybe git a mite overtaken, and we'll be needin' you to take care of us.

"You see, boys," the old judge went on, with a hitch in his voice, addressing than generally, "Press here is under a pledge to me not to touch another drop of licker till he begins servin' the sentence I imposed on him; and, boys, that means Press is goin" to be a temperance man for the balance of his days—if I know anything about the pardonin' power and the feelin's of the governor of this state!"

So, as the accommodation ran in to the Junction, where crowds were packed on the platform and pretty girls, dressed in white, with touches of red at throat and belt, waved handkerchiefs, and gimpy-legged old men in gray uniforms hobbled stiffly back and forth, and the local band blared out its own peculiar interpretation of My Old Kentucky Home, the tall old man with the gashed cheek sat in his seat, his face transfigured with a great light of joy and his throat muscles clicking with the sobs he was choking down, while little Rita Covington's fingers dabbed caressingly at his wound with a handkerchief dipped in ice water and a dozen old veterans jostled one another to shake his hand. And they hit him on the back with comradely blows—and maybe they did a little crying themselves. But Sergeant Jimmy Bagby and Corporal Jacob Smedley took no part in this. Out on the rear platform they still stood, side by side, waving the flag and firing the unfirable musket harder and faster than ever; and, as one waved and the other loaded and fired, they cheered together:

"'Rah for Jefferson Davis, the Southern Confederacy—and Pressley G. Harper!"

VII. STRATAGEM AND SPOILS

AS THE Daily Evening News, with pardonable enthusiasm, pointed out at the time, three events of practically national importance took place in town all in that one week. On Tuesday night at 9:37 there was a total eclipse of the moon, not generally visible throughout the United States; on Wednesday morning the Tri-State Steam and Hand Laundrymen's Association began a two-days annual convention at St. Clair Hall; and on Saturday at high noon Eastern capital, in the person of J. Hayden Witherbee, arrived.

And the greatest of these was Witherbee. The eclipse of the moon took place on its appointed schedule and was witnessed through opera glasses and triangular fragments of windowpane that had been smudged with candlesmoke. The Tri-State Laundrymen came and heard reports, elected officers, had a banquet at the Richland House and departed to their several homes. But J. Hayden Witherbee stayed on, occupying the bridal chamber at the hotel—the one with the private bath attached; and so much interest and speculation did his presence create, and so much space did the Daily Evening News give in its valued columns to his comings and goings and his sayings and doings, that the name of J. Hayden Witherbee speedily became, as you might say, a household word throughout the breadth and length of the Daily Evening News' circulation.

It seemed that J. Hayden Witherbee, sitting there in his lofty office building far away in Wall Street, New York, had had his keen eye upon the town for some time; and yet—such were the inscrutable methods of the man—the town hadn't known anything about it, hadn't even suspected it. However, he had been watching its growth with the deepest interest; and when, by the count of the last United States census, it jumped from seventh in population in the state to fifth he could no longer restrain himself. He got aboard the first train and came right on. He had, it would appear, acted with such promptness because, in his own mind, he had already decided that the town would make an ideal terminal point for his proposed Tobacco & Cotton States Interurban Trolley line, which would in time link together with twin bonds of throbbing steel—the words are those of the reporter for the Daily Evening News—no less-than twenty-two growing towns, ranging southward from the river. Hence his presence, exuding from every pore, as it were, the very essences of power and influence and money. The paper said he was one of the biggest men in Wall Street, a man whose operations had been always conducted upon the largest scale.

This, within the space of three or four months, had been our second experience of physical contact with Eastern capital. The first one, though, had been in the nature of a disappointment. A man named Betts—Henry Betts—had come down from somewhere in the North and, for a lump sum, had bought outright the city gasworks. It was not such a big lump sum, because the gasworks had been built right after the war and had thereafter remained untouched by the stimulating hand of improvement. They consisted in the main of a crumbly little brick engine house, full of antiquated and self-willed machinery, and just below it, on the riverbank, a round and rusted gas tank, surrounded by sloping beds of coal cinders, through which at times sluggish rivulets of molten coal tar percolated like lava on the flanks of a toy volcano. The mains took in only the old part of town—not the new part; and the quality of illumination furnished was so flickery at all seasons and so given to freezing up in winter that many subscribers, including even the leading families, used coal-oil lamps in their bedchambers until the electric power house was built. A stock company of exceedingly conservative business men had owned the gasworks prior to the advent of Henry Betts, and the general manager of the plant had been Cassius Poindexter, a fellow townsman. Cash Poindexter was a man who, in his day, had tried his 'prentice hand at many things. At one time he traveled about in a democrat wagon, taking orders for enlarging crayon portraits from photographs and tintypes, and also for the frames to accompany the same.

At a more remote period he had been the authorized agent, on commission, for a lightning-rod company, selling rods with genuine guaranteed platinum tips; and rusty iron stringers, with forked tails, which still adhered to outlying farm buildings here and there in the county, testified to his activities in this regard. Again, Cash Poindexter had held the patent rights in four counties for an improved cream separator. In the early stages of the vogue for Belgian-hare culture in this country he was the first to import a family group of these interesting animals into our section. He had sold insurance of various sorts, including life, fire and cyclone; he was a notary public; he had tried real estate, and he had once enjoyed the distinction of having read lawbooks and works on medicine simultaneously. But in these, his later years, he had settled down more or less and had become general manager of the gasworks, which position also included the keeping of the books, the reading of meters and the making out and collecting of the monthly accounts. Nevertheless, he was understood to be working at spare moments on an invention that would make him independently wealthy for life. He was a tall, thin, sad man, with long, drooping aide whiskers; and he was continually combing back his side whiskers with both hands caressingly, and this gave him the appearance of a man parting a pair of string portières and getting ready to walk through them, but never doing so.

When this Mr. Betts came down from the North and bought the gasworks it was the general expectation that he would extensively overhaul and enlarge the plant; but he did nothing of the sort, seeming, on the contrary, to be amply satisfied with things as they were. He installed himself as general manager, retained Cash Poindexter as his assistant, and kept right on with the two Kettler boys as his engineers and the two darkies, Ed Greer and Lark Tilghman, as his firemen. He was a man who violated all traditions and ideals concerning how Northern capitalists ought to look. He neither wore a white piqué vest nor smoked long, black cigars; in fact, he didn't smoke at all. He was a short, square, iron-gray person, with a sort of dead and fossilized eye. He looked as though he might have been rough-hewn originally from one of those soapstone days which grow the harder with age and exposure. He had a hard, exact way of talking, and he wore a hard, exact suit of clothes which varied not, weekdays or Sundays, in texture or in cut.

Back Home

In short, Mr. Henry Betts, the pioneer Eastern investor in those parts, was a profound disappointment as to personality and performances. Not so with J. Hayden Witherbee. From his Persian-lamb lapels to his patent-leather tips he was the physical embodiment of all the town had learned to expect of a visiting Wall Street capitalist. And he liked the town—that was plain. He spoke enthusiastically of the enterprise which animated it; he referred frequently and with praise to the awakening of the New South, and he was even moved to compliment publicly the cooking at the Richland House. It was felt that a stranger and a visitor could go no further.

Also, he moved fast, J. Hayden Witherbee did, showing the snap and push so characteristic of the ruling spirits of the great moneymarts of the East. Before he had been in town a week he had opened negotiations for the purchase outright of the new Light and Power Company, explaining frankly that if he could come to terms he intended making it a part of his projected interurban railway. Would the present owners care to sell at a fair valuation?—that was what Mr. Witherbee desired to know.

Would a drowning man grasp at a life-preserver? Would a famished colt welcome the return of its maternal parent at eventide? Would the present owners, carrying on their galled backs an unprofitable burden which local pride had forced upon them—would they sell? Here, as manna sent from Heaven by way of Wall Street, as you might say, was a man who would buy from them a property which had never paid and which might never pay; and who, besides, meant to do something noble and big for the town. Would they sell? Ask them something hard!

There was a series of conferences—if two conferences can be said to constitute a series—one in Mr. Witherbee's room at the hotel, where cigars of an unknown name but an impressive bigness were passed round freely; and one in the office of the president of the Planters' National Bank. Things went well and swimmingly from the first; Mr. J. Hayden Witherbee had a most clear and definite way of putting things; and yet, with all that, he was the embodiment of cordiality and courtesy. So charmed was Doctor Lake with his manner that he asked him, right in the midst of vital negotiations, if he were not of Southern descent; and when he confessed that his mother's people had come from Virginia Doctor Lake said he had felt it from the first moment they met, and insisted on shaking hands with Mr. Witherbee again.

"Gentlemen," said Mr. Witherbee—this was said at the first meeting, the one in his room—"as I have already told you, I need this town as a terminal for my interurban road and I need your plant. I expect, of course, to enlarge it and to modernize it right up to the minute; but, so far as it goes, it is a very good plant and I want it. I suggest that you gentlemen, constituting the directors and the majority stockholders, get together between now and tomorrow—this evening, say—and put a price on the property. Tomorrow I will meet you again, here in this hotel or at any point you may select; and if the price you fix seems fair, and the papers prove satisfactory to my lawyers, I know of no reason why we cannot make a trade. Gentlemen, good day. Take another cigar all round before leaving."

They went apart and confabbed industriously—old Major Covington, who was the president of the Light and Power Company Doctor Lake and Captain Woodward, the two heaviest stockholders, Colonel Courtney Cope, the attorney for the company and likewise a director, and sundry others. Between themselves, being meanwhile filled with sweet and soothing thoughts, they named a price that would let them out whole, with a margin of interest on the original venture, and yet one which, everything considered—the growing population, the new suburbs and all that—was a decent enough price. They expected to be hammered down a few thousand and were prepared to concede something; but it would seem that the big men of the East did not do business in that huckstering, cheese-trimming way. Time to them was evidently worth more than the money to be got by long chaffering over a proposition.

75

Back Home

"Gentlemen," J. Hayden Witherbee had said right off, "the figures seem reasonable and moderate. I think I will buy from you." A warm glow visibly lit up the faces of those who sat with him. It was as though J. Hayden Witherbee was an open fireplace and threw off a pleasant heat.

"I will take over these properties," repeated Mr. J. Hayden Witherbee; "but on one condition—I also want the ownership of your local gasworks."

There was a little pause and the glow died down a trifle—just the merest trifle. "But, sir, we do not own those gasworks," said the stately Major Covington.

"I know that," said Mr. Witherbee; "but the point is—can't you acquire them?"

"I suppose we might," said the major; "but, Mr. Witherbee, that gasworks concern is worn out—our electric-light plant has nearly put it out of business."

"I understand all that too," Mr. Witherbee went on, "perfectly well. Gentlemen, where I come from we act quickly, but we look before we leap. During the past twenty-four hours I have examined into the franchise of those gasworks. I find that nearly forty years ago your common council issued to the original promoters and owners of the gas company a ninety-year charter, giving the use of any and all of your streets, not only for the laying of gas mains, but for practically all other purposes. It was an unwise thing to do, but it was done and it stands to today. Gentlemen, this is a growing community in the midst of a rich country. I violate no confidence in telling you that capital is looking this way. I am merely the forerunner—the first in the field. The Gatins crowd, in Chicago, has its eyes upon this territory, as I have reason to know. You are, of course, acquainted with the Gatins crowd?" he said in a tone of putting a question.

Major Covington, who made a point of never admitting that he didn't know everything, nodded gravely and murmured the name over to himself as though he were trying to remember Gatins' initials. The others sat silent, impressed more than ever with the wisdom of this stranger who had so many pertinent facts at his finger tips.

"Suppose now," went on Mr. Witherbee—"suppose, now, that Ike Gratins and his crowd should come down here and find out what I have found out and should buy out that gas company. Why, gentlemen, under the terms of that old franchise, those people could actually lay tracks right through the streets of this little city of yours. They could parallel our lines—they could give us active opposition right here on the home ground. It might mean a hard fight. Therefore I need those gasworks. I may shut them up or I may run them—but I need them in my business.

"I have inquired into the ownership of this concern," continued Mr. Witherbee before any one could interrupt him, "and I find it was recently purchased outright by a gentleman from somewhere up my way named—named—" He snapped his fingers impatiently.

"Named Betts," supplied Doctor Lake—"named Henry Betts."

"Quite so," Mr. Witherbee assented. "Thank you, doctor—Betts is the name. Now the fact that the whole property is vested in one man simplifies the matter—doesn't it? Of course I would not care to go to this Mr. Betts in person. You understand that." If they didn't understand they let on they did, merely nodding and waiting for more light to be let in.

"Once let it be known that I was personally interested in a consolidation of your lighting plants, and this Mr. Betts, if I know anything about human nature, would advance his valuation far beyond its proper figure. Therefore I cannot afford to be known in the matter. You see that?"

They agreed that they saw.

"So I would suggest that all of you—or some of you—go and call upon Mr. Betts and endeavor to buy the gasworks from him outright. If you can get the plant for anything like its real value you may include the amount in the terms of the proposition you have today made me and I will take over all of the properties together.

"However, remember this, gentlemen—there is need of haste. Within forty-eight hours I should be in Memphis, where I am to confer with certain of my associates—Eastern men like myself, but who, unlike me, are keeping under cover—to confer with them concerning our rights-of-way through the cotton-raising country. I repeat, then, that there is pressing need for immediate action. May I offer you gentlemen fresh cigars?" and he reached for a well-stuffed, silver-mounted case of dull leather.

But they were already going—going in a body to see Mr. Henry Betts, late of somewhere up North. Mr. J. Hayden Witherbee's haste, great though it might be, could be no greater than theirs. On their way down Market Street to the gashouse it was decided that, unless the exigencies of the situation demanded a chorus of argument, Major Covington should do the talking. Indeed it was Major Covington who suggested this. Talking, with financial subjects at the back of the talk, was one of the things at which the major fancied himself a success.

Mr. Betts sat in the clutter of his small, untidy office like an elderly and reserved gray rat in a paper nest behind a wainscoting. His feet, in square-toed congress gaiters, rested on the fender of a stove that was almost small enough to be an inkstand, and his shoulders were jammed back against a window-ledge. By merely turning his head he commanded a view of his entire property, with the engine house in the near distance and the round tunlike belly of the gas tank rising just beyond it. He was alone.

As it happened, he knew all of his callers, having met them in the way of business—which was the only way he ever met anybody. To each man entering he vouchsafed the same greeting—namely, "How-do?"—spoken without emotion and mechanically.

Major Covington had intended to shake hands with Mr. Betts, but something about Mr. Betts' manner made him change his mind. He cleared his throat impressively; the major did nearly everything impressively.

"A fine day, sir," said the major.

Mr. Betts turned his head slightly to the left and peered out through a smudged pane as if seeking visual confirmation of the statement before committing himself. A look seemed to satisfy him.

"It is," he agreed, and waited, boring his company with his geologic gaze.

"Ahem!" sparred Major Covington—"think I will take a chair."

As Mr. Betts said nothing to this, either one way or the other, the major took a chair, it being the only chair in sight, with the exception of the chair in which Mr. Betts was slumped down and from which Mr. Betts had not stirred. Doctor Lake perched himself upon a bookkeeper's tall stool that wabbled precariously. Three other anxious local capitalists stood where they could find room, which was on the far side of the stove.

"Very seasonable weather indeed," ventured the old major, still fencing for his start.

"So you remarked before, I believe," said Mr. Betts dryly. "Did you wish to see me on business?"

Inwardly 'the major was remarking to himself how astonishing it was that one section of the country—to wit, the North—could produce men of such widely differing types as this man and the man whose delightful presence they had just quitted; could produce a gentleman like J. Hayden Witherbee, with whom it was a positive pleasure to discuss affairs of moment, and a dour, sour, flinty person like this Betts, who was lacking absolutely in the smaller refinements that should govern intercourse between gentlemen—and wasn't willing to learn them either. Outwardly the major, visibly flustered, was saying: "Yes—in a measure. Yes, we came on a matter of business." He pulled up somewhat lamely. Really the man's attitude was almost forbidding. It verged on the sinister.

"What was the business?" pressed Mr. Betts in a colorless and entirely disinterested tone of voice.

"Well, sir," said Major Covington stiffly, and his rising temper and his sense of discretion were now wrestling together inside of him—"well, sir, to be brief and to put it in as few words as possible, which from your manner and conversation I take to be your desire, I—we—my associates here and myself—have called in to say that we are interested naturally in the development of our little city and its resources and its industries; and with these objects in view we have felt, and, in fact, we have agreed among ourselves, that we would like to enter into negotiations with you, if possible, touching, so to speak, on the transfer to us of the property which you control here. Or, in other words, we—"

"Do you mean you want to buy these gasworks?"

"Yes," confessed the major; "that—that is it. We would like to buy these gasworks."

"Immediately!" blurted out Doctor Lake, teetering on his high perch. The major shot a chiding glance at his compatriot. Mr. Betts looked over the top of the stove at the major, and then beyond him at the doctor, and then beyond the doctor at the others. Then he looked out of the window again.

"They are not for sale," he stated; and his voice indicated that he regarded the subject as being totally exhausted.

"Yes, quite so; I see," said Major Covington suavely; "but if we could agree on a price now—a price that would be satisfactory to you—and to us—"

"We couldn't agree on a price," said Mr. Betts, apparently studying something in connection with the bulging side of the gas tank without, "because there isn't any price to agree on. I bought these gasworks and I own them, and I am satisfied to go on owning them. Therefore they are not for sale. Did you have any other business with me?"

There was something almost insulting in the way this man rolled his r's when he said "therefore." Checking an inclination to speak on the part of Doctor Lake the major controlled himself with an effort and said:

"Nevertheless, we would appreciate it very much, sir, if you could and would go so far as to put a figure—any reasonable figure—on this property.. We would like very much to get an expression from you—a suggestion—or—or—something of that general nature," he tailed off.

"Very well," said Mr. Betts, biting the words off short and square, "very well. I will What you want to know is my price for these gasworks?"

"Exactly so," said the major, brightening up.

"Very well," repeated Mr. Betts. "Sixty thousand."

Doctor Lake gave such a violent start that he lost his hat out of his lap. Captain Woodward's jaw dropped.

"Sixty thousand!" echoed Major Covington blankly. "Sixty thousand what?"

"Sixty thousand dollars," said Mr. Betts, "in cash."

Major Covington fairly sputtered surprise and chagrin.

"But, Mr. Betts, sir," he protested, "I happen to know that less than four months ago you paid only about twenty-seven thousand dollars for this entire business!"

"Twenty-six thousand five hundred, to be exact," corrected Mr. Betts.

Back Home

"And since that time you have not added a dollar's worth of improvement to it," added the dismayed major.

"Not one cent—let alone a dollar," assented this most remarkable man.

"But surely you don't expect us to pay such a price as that?" pleaded tie major.

"I do not," said Mr. Betts.

"We couldn't think of paying such a price as that."

"I don't expect you to," said Mr. Betts. "I didn't ask you to. As I said before, these gasworks are not for sale. They suit me just as they are. They are not on the market; but you insist that I shall name a price and I name it—sixty thousand in cash. Take it or leave it."

Having concluded this, for him, unusually long speech, Mr. Betts brought his fingertips together with great mathematical exactness, matching each finger and each thumb against its fellow as though they were all parts of a sum in addition that he was doing. With his fingers added up to his satisfaction and the total found correct, he again turned his gaze out of the smudgy window. This time it was something on the extreme top of the gas tank which seemed to engage his attention. Cassius Poindexter opened the street door and started in; but at the sight of so much company he checked himself on the threshold, combed back his side whiskers nervously, bowed dumbly and withdrew, closing the door softly behind him.

"If we could only reach some reasonable basis of figuring now," said the major, addressing Mr. Betts' left ear and the back of Mr. Betts' head—"say, forty thousand, now?" Mr. Betts squinted his Stone Age eyes the better to see out of the dirty window.

"Or even forty-five?" supplemented Doctor Lake, unable to hold in any longer. "Why, damn it, sir, forty-five thousand is a fabulous price to pay for this junkpile."

"Sixty thousand—in cash!" The ultimatum seemed to issue from the rear of Mr. Betts' collar.

Major Covington glanced about him, taking toll of the expressions of his associates. On their faces sorrowful capitulation was replacing chagrin. He nodded toward them and together they nodded back sadly.

"How much did you say you wanted down?" gulped the major weakly.

"All down," announced Mr. Betts in a tone of finality; "all in cash. Those are my terms."

"But it isn't regular!" babbled Colonel Cope.

"It isn't regular for a man to sell something he doesn't want to sell either," gulped Mr. Betts. "I bought for cash and I sell for cash. I never do business any other way."

"How much time will you give us?" asked the major. The surrender was complete and unconditional.

"Until this time tomorrow," said Mr. Betts; "then the deal is off." Doctor Lake slid off his stool, or else he fell off. At any rate, he descended from it hurriedly. His face was very red.

"Well, of all the—" he began; but the major and the colonel had him by the arms and were dragging him outside. When they were gone—all of them—Mr. Betts indulged himself in the luxury of a still, small smile—a smile that curled his lips back just a trifle and died of frostbite before it reached his fossilized eyes.

"Gentlemen," Mr. Witherbee was saying in his room at the Richland House ten minutes later, "the man has you at his mercy and apparently he knows it. I wouldn't be surprised if he had not already been in communication with the Gatins crowd. His attitude is suspicious. As I view it, it is most certainly suspicious. Gentlemen, I would advise you to close with him. He is asking a figure far in excess of the real value of the works—but what can you do?"

"And will you take the gasworks at sixty thousand?" inquired Major Covington hopefully.

"Ah, gentlemen," said Mr. Witherbee, and his smile was sympathetic and all-embracing, "that, I think, is asking too much; but, in view of the circumstances, I will do this—I will take them at"—he paused to consider—"I will take them, gentlemen, at fifty thousand. In time I think I can make them worth that much to me; but fifty thousand is as far as I can go—positively. You stand to lose ten thousand on your deal for the gasworks, but I presume you will make that back and more on your sale to me of the light and power plant. Can't I offer you fresh cigars, gentlemen?"

If for any reason a run had started on any one of the three local banks the next day there would have been the devil and all to pay, because there was mighty little ready money in any one of them. Their vaults had been scraped clean of currency; and that currency, in a compact bundle, was rapidly traveling eastward in the company of a smallish iron-gray man answering to the name of Betts. At about the same moment Mr. Witherbee, with the assistance of the darky porter of the Richland House, was packing his wardrobe into an ornate traveling kit. As he packed he explained to Doctor Lake and Major Covington:

"I am called to Memphis twenty-four hours sooner than I had expected. Tomorrow we close a deal there involving, I should say, half a million dollars. Let us see—this is Wednesday—isn't it? I will return here on Friday morning. Meanwhile you may have the papers drawn by your attorney and ready for submission to my lawyer, Mr. Sharkey, who should arrive tomorrow from Cincinnati. If he finds them all shipshape, as I have every reason to expect he will find them, then, on Friday morning, gentlemen, we will sign up and I will pay the binder, amounting to—how much?—ninety thousand, I believe, was the figure we agreed upon. Quite so. Gentlemen, you will find a box of my favorite cigars on that bureau yonder. Help yourselves."

No lawyer named Sharkey arrived from Cincinnati on Thursday; no J. Hayden Witherbee returned from Memphis on Friday,—nor was there word from him by wire or mail. The papers, drawn in Colonel Cope's best legal style, all fringed and trimmed with whereases and wherefores, waited—and waited. Telegrams which Major Covington sent to Memphis remained unanswered; in fact, undelivered. Major Covington suddenly developed a cold and sinking sensation at the pit of his stomach. In his associates he discerned signs of the same chilling manifestation. It seemed to occur to all of them at once that nobody had asked J. Hayden Witherbee for his credentials or had inquired into his antecedents. Glamoured by the grandeur of his person, they had gone along with him—had gone along until now blindly. Saturday, hour by hour, darkling suspicion grew in each mind and reared itself like a totem pole adorned with snake-headed, hawk-clawed figments of dread. And on Saturday, for the first time in a solid week the Daily Evening News carried no front-page account of the latest doings and sayings of J. Hayden Witherbee.

Upon a distracted conference, taking place Saturday night in the directors' room of the bank, intruded the sad figure of Cassius Poindexter, combing back his side whiskers like a man eternally on the point of parting a pair of lace curtains and never coming through them.

"Excuse me," he said, "but I've got something to say that I think you gentlemen oughter hear. If you thought those two—Witherbones, or whatever his name is, and my late employer, Henry Betts—if you all thought those two were strangers to one another you were mistaken—that's all. Two weeks ago I saw a letter on Betts' desk signed by this man

Witherbee—if that's his name. And Tuesday when Betts told me he was goin' to sell out, I remembered it."

The major was the first to get his voice back; and it was shaky with rage and—other emotions.

"You—you saw us all there Tuesday morning," he shouted, "didn't you? And when Betts told you he was going to sell and you remembered about Witherbee why didn't you have sense enough to put two and two together?"

"I did have sense enough to put two and two together," answered Cassius Poindexter in hurt tones. "That's exactly what I did."

"Then why in the name of Heaven didn't you come to us—to me—and tell us?" demanded the major.

"Well, sirs," said the intruder, "I was figurin' on doin' that very thing, but it sort of slipped out of my mind. You see, I've been thinkin' right stiddy lately about an invention that I'm workin' on at odd times—I'm perfectin' a non-refillble bottle," he explained—"and somehow or other this here other matter plum' escaped me."

The door closed upon the inventor. Stunned into silence, they sat mute for a long, ghastly half minute. Doctor Lake was the first to speak:

"If could afford it," he said softly—"if at present I could afford it I'd put a dynamite bomb under that gashouse and blow it up! And I'd do it anyhow," he went on, warming to his theme, "if I was only right certain of blowing up that idiot and his non-refillable bottle along with it!"

Malley, of the Sun, was doing the hotel run this night. He came up to the room clerk's wicket at the desk of the Royal.

"Say, Mac," he hailed, "what's the prospect? So far, all I've got is one rubber magnate from South America—a haughty hidalgo with an Irish name and a New England accent, who was willing to slip me a half-column interview providing I'd run in the name of his company eight or nine times—him, and an Oklahoma Congressman, with the makings of a bun, and one of Sandusky, Ohio's well-known and popular merchant princes, with a line of talk touching on the business revival in the Middle West. If that's not slim pickings I don't want a cent! Say, help an honest working lad out—can't you?"

This appeal moved the room clerk.

"Let's see now," he said, and ran a highly polished fingernail down a long column of names. Halfway down the finger halted.

"Here's copy for you, maybe," he said. "The name is Priest—William Pitman Priest is the way he wrote it. He got in here this morning, an old-time Southerner; and already he's got every coon bellhop round the place fighting for a chance to wait on him. He's the real thing all right, I guess—looks it and talks it too. You ought to be able to have some fun with him."

"Where's he registered from?" asked Malley hopefully.

"From Kentucky—that's all; just Kentucky, with no town given," said Mac, grinning.

"There're still a few of those old Southerners left that'll register from a whole state at large. Why, there he goes now!" said the room clerk, and he pointed.

Across the lobby, making slow headway against weaving tides of darting, hurrying figures, was moving a stoutish and elderly form clad in a fashion that made it look doubly and trebly strange among those marble and onyx precincts. A soft black hat of undoubted age and much shapelessness was jammed down upon the head, and from beneath its wide brim at the rear escaped wisps of thin white hair that curled over the upturned coat collar. The face the hat shaded was round and pink, chubby almost, and ended in a white chin beard which, as Malley subsequently said in his story, flowed down its owner's chest like a point-lace jabot. There was an ancient caped overcoat of a pattern that had been fashionable perhaps twenty years ago and would be fashionable again, no doubt, twenty years hence; there were gray trousers that had never been pressed apparently; and, to finish off with, there was a pair of box-toed, high-heeled boots of a kind now seen mostly in faded full-length photographs of gentlemen taken in the late seventies—boots with wrinkled tops that showed for four inches or more and shined clear up to the trouser-line with some sort of blacking that put a dull bluish iridescent blush upon the leather, almost like the colors on a dove's breast feathers.

"Thanks for the tip, Mac," said Malley, and he made off after the old man, who by now had turned and was maneuvering down the corridor toward where a revolving door turned unceasingly, like a wheel in a squirrel's cage. "Oh, colonel!" called out Malley on a venture, jibing through the human currents and trying to overtake the stout, broad figure ahead of him. An exceedingly young, exceedingly important person, who looked as though he might be prominent in the national guard or on some governor's staff, half rose from a leather lounge and glanced about inquiringly, but the old man in the cape and boots kept on.

"Major!" tried Malley vainly. "Major! Just a minute, please." And then, "Judge! Oh, judge!" he called as a last resort, and at that his quarry swung about on his heels and stopped, eying him with whimsical, mild blue eyes under wrinkly lids.

"Son," he said in a high, whiny voice which instantly appealed to Malley's sense of the picturesque, "was it me that you've been yellin' at?"

Malley answered, telling his name and his business. A moment later he was surprised to find himself shaking hands warmly with the older man.

"Malley, did you say?" the judge was inquiring almost eagerly. "Well, now, son, I'm glad to meet up with you. Malley is a fairly familiar name and a highly honored one down in our part of the country. There was a captain in Forrest's command of your name—Captain Malley—a mighty gallant soldier and a splendid gentleman! You put me right sharply in mind of him too—seem to favor him considerable round the eyes. Are you closely related to the Southern branch of the family, suh?"

Malley caught himself wishing that he could say Yes. The old judge showed almost a personal disappointment when Malley confessed that none of his kinspeople, so far as he knew, ever resided south of Scranton, Pennsylvania.

"No doubt a distant connection," amended the judge, as though consoling both himself and Malley; "the family resemblance is there shorely." He laid a pudgy pink hand on Malley's arm. "You'll pardon me for presumin' on such short acquaintance, but down where I come from it is customary, when two gentlemen meet up together at about this hour of the evenin'"—it was then three o'clock p.m., Eastern time, as Malley noted—"it is customary for them to take a dram. Will you join me?"

Scenting his story, Malley fell into step by the old judge's side; but at the door of the café the judge halted him.

"Son," he said confidentially, "I like this tavern mightily—all but the grocery here. I must admit that I don't much care for the bottled goods they're carryin' in stock. I sampled 'em and I didn't enthuse over 'em. They are doubtless excellent for cookin' purposes, but as beverages they sort of fall short.

"I wish you'd go up to my chamber with me and give me the benefit of your best judgment on a small vial of liquor I brought with me in my valise. It's an eighteen-year-old sour mash, mellowed in the wood, and I feel that I can recommend it to your no doubt dis-criminatin' palate. Will you give me the pleasure of your company, suh?"

As Malley, smiling to himself, went with the judge, it struck him with emphasis that, for a newly arrived transient, this old man seemed to have an astonishingly wide

Back Home

acquaintance among the house staff of the Hotel Royal. A page-boy, all buttons and self-importance, sidestepped them, smiling and ducking at the old judge's nod; and the elevator attendant, a little, middle-aged Irishman, showed unalloyed pleasure when the judge, after blinking slightly and catching his breath as the car started upward with a dart like a scared swallow, inquired whether he'd had any more news yet of the little girl who was in the hospital. Plainly the old judge and the elevator man had already been exchanging domestic confidences.

Into his small room on the seventeenth floor Judge Priest ushered the reporter with the air of one dispensing the hospitalities of a private establishment to an honored guest, made him rest his hat and overcoat—"rest" was the word the judge used—and sit down in the easiest chair and make himself comfortable.

In response to a conversation which the judge had over the telephone with some young person of the feminine gender, whom he insisted on addressing as Miss Exchange, there presently came knocking at the door a grinning negro boy bearing the cracked ice, the lump sugar and the glasses the old judge had ordered. Him the judge addressed direct.

"Look here," asked the judge, looking up from where he was rummaging out a flat quart flask from the depths of an ancient and much-seamed valise, "ain't you the same boy that I was talkin' to this mornin'?"

"Yas, suh," said the boy, snickering, "Horace."

"Where you came from they didn't call you Horace, did they?" inquired the old man.

"Naw, suh, that they didn't," admitted Horace, showing all his teeth except the extremely rearmost ones.

"What was it they called you—Smoke or Rabbit?"

"Ginger," owned up Horace delightedly, and vanished, still snickering. Malley noticed that the coin which the old man had extracted from the depths of a deep pocket and tossed to the darky was a much smaller coin than guests in a big New York hotel customarily bestowed upon bellhoys for such services as this; yet Horace had accepted it with every outward evidence of a deep and abiding satisfaction.

With infinite pains and a manner almost reverential, as though he were handling sacred vessels, the old judge compiled two dark reddish portions which he denominated toddies. Malley, sipping his, found it to be a most smooth and tasty mixture. And as he sipped, the old judge, smiling blandly, bestowed himself in a chair, which he widely overflowed, and balancing his own drink on the chair arm he crossed his booted feet and was ready, he said, to hear what his young friend might have to say.

As it turned out, Malley didn't have much to say, except to put the questions by which a skilled reporter leads on the man he wants to talk. And the old judge was willing enough to talk. It was his first visit to New York; he had come reluctantly, at the behest of certain friends, upon business of a more or less private nature; he had taken a walk and a ride already; he had seen a stretch of Broadway and some of Fifth Avenue, and he was full of impressions and observations that tickled Malley clear down to the core of his reportorial soul.

So Malley, like the wise newspaper man he was, threw away his notes on the Brazilian rubber magnate and the merchant prince of Sandusky; and at dark he went back to the office and wrote the story of old Judge Priest, of Kentucky, for a full column and a quarter. Boss Clark, the night city editor, saw the humor value of the story before he had run through the first paragraph; and he played it up hard on the second page of the Sun, with a regular Sun head over it.

It was by way of being a dull time of news in New York. None of the wealthiest families was marrying or giving in marriage; more remarkable still, none of them was divorcing or giving in divorce. No subway scandal was emerging drippingly from the bowels of the earth; no aviator was descending abruptly from aloft with a dull and lethal thud. Malley's story, with the personality of the old judge deftly set forward as a foil for his homely simplicity and small-town philosophy, arched across the purview of divers saddened city editors like a rainbow spanning a leadish sky. The craft, in the vernacular of the craft, saw the story and went to it. Inside of twenty-four hours Judge Priest, of Kentucky, was Broadway's reigning favorite, for publicity purposes anyhow. The free advertising he got could not have been measured in dollars and cents if a prima donna had been getting it.

The judge kept open house all that next day in his room at the Hotel Royal, receiving regular and special members of various city staffs. Margaret Movine, the star lady writer of the Evening Journal, had a full-page interview, in which the judge, using the Southern accent as it is spoken in New York exclusively, was made to discuss, among other things, the suffragette movement, women smoking in public, Fifth Avenue, hobble skirts, Morgan's raid, and the iniquity of putting sugar in corn bread. The dialect was the talented Miss Margaret Movine's, but the thoughts and the words were the judge's, faithfully set forth. The Times gave him a set of jingles on its editorial page and the Evening Mail followed up with a couple of humorous paragraphs; but it was the Sunday World that scored heaviest.

McCartwell, of the Sunday, went up and secured from the judge his own private recipe for mint juleps—a recipe which the judge said had been in his family for three generations—and he thought possibly longer, it having been brought over the mountains and through the Gap from Virginia by a grandsire who didn't bring much of anything else of great value; and the World, printing this recipe and using it as a starter, conducted through its correspondents southward a telegraphic symposium of mint-julep recipes. Private John Allen, of Mississippi; Colonel Bill Sterritt, of Texas; Marse Henry Watterson and General Simon Bolivar Buckner, of Kentucky; Senator Bob Taylor, of Tennessee, and others, contributed. A dispute at once arose in the South concerning the relative merits oi mint bruised and mint crushed. An old gentleman in Virginia wrote an indignant letter to the Richmond Times-Dispatch—he said it should be bruised only— and a personal misunderstanding between two veteran members oi the Pendennis Club, of Louisville, was with difficulty averted by bystanders. For the American, Tom Powers drew a cartoon showing the old judge, with a julep in his hand, marching through the Prohibition belt of the South, accompanied by a procession of jubilant Joys, while hordes of disconcerted Glooms fled ahead oi them across the map.

In short, for the better part of a week Judge Priest was a celebrity, holding the limelight to the virtual exclusion of grand opera stars, favorite sons, white hopes, debutantes and contributing editors of the Outlook Magazine. And on the fourth day the judge, sitting in the privacy of his chamber and contemplating his sudden prominence, had an idea—and this idea was the answer to a question he had been asking himself many times since he left home. He spent half an hour and seventy cents telephoning to various newspaper offices. When finally he hung up the receiver and wriggled into his caped overcoat a benevolent smile illumined his broad, pink face. The smile still lingered there as he climbed into a cab at the curb and gave the driver a certain Wall Street address, which was the address ci one J. Hayden Witherbee.

J. Hayden Witherbee, composing the firm of Witherbee & Company, bankers, had a cozy flytrap or office suite in one of the tallest and most ornate of the office buildings or spider-webs in the downtown financial district. This location was but a natural one, seeing that Mr. J. Hayden Witherbee's interests were widely scattered and diversified, including as they did the formation and construction—on paper and with paper—of trolley lines; the floating of various enterprises, which floated the more easily by reason of the fact that water was their native element; and the sale of what are known in the West as holes in the ground and in the East as permanent mining investments. He rode to and from business in a splendid touring car trained to stop automatically at at least three cafés on the way up town of an evening; and he had in his employ a competent staff, including a grayish gentle-man of a grim and stolid aspect, named Betts.

Being a man of affairs, and many of them, Mr. Witherbee had but small time for general newspaper reading, save and except only the market quotations, the baseball scores in season and the notices of new shows for tired business men, though keeping a weather eye ever out for stories touching on the pernicious activities of the Federal Grand Jury, with its indictments and summonses and warrants, and of the United States Post-Office Department, with its nasty habit of issuing fraud orders and tying up valuable personal mail. Nevertheless, on a certain wintry afternoon about two o'clock or half-past two, when his office boy brought to him a small card, engraved—no, not engraved; printed—smudgily printed with the name of William Pitman Priest and the general address of Kentucky, the sight of the card seemed to awaken within him certain amusing stories which had lately fallen under his attention in the printed columns; and, since he never overlooked any bets—even the small ones—he told the boy to show the gentleman in.

The reader, I take it, being already acquainted with the widely varying conversational characteristics of Judge Priest and Mr. J. Hayden Witherbee, it would be but a waste of space and time for me to undertake to describe in detail the manner of their meeting on this occasion. Suffice it to say that the judge was shown into Mr. J. Hayden Witherbee's private office; that he introduced himself, shook hands with Mr. Witherbee, and in response to an invitation took a seat; after which he complimented Mr. Witherbee upon the luxury and good taste of his surroundings, and remarked that it was seasonable weather, considering the Northern climate and the time of the year. And then, being requested to state the nature of his business, he told Mr. Witherbee he had called in the hope of interesting him in an industrial property located in the South. It was at this juncture that Mr. Witherbee pressed a large, dark cigar upon his visitor.

"Yes," said Mr. Witherbee, "we have been operating somewhat extensively in the South of late, and we are always on the lookout for desirable properties of almost any character. Er—where is this particular property you speak of located and what is its nature?"

When Judge Priest named the town Mr. Witherbee gave a perceptible start, and when Judge Priest followed up this disclosure by stating that the property in question was a gasworks plant which he, holding power of attorney and full authority to act, desired to sell to Mr. Witherbee, complete with equipment, accounts, franchise and good will, Mr. Witherbee showed a degree of heat and excitement entirely out of keeping with the calmness and deliberation of Judge Priest's remarks. He asked Judge Priest what he—the judge—took him—Witherbee—for anyhow? Judge Priest, still speaking slowly and choosing his words with care, then told him—and that only seemed to add to Mr. Witherbee's state of warmth. However, Judge Priest drawled right on.

"Yes, suh," he continued placidly, "accordin' to the best of my knowledge and belief, you are in the business of buyin' and sellin' such things as gasworks, and so I've come to you to sell you this here one. You have personal knowledge of the plant, I believe, havin' been on the ground recently."

"Say," demanded Mr. Witherbee with a forced grin—a grin that would have reminded you of a man drawing a knife—"say, what do you think you're trying to slip over on me?

I did go to your measly little one-horse town and I spent more than a week there; and I did look over your broken-down little old gashouse, and I concluded that I didn't want it; and then I came away. That's the kind of a man I am—when I'm through with a thing I'm through with it! Huh! What would I do with those gasworks if I bought 'em?"

"That, suh, is a most pertinent point," said Judge Priest, "and I'm glad you brought it up early. In case, after buyin' this property, you do not seem to care greatly for it, I am empowered to buy it back from you at a suitable figure. For example, I am willin' to sell it to you for sixty thousand dollars; and then, providin' you should want to sell it back to me, I stand prepared to take it off your hands at twenty-six thousand five hundred. I name those figures, suh, because those are the figures that were lately employed in connection with the proposition."

"Blackmail—huh!" sneered Mr. Witherbee. "Cheap blackmail and nothing else. Well, I took you for a doddering old pappy guy; but you're a bigger rube even than I thought. Now you get out of here before you get thrown out—see?"

"Now there you go, son—fixin' to lose your temper already," counseled the old judge reprovingly.

But Mr. Witherbee had already lost it—completely lost it. He jumped up from his desk as though contemplating acts of violence upon the limbs and body of the broad, stoutish old man sitting in front of him; but he sheered off. Though old Judge Priest's lips kept right on smiling, his eyelids puckered down into a disconcerting little squint; and between them little menacing blue gleams flickered. Anyway, personal brawls, even in the sanctity of one's office, were very bad form and sometimes led to that publicity which is so distasteful to one engaged in large private enterprises. Mr. Witherbee had known the truth of this when his name had been Watkins and when it had been the Bland. Brothers' Investment Company, limited; and he knew it now when he was Witherbee & Company. So, as aforesaid, he sheered off. Retreating to his desk, he felt for a button. A buzzer whirred dimly in the wall like a rattlesnake's tail. An officeboy poked his head in instantly.

"Herman," ordered Mr. Witherbee, trembling with his passion, "you go down to the superintendent's office and tell him to send a special building officer here to me right away!"

The boy's head vanished, and Mr. Witherbee swung back again on the judge, wagging a threatening forefinger at him.

"Do you know what I'm going to do?" he asked. "Well, I'll tell you what I'm going to do—I'm going to have you chucked out of here bodily—that's what!"

But he couldn't keep the quaver out of the threat. Somehow he was developing a growing fear of this imperturbable old man.

"Now, son," said Judge Priest, who hadn't moved, "I wouldn't do that if I was you. It might not be so healthy for you."

"Oh, you needn't be trying any of your cheap Southern gunplays round here," warned Mr. Witherbee; but, in spite of his best efforts at control, his voice rose quivering at the suggestion.

"Bless your heart, son!" said the judge soothingly, "I wouldn't think of usin' a gun on you any more'n I'd think of takin' a Winchester rifle to kill one of these here cockroaches! Son," he said, rising now for the first time, "you come along here with me a minute—I want to show you something you ain't seen yet."

He walked to the door and opened it part way. Witherbee, wondering and apprehensive, followed him and looked over the old judge's shoulder into the anteroom.

Back Home

For J. Hayden Witherbee, one quick glance was enough. Four—no, five—five alert-looking young men, all plainly marked with the signs of a craft abhorrent to Mr. Witherbee, sat in a row of chairs beyond a railing; and beyond them was a sixth person, a young woman with a tiptilted nose and a pair of inquisitive, expectant gray eyes. Mr. Witherbee would have known them anywhere by their backs—jackals of the press, muckrakers, sworn enemies to Mr. Witherbee and all his kith and kind!

It was Mr. Witherbee who slammed the door shut, drawing Judge Priest back into the shelter of the closed room; and it was Mr. Witherbee who made inquiry, tremulously, almost humbly:

"What does this mean? What are these people doing there? What game is this?" He sputtered out the words, one question overlapping the next.

"Son," said Judge Priest, "you seem flustered. Ca'm yourself. This is no game as I know of. These are merely friends of mine—representatives of the daily press of your city."

"But how did they come to be here?"

"Oh!" said the judge. "Why, I tele-phoned 'em. I telephoned 'em that I was comin' down here on a matter of business, and that maybe there might be a sort of an item for them if they'd come too. I've been makin' what they call copy for them, and we're all mighty sociable and friendly; and so they came right along. To tell you the truth, we all arrived practically together. You see, if I was sort of shoved out of here against my will and maybe mussed up a little those boys and that there young lady there—her name Is Miss Margaret Movine—they'd be sure to put pieces in their papers about it; and if it should come out incidentally that the cause of the row was a certain gasworks transaction, in a certain town down in Kentucky, they'd probably print that too. Why, those young fellows would print anything almost if I wanted them to. You'd be surprised!

"Yes, suh, you'd be surprised to see how much they'd print for me," he went on, tapping J. Hayden Witherbee upon his agitated chest with a blunt forefinger. "I'll bet you they'd go into the full details."

As Mr. Witherbee listened, Mr. Witherbee perspired freely. At this very moment there were certain transactions pending throughout the country—he had a telegram in his desk now from Betts, sent from a small town in Alabama—and newspaper publicity of an unpleasant and intimate nature might be fatal in the extreme. Mr. Witherbee had a mind trained to act quickly.

"Wait a minute!" he said, mopping his brow and wetting his lips, they being the only dry things about him. "Wait a minute, please. If we could settle this—this matter—just between ourselves, quietly—and peaceably—-there wouldn't be anything to print—would there?"

"As I understand the ethics of your Eastern journalism, there wouldn't be anything to print," said Judge Priest. "The price of them gasworks, accordin' to the latest quotations, was sixty thousand—but liable to advance without notice."

"And what—what did you say you'd buy 'em back at?"

"Twenty-six thousand five hundred was the last price," said the judge, "but subject to further shrinkage almost any minute."

"I'll trade," said Mr. Witherbee.

"Much obliged to you, son," said Judge Priest gratefully, and he began fumbling in his breast pocket. "I've got the papers all made out."

Mr. Witherbee regained his desk and reached for a checkbook just as the officeboy poked his head in again.

"Special officer's cornin' right away, sir," he said.

"Tell him to go away and keep away," snarled the flurried Mr. Witherbee; "and you keep that door shut—tight! Shall I make the check out to you?" he asked the judge.

"Well, now, I wouldn't care to bother with checks," said the judge. "All the recent transactions involvin' this here gashouse property was by the medium of the common currency of the country, and I wouldn't care to undertake on my own responsibility to interfere with a system that has worked heretofore with such satisfaction. I'll take the difference in cash—if you don't mind."

"But I can't raise that much cash now," whined Witherbee. "I haven't that much in my safe. I doubt if I could get it at my bank on such short notice."

"I know of a larger sum bein' gathered together in a much smaller community than this—oncet!" said the judge reminiscently. "I would suggest that you try."

"I'll try," said Mr. Witherbee desperately. "I'll send out for it—on second thought, I guess I can raise it."

"I'll wait," said the judge; and he took his seat again, but immediately got up and started for the door. "I'll ask the boys and Miss Margaret Movine to wait too," he explained. "You see, I'm leavin' for my home tomorrow and we're all goin' to have a little farewell blowout together tonight."

Upon Malley, who in confidence had heard enough from the judge to put two and two together and guess something of the rest, there was beginning to dawn a conviction that behind Judge William Pitman Priest's dovelike simplicity there lurked some part of the wisdom that has been commonly attributed to the serpent of old. His reporter's instinct sensed out a good story in it, too, but his pleadings with the old judge to stay over for one more day, anyhow, were not altogether based on a professional foundation. They were in large part personal.

Judge Priest, caressing a certificate of deposit in a New York bank doing a large Southern business, insisted that he had to go. So Malley went with him to the ferry and together they stood on the deck of the ferryboat, saying good-by. For the twentieth time Malley was promising the old man that in the spring he would surely come to Kentucky and visit him. And at the time he meant it.

In front of them as they faced the shore loomed up the tall buildings, rising jaggedly like long dog teeth in Manhattan's lower jaw. There were pennons of white steam curling from their eaves. The Judge's puckered eyes took in the picture, from the crowded streets below to the wintry blue sky above, where mackerel-shaped white clouds drifted by, all aiming the same way, like a school of silver fish.

"Son," he was saying, "I don't know when I've enjoyed anything more than this here little visit, and I'm beholden to you boys for a lot. It's been pleasant and it's been profitable, and I'm proud that I met up with all of you."

"When will you be coming back, judge?" asked Malley.

"Well, that I don't know," admitted the old judge. "You see, son, I'm gettin' on in years, considerably; and it's sort of a hard trip from away down where I live plum' up here to New York. As a matter of fact," he went on, "this was the third time in my life that I started for this section of the country. The first time I started was with General Albert Sidney Johnston and a lot of others; but, owin' to meetin' up with your General Grant at a place called Pittsburg Landing by your people and Shiloh by ours, we sort of altered our plans. Later on I started again, bein' then temporarily in the company of General John Morgan, of my own state; and that time we got as far as the southern part of the state of Ohio before we run into certain insurmountable obstacles; but this time I managed to git through. I was forty-odd years doin' it—but I done it! And, son," he called out as the ferryboat began to quiver and Malley stepped ashore, "I don't mind tellin' you in strict confidence that while the third Confederate invasion of the North was a long time gittin' under way, it proved a most complete success in every particular when it did. Give my best reguards to Miss Margaret Movine."

VIII. THE MOB FROM MASSAC

YOU might call it a tragedy—this thing that came to pass down in our country here a few years back. For that was exactly what it was—a tragedy, and in its way a big one. Yet at the time nobody thought of calling it by any name at all. It was just one of those shifts that are inevitably bound to occur in the local politics of a county or a district; and when it did come, and was through and over with, most people accepted it as a matter of course.

There were some, however, it left jarred and dazed and bewildered—yes, and helpless too; men too old to readjust their altered fortunes to their altered conditions even if they had the spirit to try, which they hadn't. Take old Major J. Q. A. Pickett now. Attaching himself firmly to a certain spot at the far end of Sherrill's bar, with one leg hooked up over the brass bar-rail—a leg providentially foreshortened by a Minie ball at Shiloh, as if for that very purpose—the major expeditiously drank himself to death in a little less than four years, which was an exceedingly short time for the job, seeing he had always been a most hale and hearty old person, though grown a bit gnarly and skewed with the coming on of age. The major had been county clerk ever since Reconstruction; he was a gentleman and a scholar and could quote Latin and Sir Walter Scott's poetry by the running yard. Toward the last he quoted them with hiccups and a stutter.

Also there was Captain Andy J. Redcliffe, who was sheriff three terms handrunning and, before that, chief of police. Going out of office he went into the livery-stable business; but he didn't seem to make much headway against the Farrell Brothers, who 'owned the other livery stable and were younger men and spry and alert to get trade. He spent a few months sitting at the front door of his yawning, half-empty stables, nursing a grudge against nearly everything and plaintively garrulous on the subject of the ingratitude of republics in general and this republic in particular; and presently he sickened of one of those mysterious diseases that seem to attack elderly men of a full habit of life and to rob them of their health without denuding them of their flesh. His fat sagged on his bones in unwholesome, bloated folds and he wallowed unsteadily when he walked. One morning one of his stable hands found him dead in his office, and the Gideon K. Irons Camp turned out and gave him a comrade's funeral, with full military honors.

Also there were two or three others, including ex-County Treasurer Whitford, who shot himself through the head when a busy and conscientious successor found in his accounts a seeming shortage of four hundred and eighty dollars, which afterward turned out to be more a mistake in bookkeeping than anything else. Yet these men—all of them—might have seen what was coming had they watched. The storm that wrecked them was a long time making up—four years before it had threatened them.

There had grown up a younger generation of men who complained—and perhaps they had reason for the complaint—that they did nearly all the work of organizing and campaigning and furnished most of the votes to carry the elections, while a close combine of aging, fussy, autocratic old men held all the good county offices and fatted themselves on the spoils of county politics. These mutterings of discontent found shape in a sort of semi-organized revolt against the county ring, as the young fellows took to calling it, and for the county primary they made up a strong ticket among themselves—a ticket that included two smart young lawyers who could talk on their feet, and a popular young farmer for sheriff, and a live young harnessmaker as a representative of union labor, which was beginning to be a recognized force in the community with the coming of the two big tanneries. They made a hard fight of it, too, campaigning at every fork in the big road and every country store and blacksmith shop, and spouting arguments and oratory like so many inspired human spigots. Their elderly opponents took things easier. They rode about in top buggies and democrat wagons from barbecue to rally and from rally to schoolhouse meeting, steadfastly refusing the challenges of the younger men for a series of joint debates and contenting themselves with talking over old days with fading, grizzled men of their own generation. These elders, in turn, talked with their sons and sons-in-law and their nephews and neighbors; and so, when the primaries came, the young men's ticket stood beaten—but not by any big margin. It was close enough to be very close.

"Well, they've licked us this time!" said Dabney Prentiss, who afterward went to Congress from the district and made a brilliant record there. Dabney Prentiss had been the younger element's candidate for circuit-court judge against old Judge Priest. "They've licked us and the Lord only knows how they did it. Here we thought we had 'em out-organized, outgeneraled and outnumbered. All they did was to go out in the back districts and beat the bushes, and out crawled a lot of old men that everybody else thought were dead twenty years ago. I think they must hide under logs in the woods and only come out to vote. But, fellows"—he was addressing some of his companions in disappointment—"but, fellows, we can afford to wait and they can't. The day is going to come when it'll take something more than shaking an empty sleeve or waving a crippled old leg to carry an election in this county. Young men keep growing up all the time, but all that old men can do is to die off. Four years from now we'll win sure!" The four years went by, creakingly slow of passage to some and rolling fast to others; and in the summer of the fourth year another campaign started up and grew hot and hotter to match the weather, which was blazing hot. The August drought came, an arid and a blistering visitation. Except at dusk and at dawn the birds quit singing and hung about in the thick treetops, silent and nervous, with their bills agape and their throat feathers panting up and down. The roasting ears burned to death on the stalk and the wide fodder blades slowly cooked from sappy greenness to a brittle dead brown. The clods in the cornrows wore dry as powder and gave no nourishment for growing, ripening things. The dust powdered the blackberry vines until they lost their original color altogether, and at the roadside the medicinal mullein drooped its wilted long leaves, like lolling tongues that were all furred and roiled, as though the mullein suffered from the very fevers that its steeped juices are presumed to cure. At its full the moon shone hot and red, with two rings round it; and the two rings always used to mean water in our country—two rings for drinking water at the hotel, and for rainwater two rings round the moon—but week after week no rain fell and the face of the earth just seemed to dry up and blow away. Yet the campaign neither lost its edge nor abated any of its fervor by reason of the weather. Politics was the chief diversion and the main excitement in our county in those days—and still is.

One morning near the end of the month a dust-covered man on a sorely spent horse galloped in from Massac Creek, down in the far edge of the county; and when he had changed horses at Farrell Brothers' and started back again there went with him the sheriff, both of his deputies and two of the town policemen, the sheriff taking with him in his buckboard a pair of preternaturally grave dogs of a reddish-brown aspect, with long, drooping ears, and long, sad, stupid faces and eyes like the chief mourners' at a funeral. They were bloodhounds, imported at some cost from a kennel in Tennessee and reputed to be marvelously wise in the tracking down of criminals. By the time the posse was a mile away and headed for Massac a story had spread through the town that made men grit their teeth and sent certain armed and mounted volunteers hurrying out to join the manhunt.

Late that same afternoon a team of blown horses, wet as though they had wallowed in the river and drawing a top buggy, panted up to the little red-brick jail, which stood on the county square alongside the old wooden white courthouse, and halted there. Two men—a constable and a deputy sheriff—sat back under the overhanging top of the buggy, and between them something small was crushed, huddled down on the seat and almost hidden by their broad figures. They were both yellowed with the dust of a hard drive. It lay on their shoulders like powdered sulphur and was gummed to their eyelashes, so that when they batted their eyelids to clear their sight it gave them a grotesque, clownish look. They climbed laboriously out and stretched their limbs.

The constable hurried stiffly up the short gravel path to the jail and rapped on the door and called out something. The deputy sheriff reached in under the buggy top and hauled out a little negro, skinny and slight and seemingly not over eighteen years old. He hauled him out as though he was handling a sack of grits, and the negro came out like a sack of grits and fell upon his face on the pavement, almost between the buggy wheels. His wrists were held together by a pair of iron handcuffs heavy enough to fetter a bear, and for further precaution his legs had been hobbled with a plowline, and his arms were tied back with another length of the plowline that passed through his elbows and was knotted behind. The deputy stooped, took a grip on the rope across the prisoner's back and heaved him up to his feet. He was ragged, barefooted and bareheaded and his face was covered with a streaky clayish-yellow caking, where the sweat had run down and wetted the dust layers. Through this muddy mask his pop-eyes stared with a dulled animal terror.

Thus yanked upright the little negro swayed on his feet, shrinking up his shoulders and lurching in his tethers. Then his glazed stare fell on the barred windows and the hooded door of the jail, and he realized where he had been brought and hurried toward it as toward a welcome haven, stretching his legs as far as the ropes sawing on his naked ankles would let him. Willing as he was, however, he collapsed altogether as he reached the door and lay on his face kinking and twisting up in his bonds like a stricken thing. The deputy and the constable dragged him up roughly, one lifting him by his arm bindings and the other by the ropes on his legs, and they pitched him in flat on the floor of the little jail office. He wriggled himself under a table and lay there, sniffling out his fear and relief. His tongue hung out of his mouth like the tongue of a tied calf, and he panted with choky, slobbering sounds.

The deputy sheriff and the constable left him lying and went to a water bucket in the corner and drank down brimming dippers, turn and turn about, as though their thirst was unslakable. It was Dink Bynum, the deputy jailer, who had admitted them and in the absence of his superior he was in charge solely. He waited until the two had lowered the water line in the cedar bucket by a matter of inches.

"Purty quick work, boys," he said professionally, "if this is the right nigger."

"I guess there ain't much doubt about him bein' the right one," said the constable, whose name was Quarles. "Is there, Gus?" he added.

"No doubt at all in my mind," said the deputy. He wiped his mouth on his sleeve, which smeared the dust across his face in a sort of pattern.

"How'd you fellers come to git him?" asked Bynum.

Back Home

"Well," said the deputy, "we got out to the Hampton place about dinner time I reckin it was. Every man along the creek and every boy that was big enough to tote a gun was out scourin' the woods and there wasn't nobody round the place exceptin' a passel of the womenfolks. Just over the fence where the nigger was s'posed to have crossed we found his old wool hat layin' right where he'd run out from under it and we let the dogs smell of it, and inside of five minutes they'd picked up a trail and was openin' out on it. It was monstrous hot going through them thick bottoms afoot, and me and Quarles here outrun the sheriff and the others. Four miles back of Florence Station, and not more'n a mile from the river, we found this nigger treed up a hackberry with the dogs bayin' under him. I figure he'd been hidin' out in the woods all night and was makin' for the river, aimin' to cross, when the dogs fetched up behind him and made him take to a tree."

"Did you carry him back for the girl to see?"

"No," said the deputy sheriff. "Me and Quarles we talked it over after we'd got him down and had him roped up. In the first place she wasn't in no condition to take a look at him, and besides we knewed that them Massac people jest natchelly wouldn't listen to nothin' oncet they laid eyes on him. They'd 'a' tore him apart bodily."

The bound figure on the floor began moaning in a steady, dead monotone, with his lips against the planking.

"So, bein' as me and Quarles wanted the credit for bringin' him in, not to mention the reward," went on the deputy, without a glance at the moaning negro, "we decided not to take no chances. I kept him out of sight until Quarles could go over to the river and borrow a rig, and we driv in with him by the lower road, acrost the iron bridge, without goin' anywhere near Massac."

"What does the nigger say for himself?" asked Bynum, greedy for all the details.

"Huh!" said the deputy. "He's been too scared to say much of anything. Says he'd tramped up here from below the state line and was makin' for Ballard County, lookin' for a job of work. He's a strange nigger all right. And he as good as admits he was right near the Hampton place yistiddy evenin' at milkin' time, when the girl was laywaid, and says he only run because the dogs took out after him and scared him. But here he is. We've done our duty and delivered him, and now if the boys out yonder on Massac want to come in and take him out that's their lookout and yourn, Dink."

"I reckon you ain't made no mistake," said Bynum. Cursing softly under his breath he walked over and spurned the prisoner with his heavy foot. The negro writhed under the pressure like a crushed insect. The under jailer looked down at him with a curious tautening of his heavy features.

"The papers call 'em burly black brutes," he said, "and I never seen one of 'em yit that was more'n twenty years old or run over a hundred and thirty pound." He raised his voice: "Jim—oh, Jim!"

An inner door of sheet-iron opened with a suspicious instantaneousness, and in the opening appeared a black jail trusty, a confirmed chicken thief. He ducked his head in turn toward each of the white men, carefully keeping his uneasy gaze away from the little negro lying between the table legs in the corner.

"Yas, suh, boss—right here, suh," said the trusty.

"Here, Jim"—the deputy jailer was opening his pocketknife and passing it over—"take and cut them ropes off that nigger's arms and laigs."

With a ludicrous alacrity the trusty obeyed.

"Now pull him up on his feet!" commanded Bynum. "I guess we might as well leave them cuffs on him—eh?" he said to the deputy sheriff. The deputy nodded. Bynum took down from a peg over the jailer's desk a ring bearing many jingling keys of handwrought iron. "Bring him in here, Jim," he bade the trusty.

He stepped through the inner door and the negro Jim followed him, steering the manacled little negro. Quarles, the constable, and the deputy sheriff tagged behind to see their catch properly caged. They went along a short corridor, filled with a stifling, baked heat and heavy with the smell of penned-up creatures. There were faces at the barred doors of the cells that lined one side of this corridor—all black or yellow faces except one white one; and from these cells came no sound at all as the three white men and the two negroes passed. Only the lone white prisoner spoke out.

"Who is he, Dink?" he called eagerly. "What's he done?"

"Shut up!" ordered his keeper briefly, and that was the only answer he made. At the far end of the passage Bynum turned a key in a creaky lock and threw back the barred door of an inner cell, sheathed with iron and lacking a window. The trusty shoved in the little handcuffed negro and the negro groveled on the wooden floor upon all fours. Bynum locked the door and the three white men tramped back through the silent corridor, followed by the sets of white eyes that stared out unwinkingly at them through the iron-latticed grills. It was significant that from the time of the arrival at the jail not one of the whites had laid his hands actually upon the prisoner. "Well, boys," said Bynum to the others by way of a farewell, "there he is and there he'll stay—unless than Massac Creek folks come and git him. You've done your sworn duty and I've done mine. I locked him up and I won't be responsible for what happens now. I know this much—I ain't goin' to git myself crippled up savin' that nigger. If a mob wants to come let 'em come on!"

No mob came from Massac that night or the next night either; and on the second day there was a big basket picnic and rally under a brush arbor at the Shady Grove schoolhouse—the biggest meeting of the whole campaign it was to be, with speaking, and the silver cornet band out from town to make music, and the oldest living Democrat in the county sitting on the platform, and all that. Braving the piled-on layers of heat that rode the parched country like witch-hags half the town went to Shady Grove. Nearly everybody went that could travel. All the morning wagons and buggies were clattering out of town, headed toward the west. And in the cooking dead calm of the midafternoon the mob from Massac came.

They came by roundabout ways, avoiding those main traveled roads over which the crowds were gathering in toward the common focus of the Shady Grove schoolhouse; and coming so, on horseback by twos and threes, and leaving their horses in a thicket half a mile out, they were able to reach the edge of the town unnoticed and unsuspected. The rest, their leader figured, would be easy. A mistake in judgment by the town fathers in an earlier day had put the public square near the northern boundary, and the town, instead of growing up to it, grew away from it in the opposite direction, so that the square stood well beyond the thickly settled district.

All things had worked out well for their purpose. The sheriff and the jailer, both candidates for renomination, were at Shady Grove, and the sheriff had all his deputies with him, electioneering for their own jobs and his. Legal Row, the little street of lawyers' offices back of the square, might have been a byroad in old Pompeii for all the life that showed along its short and simmering length. No idlers lay under the water maples and the red oaks in the square. The jail baked in the sunlight, silent as a brick tomb, which indeed it somewhat resembled; and on the wide portico of the courthouse a loafer dog of remote hound antecedents alternately napped and roused to snap at the buzzing flies. The door of the clerk's office stood agape and through the opening came musty, snuffy smells of old leather and dry-rotted deeds. The wide hallway that ran from end to end of the old building was empty and echoed like a cave to the frequent thump of the loafer dog's leg joints upon the planking.

Back Home

Indeed, the whole place had but a single occupant. In his office back of the circuit-court room Judge Priest was asleep, tilted back in a swivel chair, with his short, plump legs propped on a table and his pudgy hands locked across his stomach, which gently rose and fell with his breathing. His straw hat was on the table, and in a corner leaned his inevitable traveling companion in summer weather—a vast and cavernous umbrella of a pattern that is probably obsolete now, an unkempt old drab slattern of an umbrella with a cracked wooden handle and a crippled rib that dangled away from its fellows as though shamed by its afflicted state. The campaigning had been hard on the old judge. The Monday before, at a rally at Temple's Mills, he had fainted, and this day he hadn't felt equal to going to Shady Grove. Instead he had come to his office alter dinner to write some letters and had fallen asleep. He slept on for an hour, a picture of pink and cherubic old age, with little headings of sweat popping out thickly on his high bald head and a gentle little snoring sound, of first a drone and then a whistle, pouring steadily from his pursed lips.

Outside a dry-fly rasped the brooding silence up and down with its fret-saw refrain. In the open spaces the little heat waves danced like so many stress marks, accenting the warmth and giving emphasis to it; and far down the street, which ran past the courthouse and the jail and melted into a country road so imperceptibly that none knew exactly where the street left off and the road began, there appeared a straggling, irregular company of men marching, their shapes more than half hid in a dust column of their own raising. The Massac men were coming.

I believe there is a popular conception to the effect that an oncoming mob invariably utters a certain indescribable, sinister, muttering sound that is peculiar to mobs. For all I know that may be true of some mobs, but certain it was that this mob gave vent to no such sounds. This mob came on steadily, making no more noise than any similar group of seventy-five or eighty men tramping over a dusty road might be expected to make.

For the most part they were silent and barren of speech. One youngish man kept repeating to himself a set phrase as he marched along. This phrase never varied in word or expression. It was: "Goin' to git that nigger! Goin' to git that nigger!"—that was all—said over and over again in a dull, steady monotone. By its constant reiteration he was working himself up, just as a rat-terrier may be worked up by constant hissed references to purely imaginary rats.

Their number was obscured by the dust their feet lifted. It was as if each man at every step crushed with his toe a puffball that discharged its powdery particles upward into his face. Some of them carried arms openly—shotguns and rifles. The others showed no weapons, but had them. It seemed that every fourth man, nearly, had coiled upon his arm or swung over his shoulder a rope taken from a plow or a well-bucket. They had enough rope to hang ten men or a dozen—yes, with stinting, to hang twenty. One man labored under the weight of a three-gallon can of coal-oil, so heavy that he had to shift it frequently from one tired arm to the other. In that weather the added burden made the sour sweat run down in streaks, furrowing the grime on his face. The Massac Creek blacksmith had a sledge-hammer over his shoulder and was in the front rank. Not one was masked or carried his face averted. Nearly all were grown men and not one was under twenty. A certain definite purpose showed in their gait. It showed, also, in the way they closed up and became a more compact formation as they came within sight of the trees fringing the square.

Down through the drowsing town edge they stepped, giving alarm only to the chickens that scratched languidly where scrub-oaks cast a skimpy shade across the road; but as they reached the town line they passed a clutter of negro cabins clustering about a little doggery. A negro woman stepped to a door and saw them. Distractedly, fluttering like a hen, she ran into the bare, grassless yard, setting up a hysterical outcry. A negro man came quickly from the cabin, clapped his hand over her mouth and dragged her back inside, slamming the door to behind him with a kick of his bare foot. Unseen hands shut the other cabin doors and the woman's half-smothered cries came dimly through the clapboarded wall; but a slim black darky darted southward from the doggery, worming his way under a broken, snaggled fence and keeping the straggling line of houses and stables between him and the marchers. This fleeing figure was Jeff, Judge Priest's negro bodyservant, who had a most amazing faculty for always being wherever things happened.

Jeff was short and slim and he could run fast. He ran fast now, snatching off his hat and carrying it in his hand—the surest of all signs that a negro is traveling at his top gait. A good eighth of a mile in advance of the mob, he shot in at the back door of the courthouse and flung himself into his employer's room.

"Jedge! Jedge!" he panted tensely. "Jedge Priest, please, suh, wake up—the mobbers is comin'!"

Judge Priest came out of his nap with a jerk that uprighted him in his chair.

"What's that, boy?"

"The w'ite folks is conin' after that there little nigger over in the jail. I outrun 'em to git yere and tell you, suh."

"Ah-hah!" said Judge Priest, which was what Judge Priest generally said first of all when something struck him forcibly. He reared himself up briskly and reached for his hat and umbrella.

"Which way are they comin' from?" he asked as he made for the hall and the front door.

"Comin' down the planin'-mill road into Jefferson Street," explained Jeff, gasping out the words.

As the old judge, with Jeff in his wake, emerged from the shadows of the tall hallway into the blinding glare of the portico they met Dink Bynum, the deputy jailer, just diving in. Dink was shirtsleeved. His face was curiously checkered with red-and-white blotches. He cast a backward glance, bumped into the judge's greater bulk and caromed off, snatching at the air to recover himself.

"Are you desertin' your post, Dink?" demanded the judge.

"Jedge, there wasn't no manner of use in my stayin'," babbled Bynum. "I'm all alone and there's a whole big crowd of 'em comin' yonder. There'll git that nigger anyhow—and he deserves it!" he burst out.

"Dink Bynum, where are the keys to that jail?" said Judge Priest, speaking unusually fast for him.

"I clean forgot 'em!" he quavered. "I left 'em hangin' in the jail office."

"And also I note you left the outside door of the jail standin' wide open," said the judge, glancing to the left. "Where's your pistol?"

"In my pocket—in my pocket, here."

"Git it out!"

"Jedge Priest, I wouldn't dare make no resistance single-handed—I got a family—I—" faltered the unhappy deputy jailer.

The moving dustcloud, with legs and arms showing through its swirling front, was no more than a hundred yards away. You could make out details—hot, red, resolute faces; the glint of the sun on a gunbarrel; the polished nose of the blacksmith's sledge; the round curve of a greasy oilcan.

"Dink Bynum," said Judge Priest, "git that gun out and give it to me—quick!"

"Jedge, listen to reason!" begged Bynum. "You're candidate yourse'f. Sentiment is aginst that nigger—strong. You'll hurt your own chances if you interfere."

The judge didn't answer. His eyes were on the dustcloud and his hand was extended. His pudgy fingers closed round the heavy handful of blued steel that Dink Bynum passed over and he shoved it out of sight. Laboring heavily down the steps he opened his umbrella and put it over his shoulder, and as he waddled down the short gravel path his shadow had the grotesque semblance of a big crawling land terrapin following him. One look Judge Priest sent over his shoulder. Dink Bynum and Jeff had both vanished. Except for the men from Massac there was no living being to be seen.

They didn't see him, either, until they were right upon him. He came out across the narrow sidewalk of the square and halted directly in their path, with his right hand raised and his umbrella tilted far back, so that its shade cut across the top of his straw hat, making a distinct line.

"Boys," he said familiarly, almost paternally—"Boys, I want to have a word with you."

Most of the Massac men knew him—some of them knew him very well. They had served on juries under him; he had eaten Sunday dinners under their rooftrees. They stopped, the rear rows crowding up closer until they were a solid mass facing him. Beyond him they could see the outer door of the jail gaping hospitably and the sight gave an edge to their purpose that was like the gnawing of physical hunger. Above all things they were sharp-set to hurry forward the thing they had it in their minds to do.

"Boys," said the judge, "most of you are friends of mine—and I want to tell you something. You mustn't do the thing you're purposin' to do—you mustn't do it!"

A snorted outburst, as of incredulity, came from the sweating clump of countrymen confronting him.

"The hell we mustn't!" drawled one of them derisively, and a snicker started.

The snicker grew to a laugh—a laugh with a thread of grim menace in it, and a tinge of mounting man-hysteria. Even to these men, whose eyes were used to resting on ungainly and awkward old men, the figure of Judge Priest, standing in their way alone, had a grotesque emphasis. The judge's broad stomach stuck far out in front and was balanced by the rearward bulge of his umbrella. His white chin-beard was streaked with tobacco stains. The legs of his white linen trousers were caught up on his shins and bagged dropsically at the knees. His righthand pocket of his black alpaca coat was sagged away down by some heavy unseen weight.

None of the men in the front rank joined in the snickering however; they only looked at the judge with a sort of respectful obstinacy.

There was nothing said for maybe twenty seconds.

"Jedge Priest," said a spokesman, a tall, spare, bony man with a sandy drooping mustache and a nose that beaked over like a butcherbird's bill—"Jedge Priest, we've come after a nigger boy that's locked up in that jail yonder and we're goin' to have him! Speaking personally, most of us here know you and we all like you, suh; but I'll have to ask you to stand aside and let us go ahead about our business."

"Gentlemen," said Judge Priest, without altering his tone, "the law of this state provides a proper——"

"The law provides—eh?" mimicked the man who had laughed first. "The law provides, does it?"

"——provides a fittin' and an orderly way of attendin' to these matters," went on the judge. "In the absence of the other sworn officials of this county I represent in my own humble person the majesty of the law, and I say to you——"

"Jedge Priest," cut in the beaky-nosed man, "you are an old man and you stand mighty high in this community—none higher. We don't none of us want to do nothin' or say nothin' to you that mout be regretted afterward; but we air goin' to have that nigger out of that jail and stretch his neck for him. He's one nigger that's lived too long already. You'd better step back!" he went on. "You're just wastin' your time and ourn."

A growling assent to this sentiment ran through the mob. It was a growl that carried a snarl. There was a surging forward movement from the rear and a restless rustle of limbs.

"Wait a minute, boys!" said the leader. "Wait a minute. There's no hurry—we'll git him! Jedge Priest," he went on, changing his tone to one of regardful admonition, "you've got a race on for reëlection and you'll need every vote you kin git. I hope you ain't goin' to do nothin' that'll maybe hurt your chances among us Massac Creekers."

"That's the second time that's been throwed up to me inside of five minutes," said Judge Priest. "My chances for election have nothin' to do with the matter now in hand—remember that!"

"All right—all right!" assented the other. "Then I'll tell you somethin' else. Us men have come in broad daylight, not hidin' our faces from the noonday sun. We air open and aboveboard about this thing. Every able-bodied, self-respectin' white man in our precinct is right here with me today. We've talked it over and we know what we air doin'. If you want to take down our names and prosecute us in the cotes you kin go ahead."

Somebody else spoke up.

"I'd admire to see the jury in this county that would pop the law to any one of us for swingin' up this nigger!" he said, chuckling at the naked folly of the notion.

"You're right, my son," said the judge, singling out the speaker with his aimed forefinger. "I ain't tryin' to scare grown men I like you with such talk as that. I know how you feel. I can understand how you feel—every man with white blood in his veins knows just what your feelin's are. I'm not trying to threaten you. I only want to reason with you and talk sense with you. This here boy ain't been identified yet—remember that!"

"We know he's guilty!" said the leader. "I'll admit that circumstances may be against him," pleaded the judge, "but his guilt remains to be proved. You can't hang any man—you can't hang even this poor, miserable little darky—jest on suspicion."

"The dogs trailed him, didn't they?"

"A dog's judgment is mighty nigh as poor as a man's sometimes," he answered back fighting hard for every shade of favor. "It's my experience that a bloodhound is about the biggest fool dog there is. Now listen here to me, boys, a minute. That boy in the jail is goin' to be tried just as soon as I can convene a special grand jury to indict him and a special term of court to try him, and if he's guilty I promise you he'll hang inside of thirty days."

"And drag that pore little thing—my own first cousin—into a cotehouse to be shamed before a lot of these town people—no!" the voice of the leader rose high. "Cotes and juries may do for some cases, but not for this. That nigger is goin' to die right now!"

He glanced back at his followers; they were ready—and more than ready. On his right a man had uncoiled a well-rope and was tying a slipknot in it. He tested the knot with both hands and his teeth, then spat to free his lips of the gritty dust and swung the rope out in long doubled coils to reeve the noose in it.

"Jedge Priest, for the last time, stand aside!" warned the beaky-nosed man. His voice carried the accent of finality and ultimate decision in it. "You've done wore our patience plum' out. Boys, if you're ready come on!"

"One minute!" The judge's shrill blare of command held them against their wills. He was lowering his umbrella. "One minute and one word more!"

Back Home

Shuffling their impatient feet they watched him backing with a sort of ungainly alertness over from right to left, dragging the battered brass ferrule of his umbrella after him, so that it made a line from one curb of the narrow street to the other. Doing this his eyes never left their startled faces. At the far side he halted and stepped over so that they faced this line from one side and he from the other. The line lay between them, furrowed in the deep dust.

"Men," he said, and his lifelong affectation of deliberately ungrammatical speech was all gone from him, "I have said to you all I can say. I will now kill the first man who puts his foot across that line!"

There was nothing Homeric, nothing heroic about it. Even the line he had made in the dust waggled, and was skewed and crooked like the trail of a blind worm. His old figure was still as grotesquely plump and misshapen as ever—the broken rib of his umbrella slanted askew like the crippled wing of a fat bat; but the pudgy hand that brought the big blue gun out of the right pocket of the alpaca coat and swung it out and up, muzzle lifted, was steady and sure. His thumb drew the hammer back and the double click broke on the amazed dumb silence that had fallen like two clangs upon an anvil. The wrinkles in his face all set into fixed, hard lines.

It was about six feet from them to where the line crossed the road. Heavily, slowly, diffidently, as though their feet were weighted with the leaden boots of a deep sea diver, yet pushed on by one common spirit, they moved a foot at a time right up to the line. And there they halted, their eyes shifting from him to the dustmark and back again, rubbing their shoulders up against one another and shuffling on their legs like cattle startled by a snake in the path.

The beaky-nosed man fumbled in the breast of his unbuttoned vest, loosening a revolver in a shoulder holster. A twenty-year-old boy, his face under its coating of dust as white as flour dough, made as if to push past him and break across the line; but the Massac blacksmith caught him and plucked him back. The leader, still fumbling inside his vest, addressed the judge hoarsely:

"I certainly don't want to have to kill you Jedge Priest!" he said doggedly.

"I don't want to have to kill anybody," answered back Judge Priest; "but, as God is my judge, I'm going to kill the first one of you that crosses that line. If it was my own brother I'd kill him. I don't know which one of you will kill me, but I know which one I'm going to kill—the first man across!"

They swayed their bodies from side to side—not forward but from side to side. They fingered their weapons, and some of them swore in a disappointed, irritated sort of way. This lasted perhaps half a minute, perhaps a whole minute—anyway it lasted for some such measurable period of time—before the crumbling crust of their resolution was broken through. The break came from the front and the center. Their leader, the lank, tall man with the down-tilted nose, was the first to give ground visibly. He turned about and without a word he began pushing a passage for himself through the scrouging pack of them. Breathing hard, like men who had run a hard race, they followed him, going away with scarcely a backward glance toward the man who—alone—had daunted them. They followed after their leader as mules follow after a bell-mare, wiping their grimy shirtsleeves across their sweaty, grimier faces and glancing toward each other with puzzled, questioning looks. One of them left a heavy can of coal-oil behind him upright in the middle of the road.

The old judge stood still until they were a hundred yards away. He uncocked the revolver and put the deadly thing back in his pocket. Mechanically he raised his umbrella, fumbling a little with the stubborn catch, and tilted it over his left shoulder; his turtlelike shadow sprang out again, but this time it was in front of him. Very slowly, like a man who was dead tired, he made his way back up the gravel path toward the courthouse. Jeff magically materialized himself out of nowhere, but of Dink Bynum there was no sign.

"Is them w'ite gen'l'men gone?" inquired Jeff, his eyes popping with the aftershock of what he had just witnessed—had witnessed from under the courthouse steps.

"Yes," said the judge wearily, his shoulders drooping. "They're gone."

"Jedge, ain't they liable to come back?"

"No; they won't come back."

"You kinder skeered 'em off, jedge!" An increasing admiration for his master percolated sweetly through Jeff's remarks like dripping honey.

"No; I didn't scare 'em off exactly," answered the judge. "They are not the kind of men who can be scared off. I merely invoked the individual equation, if you know what that means?"

"Yas, suh—that's whut I thought it wuz," assented Jeff eagerly—the more eagerly because he had no idea what the judge meant.

"Jeff," the old man said, "help me into my office and get me a dipper of drinkin' water. I reckin maybe I've got a tech of the sun." He tottered a little and groped outward with one hand.

Guided to the room, he sank inertly into his chair and feebly fought off the blackness that kept blanking his sight. Jeff fanned him with his hat.

"I guess maybe this here campaignin' has been too much for me," said the judge slowly. "It must be the weather. I reckin from now on, Jeff, I'll have to set back sort of easy and let these young fellows run things."

He sat there until the couching sun brought long, thin shadows and a false promise of coolness. Dink Bynum returned unobtrusively to his abandoned post of duty; the crowds began coming back from the Shady Grove schoolhouse; and Jeff found time to slip out and confiscate to private purposes a coal-oil can that still stood in the roadway. He knew of a market for such commodities. The telephone bell rang and the old judge, raising his sagged frame with an effort, went to the instrument and took down the receiver. Longdistance lines were beginning to creep out through the county and this was a call from Florence Station, seven miles away.

"That you, Jedge Priest?" said the voice over the wire. "This is Brack Rodgers. I've been tryin' to raise the sheriff's office, but they don't seem to answer. Well, suh, they got the nigger what done that devil-mint over at the Hampton place on Massac this evenin'. Yes, suh—about two hours ago. He was a nigger named Moore that worked on the adjoinin' place to Hampton's—a tobacco hand. Nobody suspected him until this mornin', when some of the other darkies got to talkin' round; and Buddy Quarles heard the talk and went after him. The nigger he fit back and Buddy had to shoot him a couple of times. Oh, yes, he died—died about an hour afterward; but before he died he owned up to ever'thing. I reckin, on the whole, he got off light by bein' killed. Which, Jedge?—the nigger that's there in the jail? No, suh; he didn't have nothin' a-tall to do with it—the other nigger said so while he was dyin'. I jedge it was what you mout call another case of mistaken identity on the part of them fool hounds."

To be sure of getting the full party vote out and to save the cost of separate staffs of precinct officers, the committee ordained that the Democratic primaries should be held on the regular election day. The rains of November turned the dusts of August to high-edged ridges of sticky ooze. Election day came, wet and windy and bleak. Men cutting across the yellow-brown pastures, on their way to the polling places, scared up flocks of little grayish birds that tumbled through the air like wind-driven leaves and dropped again into the bushes with small tweaking sounds, like the slicing together of shears; and as if to help out this illusion, they showed in their tails barrings of white feathers which opened and closed like scissor-blades. The night came on; and it matched the day, being raw and gusty, with clouds like clotted whey whipping over and round a full moon that resembled a chum-dasher covered with yellow clabber. Then it started raining.

The returns—county, state and national—were received at the office of the Daily Evening News; by seven o'clock the place was packed. Candidates and prominent citizens were crowded inside the railing that marked off the business department and the editorial department; while outside the railing and stretching on outdoors, into the street, the male populace of the town herded together in an almost solid mass. Inside, the air was streaky with layers of tobacco smoke and rich with the various smells of a small printing shop on a damp night. Behind a glass partition, hallway back toward the end of the building, a small press was turning out the weekly edition, smacking its metal lips over the taste of the raw ink. Its rumbling clatter, with the slobbery sputter of the arclights in the ceiling overhead, made an accompaniment to the voices of the crowd. Election night was always the biggest night of the year in our town—bigger than Christmas Eve even.

The returns at large came by telegraph, but the returns of the primaries were sent in from the various precincts of town and county by telephone; or, in cases where there was no telephone, they were brought in by hard-riding messengers. At intervals, from the telegraph office two doors away, a boy would dash out and worm his way in through the eager multitude that packed and overflowed the narrow sidewalk; and through a wicket he would fling crumpled yellow tissue sheets at the editor of the paper. Then the editor would read out:

"Seventeen election districts in the Ninth Assembly District of New York City give Schwartz, for coroner—"

"Ah, shuckin's! Fooled again!"

"St. Louis—At this hour—nine-thirty—the Republicans concede that the entire Democratic state ticket has won by substantial majorities—"

"Course it has! What did they expect Missouri to do?"

"Buffalo—Doran—for mayor, has been elected. The rest of the reform ticket is——"

"Oh, dad blame it! Henry, throw that stuff away and see if there ain't some way to get something definite from Lang's Store or Clark's River on the race for state senator!"

"Yes, or for sheriff—that's the kind of thing we're all honin' to know."

The telephone bell rang.

"Here you are, Mr. Tompkins—complete returns from Gum Spring Precinct."

"Now—quiet, boys, please, so we can all hear."

It was on this night that there befell the tragedy I made mention of in the first paragraph of this chapter. The old County Ring was smashing up. One by one the veterans were going under. A stripling youth not two years out of the law school had beaten old Captain Daniel Boone Calkins for representative; and old Captain Calkins had been representative so many years he thought the job belonged to him. Not much longer was the race for sheriff in doubt, or the race for state senator. Younger men snatched both jobs away from the old men who held them.

In a far corner, behind a barricade of backs and shoulders, sat Major J. Q. A. Pickett, a spare and knotty old man, and Judge Priest, a chubby and rounded one. Of all the old men, the judge seemingly had run the strongest race, and Major Pickett, who had been county clerk for twenty years or better, had run close behind him; but as the tally grew nearer its completion the major's chances faded to nothing at all and the judge's grew dimmed and dimmer.

"'What do you think, judge?" inquired Major Pickett for perhaps the twentieth time, dinging forlornly to a hope that was as good as gone already.

"I think, major, that you and me are about to be notified that our fellow citizens have returned us onc't more to private pursoots," said the old judge, and there was a game smile on his face. For, so far back that he hated to remember how long it was, he had had his office—holding it as a trust of honor. He was too old actively to reënter the practice of law, and he had saved mighty little out of his salary as judge. He would be an idle man and a poor one—perhaps actually needy; and the look out of his eyes by no means matched the smile on his face.

"I can't seem to understand it," said the major, crushed. "Always before, the old boys could be depended upon to turn out for us."

"Major," said Judge Priest, letting his wrinkled old hand fall on the major's sound leg, "did you ever stop to think that there ain't so many of the old boys left any more? There used to be a hundred and seventy-five members of the camp in good standin'. How many are there now? And how many of the boys did we bury this past year?"

There was a yell from up front and a scrooging forward of bodies.

Editor Tompkins was calling off something. The returns from Clark's River and from Lang's Store had arrived together. He read out the figures. These two old men, sitting side by side, at the back, listened with hands cupped behind ears that were growing a bit faulty of hearing. They heard.

Major J. Q. A. Pickett got up very painfully and very slowly. He hooked his cane up under him and limped out unnoticed. That was the night when the major established his right of squatter sovereignty over that one particular spot at the far end of Billy Sherrill's bar-rail.

Thus deserted, the judge sat alone for a minute. The bowl of his corncob pipe had lost its spark of life and he sucked absently at the cold, bitterish stem. Then he, too, got on his feet and made his way round the end of a cluttered-up writing desk into the middle of the room. It took an effort, but he bore himself proudly erect.

"Henry," he called out to the editor, in his homely whine—"Henry, would you mind tellin' me—jest for curiosity—how my race stands?"

"Judge," said the editor, "by the latest count you are forty-eight votes behind Mr. Prentiss."

"And how many more precincts are there to hear from, my son?"

"Just one—Massac!"

"Ah-hah! Massac!" said the old judge. "Well, gentlemen," he went on, addressing the company generally, "I reckin I'll be goin' on home and turnin' in. This is the latest I've been up at night in a good while. I won't wait round no longer—I reckin everything is the same as settled. I wisht one of you boys would convey my congratulations to Mr. Prentiss and tell him for me that——"

There was a bustle at the door and a newcomer broke in through the press of men's bodies. He was dripping with rain and spattered over the front with blobs of yellow mud. He was a tall man, with a drooping mustache and a nose that beaked at the tip like a butcher-bird's mandible. With a moist splash he slammed a pair of wet saddlebags down on the narrow shelf at the wicket and, fishing with his fingers under one of the flaps, he produced a scrawled sheet of paper. The editor of the Daily Evening News grabbed it from him and smoothed it out and ran a pencil down the irregular, weaving column of figures.

"Complete returns on all the county races are now in," he announced loudly, and every face turned toward him.

"The returns from Massac Precinct make no changes in any of the races——"

The cheering started in full volume; but the editor raised his hand and stilled it.

"——make no change in any of the races—except one."

All sounds died and the crowd froze to silence.

"Massac Precinct has eighty-four registered Democratic votes," went on Tompkins, prolonging the suspense. For a country editor, he had the dramatic instinct most highly developed.

"And of these eighty-four, all eighty-four voted."

"Yes; go on! Go on, Henry!"

"And all eighty-four of 'em—every mother's son of 'em—voted for the Honorable William Pitman Priest," finished Tompkins. "Judge you win by——"

Really, that sentence was not finished until Editor Tompkins got his next day's paper out. The old judge felt blindly for a chair, sat down and put his face in his two hands. Eight or ten old men pressed in toward him from all directions; and, huddling about him, they raised their several cracked and quavery voices in a yell that ripped its way up and through and above and beyond the mixed and indiscriminate whoopings of the crowd.

This yell, which is shrill and very penetrating, has been described in print technically as the Rebel yell..

IX. A DOGGED UNDER DOG

ONE or two nights a week my uncle used to take me with him when he went to spend the evening with old Judge Priest. There were pretty sure to be a half dozen or more gray heads there; and if it were good out-door weather, they would sit in a row on the wide low veranda, smoking their pipes and their cigars; and of these the cigars kept off the mosquitos even better than the pipes did, our country being notorious, then, as now, for the excellence of its domestic red liquor and the amazing potency of its domestic black cigars. Every little while, conceding the night to be hot, Judge Priest's Jeff would come bringing a tray with drinks—toddies or else mint juleps, that were as fragrant as the perfumed fountains of a fairy tale and crowned with bristling sprays of the gracious herbage. And they would sit and smoke and talk, and I would perch on the top step of the porch, hugging my bare knees together and listening.

It was on just such a night as this that I heard the story of Singin' Sandy Riggs, the Under Dog. I think it must have been in July—or maybe it was August. To the northward the sheet lightning played back and forth like a great winking lens, burning the day heat out of the air and from the dried up bed of the creek, a quarter of a mile away, came the notes of big bassooning bull frogs, baying at the night. Every now and then a black bird or a tree martin in the maple over head would have a bad dream and talk out in its sleep; and hundreds upon hundreds of birds roosting up there would rouse and utter querulous, drowsy bird-sounds, and bestir themselves until the whole top of the tree rustled and

Back Home

moved as though from a sudden breeze. In lulls of the talk, thin-shredded snatches of winging was borne to us from the little church beyond the old Enders orchard where the negroes were holding one of their frequent revivals.

It was worth any boy's while to listen to the company that assembled on Judge Priest's front porch. For one, Squire Rufus Buckley was pretty certain to be there. Possibly by reason of his holding a judicial office and possibly because he was of a conservative habit of mind, Squire Buckley was never known to give a direct answer to any question. For their own amusement, people used to try him. Catching him on a flawless morning, someone would remark in a tone of questioning that it was a fine day.

"Well now," the Squire would say, "It tis and it taint. It's clear now but you can't never tell when it'll cloud up."

He owned a little grocery store out in the edge of town and had his magistrate's office in a back room behind it. On a crowded Saturday when the country rigs were standing three deep outside and the two clerks were flying about measuring and weighing and counting up and drawing off, a waiting customer might be moved to say:

"Business pretty good, ain't it Squire?"

"It's good," the Squire would say, licking off the corn-cob stopper of a molasses jug and driving it with a sticky *plop* into its appointed orifice, "And then agin it's bad. Some things air sellin' off very well and some things ain't hardly sellin' off a'tall."

The Squire was no great shakes of a talker, but as a listener he was magnificent. He would sit silently hour after hour with his hands laced over his paunch, only occasionally spitting over the banisters with a strident tearing sound.

Nor was the assemblage complete without Captain Shelby Woodward. Captain Shelby Woodward's specialty in conversation was the Big War. From him I first heard the story of how Lieutenant Gracey of the County Battery floated down the river on a saw log and single handed, captured the Yankee gunboat and its sleepy-headed crew. From him I learned the why and wherefore of how our town although located right on the border of North and South, came in '61 to be called the Little Charleston, and from him also I got the tale of that lost legion of Illinois men, a full battalion of them, who crossing out of their own State by stealth were joyously welcomed into ours, and were mustered into the service and thereafter for four years fought their own kinspeople and neighbors—the only organized command, so Captain Shelby Woodward said, that came to the army from the outside. Frequently he used to tell about Miss Em. Garrett, who when Grant came up from Cairo on his gunboats, alone remembered what all the rest of the frightened town forgot—that the silken flag which the women had made with loving hands, was still floating from its flag pole in front of the engine house; and she drove her old rock-away down to the engine house and made her little negro house boy shin up the pole and bring the flag down to her, he greatly fearing the shells from the gunboats that whistled past his head, but fearing much more his mistress, standing down below and looking up at his bare legs with her buggy whip.

"So then," Captain Woodward would go on, "she put the flag under her dress and drove on home. But some Union sympathizer told on her when the troops landed and a crowd of them broke away and went out to her place and called on her to give it up. She was all alone except for the darkeys, but she wasn't scared, that old woman. They sassed her and she sassed 'em back, and they were swearing they'd burn the house down over her head, and she was daring 'em to do it, when an officer came up and drove 'em off. And afterwards when the warehouses and the churches and the Young Ladies' Seminary were chuck full of sick and wounded, brought down from Donaldson and Shiloh, she turned in and nursed them all alike, not caring which side they'd fought on. And so, some of the very men that had threatened her, used to salute when she passed them on the street.

"And sir, she wore that flag under her skirts for four years, and she kept it always and when she died it was her shroud. You remember, Billy,—you were one of the pall bearers?" he would say, turning to Judge Priest.

And Judge Priest would say he remembered mighty well and the talk would go swinging back and forth, but generally back, being concerned mainly with people that were dead and things that were done years and years before I was born.

Major J. Q. A. Pickett was apt to be of the company, dapper and as jaunty as his game leg would let him be, always in black with a white tube rose in his buttonhole. The Major was a born boulevaidier without a boulevard, a natural man about town without the right kind of a town to be about in, and a clubman by instinct, yet with no club except the awnings under Soule's drug store, and the screening of dishrag vines and balsam apples on Priest's front porch. Also in a far corner somewhere, little Mr. Herman Felsburg of Felsburg Brothers, our leading clothiers, might often be found. Mr. Felsburg's twisted sentences used to tickle me. I was nearly grown before I learned, by chance, what Mr. Felsburg himself never mentioned—that he, a newly landed immigrant, enlisted at the first call and had fought in half a dozen hard battles before he properly knew the English for the commands of his captain. But my favorite story-teller of them all, was old Cap'n Jasper Lawson, and he was old—old even to these other old men, older by a full twenty years than the oldest of them, a patriarch of the early times, a Forty-niner, and a veteran of two wars and an Indian Campaign. For me he linked the faded past to the present and made it glow again in vivid colors. Wherever he was, was an Arabian Nights Entertainment for me.

He lives as a memory now in the town—his lean shaven jowl, and his high heeled boots and the crimson blanket that he wore winters, draped over his shoulders and held at the throat with a pin made of a big crusty nugget of virgin California gold. Wearing this blanket was no theatrical affectation of Cap'n Jasper's—it was a part of him; he was raised in the days when men, white and red both, wore blankets for overcoats. He could remember when the Chickasaws still held our end of the State and General Jackson and Governor Shelby came down and bought it away from them and so gave to it its name of The Purchase. He could remember plenty of things like that—and what was better, could tell them so that you could see before your eyes the burnished backs of the naked bucks sitting in solemn conclave and those two old Indian fighters chaffering with them for their tribal lands. He was tall and sparse and straight like one of those old hillside pines, that I have seen since growing on the red clay slopes of the cotton country south of us; and he stayed so until he died, which was when he was away up in the nineties. It was Cap'n Jasper this night who told the story of Singin' Sandy Biggs.

Somehow or other, the talk had flowed and eddied by winding ways to the subject of cowardice, and Judge Priest had said that every brave man was a coward and every coward was a brave man—it all depended on the time and the place—and this had moved Captain Shelby Woodward to repeat one of his staple chronicles—when the occasion suited he always told it. It concerned that epic last year of the Orphan Brigade—his brigade he always called it, as though he'd owned it.

"More than five thousand of us in that brigade of mine, when we went out in '61," he said, "and not quite twelve hundred of us left on that morning in May of '64 when we marched out of Dalton—Joe Johnston's rear guard, holding Sherman back. Holding him back? Hah, feeding ourselves to him; that was it, sir—just feeding ourselves to him a bite at a time, so as to give the rest of the army a chance for its life. And what does that man Shaler say—what does he say and prove it by the figures? One hundred and twenty solid days of fighting and marching and retreating—one hundred and forty days that were like a hot red slice carved out of hell—fighting every day and mighty near every hour, hanging on Sherman's flanks and stinging at him like gadflies and being wiped out and swallowed in mouthfuls. A total, sir, of more than 1800 deadly, or disabling wounds for us in those hundred and twenty days, or more than a wound apiece if every man had been wounded, and there were less than fifty of the boys that weren't wounded at that. And in September, at the end of those hundred and twenty days, just 240 of us left out of what had been five thousand three years before—240 out of what had been nearly twelve hundred in May—240 out of a whole brigade, infantry, and artillery—but still fighting and still ready to keep right on fighting. Those are Shaler's figures, and he was a Federal officer himself, and a most gallant gentleman. And it is true, sir—every word of it is true.

"Now was that bravery? Or was it just pure doggedness? And when you come right down to it, what is the difference between the two? This one thing I do know, though—if it was bravery we were no braver than the men who fought us and chased us and killed us off on that campaign to Atlanta and then on down to the Sea and if it was doggedness, they'd have been just as dogged as we were with the conditions reversed—them losing and us winning. When you're the underdog you just naturally have to fight—there's nothing else for you to do—isn't that true in your experience, Billy?"

"Yes," said Judge Priest, "that's true as Gospel Writ. After all, boys," he added, "I reckin the bravest man that lives is the coward that wants to run and yit don't do it. And anyway, when all's said and done, the bravest fighters in every war have always been the women and not the men. I know 'twas so in that war of ours—the men could go and git what joy there was out of the fightin'; it was the women that stayed behind and suffered and waited and prayed. Boys, if you've all got a taste of your toddies left, s'posen we drink to our women before Jeff brings you your fresh glasses."

They drank with those little clucking sipping sounds that old men make when they drink, and for a bit there was a silence. The shifting shuttle play of the lightning made stage effects in yellow and black against the back-drop of the sky. From the shadows of the dishrag vine where he sat in a hickory arm chair, his pipe bowl making a glowing red smudge in the darkness, old Cap'n Jasper Lawson spoke.

"Speaking of under dogs and things, I reckon none of you young fellows"—he chuckled a little down in his throat—"can remember when this wasn't a gun-toting country down here? But I do.

"It was before your day, but I remember it. First off, there was the time when my daddy and the granddaddies of some of you gentlemen came out over the Wilderness trail with a squirrel rifle in one hand and an ax in the other, swapping shots with the Indians every step of the way. And that was the beginning of everything here. Then, years later on, the feuds started, up in the mountains—although I'm not denying but we had our share of them down here too—and some broken down aristocrats moved out from Virginia and Maryland and brought the Code and a few pairs of those old long barreled dueling pistols along with them, which was really the only baggage some of them had; and awhile after that the Big War came on; and so what with one thing and another, men took to toting guns regularly—a mighty bad habit too, and one which we've never been entirely cured of yet, as Billy's next court docket will show, eh, Billy?"

Judge Priest made an inarticulate sound of regretful assent and Squire Buckley spat out into the darkness with a long-drawn syrupy swish.

"But in between, back in the twenties and the thirties, there was a period when gun toting wasn't so highly popular. Maybe it was because pistols hadn't got common yet and squirrel rifles were too heavy to tote around, and maybe it was because people were just tired of trouble. I won't pretend to say exactly what the cause of it was, but so it was— men settled their differences with their fists and their feet—with their teeth too, sometimes. And if there were more gouged eyes and more teeth knocked out, there were fewer widows and not so many orphans either.

Back Home

"I notice some of you younger fellows have taken here lately to calling this town a city, but when I first came here, it wasn't even a town—just an overgrown wood landing, in the river bottom, with the shacks and houses stuck up on piles to keep 'em out of the river mud. There were still Indians a plenty too—-Chickasaws and Creeks and some Shawnees—-and some white folks who were mighty near as ignorant as the Indians. Why it hadn't been but a few years before—three or four at most, I reckon—since they'd tried to burn the widow woman Simmons as a witch. As boys, some of you must have heard tell of old Marm Simmons. Well, I can remember her and that's better. She lived alone with an old black cat for company, and she was poor and friendless and sort of peculiar in her ways and that started it. And one spring, when the high-water went down, the children got sickly and begun dying off of this here spotted fever. And somebody started the tale that old Marm Simmons was witching 'em to make 'em die—that she'd look at a child and then the child would take down sick and die. It was Salem, Massachusetts, moved up a couple of hundred years, but they believed it—some of them did. And one night a dozen men went to her cabin and dragged her out along with her cat—both of them spitting and yowling and scratching like blood sisters—and they had her flung up onto a burning brush pile and her apron strings had burnt in two when three or four men who were still sane came running up and broke in and kicked the fire apart and saved her. But her old cat went tearing off through the woods like a Jack-mer-lantern with his fur all afire."

He paused a moment to suck deliberately at his pipe, and I sat and thought about old Marm Simmons and her blazing tom cat, and was glad clear down to my wriggling toes that I didn't have to go home alone. In a minute or so Cap'n Jasper was droning on again:

"So you can tell by that, that this here city of yours was a pretty tolerable rough place In its infancy, and full of rough people as most all new settlements are. You've got to remember that this was the frontier in those days. But the roughest of them all, as I recollect, rougher even than the keel-boaters and the trappers and even the Indian traders—was Harve Allen. He set himself up to be the bully of this river country.

"Well, he was. He was more than six feet tall and built like a catamount, and all the whiskey he'd drunk—you could get a gallon then for what a dram'll cost you now—hadn't burnt him out yet. He fought seemingly just for the pure love of fighting. Come a muster or a barn raising or an election or anything, Harve Allen fought somebody—and licked him. Before he had been here a year he had beat up half the men in this settlement, and the other half were pretty careful to leave him alone, even those that weren't afraid of him. He never used anything though except his fists, and his feet and his teeth—he never needed anything else. So far as was known, he'd never been licked in his whole life.

"You see, there was nobody to stop him. The sheriff lived away down at the other end of the county, and the county was five times as big as it is now. There were some town trustees—three of them—and they'd appointed a long, gangling, jimpy-jawed fellow named Catlett to be the first town constable, but even half grown boys laughed at Catlett, let alone Harve Allen. Harve would just look at Catlett sort of contemptuously and Catlett would slide off backwards like a crawfish. And when Harve got a few drams aboard and began churning up his war medicine, Catlett would hurry right straight home, and be taken down sick in bed and stay there until Harve had eased himself, beating up people.

"So Harve Allen ran a wood yard for the river people and had things pretty much his own way. Mainly people gave him the whole road. There was a story out that he'd belonged to the Ford's Ferry gang before they broke up the gang. That's a yarn I'll have to tell this boy here some of these days when I get the time—how they caught the gang hiding in Cave-In-Rock and shot some of them and drowned the rest, all but the two head devils—Big Harp and Little Harp who were brothers—and how they got back across the river in a dug out and were run down with dogs and killed too; and the men that killed them cut off their heads and salted them and packed them in a piggin of brine and sent the piggin by a man on horseback up to Frankfort to collect the reward. Yes, that's what they did, and it makes a tale that ought to be written out some time."

That was old Cap'n Jasper's way. His mind was laden like Aladdin's sumter-mule, with treasures uncountable, and often he would drop some such glittering jewel as this and leave it and go on. I mind now how many times he started to tell me the full story of the two dissolute Virginians, nephews of one of the first Presidents, who in a fit of drunken temper killed their slave boy George, on the very night that the great Earthquake of 1811 came—and taking the agues and the crackings of the earth for a judgment of God upon their heads, went half mad with terror and ran to give themselves up. But I never did find out, and I don't know yet what happened to them after that. Nor was I ever to hear from Cap'n Jasper the fuller and gory details of the timely taking-off of Big Harp and little Harp. He just gave me this one taste of the delightful horror of it and went on.

"Some of them said that Harve Allen had belonged to the Ford's Ferry gang and that he'd got away when the others were trapped. For a fact he did come down the river right after the massacre at the cave, and maybe that was how the story started. But as for myself, I never believed that part of it at all. Spite of his meanness, Harve Allen wasn't the murdering kind and it must have taken a mighty seasoned murderer to keep steady company with Big Harp and Little Harp.

"But he looked mean enough for anything—just the way he would look at a man won half his fights for him. It's rising of sixty years since I saw him, but I can shut my eyes and the picture of him comes back to me plain as a painted portrait on a wall. I can see him now, rising of six feet-three, as I told you, and long-legged and raw-boned. He didn't have any beard on his face—he'd pulled it out the same as the Indian bucks used to do, only they'd use mussel shells, and he used tweezers, but there were a few hairs left in his chin that were black and stiff and stood out like the bristles on a hog's jowl. And his under lip lolled down as though it'd been sagged out of plumb by the weight of all the cuss-words that Harve had sworn in his time, and his eyes were as cold and mean as a catfish's eyes. He used to wear an old deer skin hunting vest, and it was gurmed and smeared with grease until it was as slick as an otter-slide; and most of the time he went bare foot. The bottoms of his feet were like horn.

"That was the way he looked the day he licked Singin' Sandy the first time—and likewise the way he looked all the other times too, for the matter of that. But the first time was the day they hanged Tallow Dave, the half breed, for killing the little Cartright girl. It was the first hanging we ever had in this country—the first legal hanging I mean—and from all over the county, up and down the river, and from away back in the oak barrens, the people came to see it. They came afoot and ahorseback, the men bringing their rifles and even old swords and old war hatchets with them, with the women and children riding on behind them. It made the biggest crowd that'd ever been here up to then. Away down by the willows stood the old white house that washed away in the rise of '54, where old Madame La Farge, the old French woman, used to gamble with the steamboat captains, and up where the Market Square is now, was the jail, which was built of logs; and in between stretched a row of houses and cabins, mainly of logs too, all facing the river. There was a road in front, running along the top of the bank, and in summer it was knee deep in dust, fit to choke a horse, and in winter it was just one slough of mud that caked and balled on your feet until it would pull your shoes off. I've seen teams mired down many a time there, right where the Richland House is now. But on this day the mud was no more than shoe-throat deep, which nobody minded; and the whole river front was just crawling with people and horses.

"They brought Tallow Dave out of the jail with his arms tied back, and put him in a wagon, him sitting on his coffin, and drove him under a tree and noosed him round the neck, and then the wagon pulled out and left him swinging and kicking there with the people scrooging up so close to him they almost touched his legs. I was there where I could see it all, and that's another thing in my life I'm never going to forget. It was pretty soon after they'd cut him down that Harve Allen ran across Singin' Sandy. This Sandy Biggs was a little stumpy man with sandy hair and big gray eyes that would put you in mind of a couple of these here mossy agates, and he was as freckled as a turkey egg, in the face. He hadn't been here very long and people had just begun calling him Singin' Sandy on account of him going along always humming a little tune without any words to it and really not much tune, more like a big blue bottle fly droning than anything else. He lived in a little clearing that he'd made about three miles out, back of the Grundy Hill, where that new summer park, as they call it, stands now. But then it was all deep timber—oak barrens in the high ground and cypress slashes in the low—with a trail where the gravel road runs, and the timber was full of razor back hogs stropping themselves against the tree boles and up above there were squirrels as thick as these English sparrows are today. He had a cub of a boy that looked just like him, freckles and sandy head and all; and this boy—he was about fourteen, I reckon—had come in with him on this day of the Tallow Dave hanging.

"Well, some way or other, Singin' Sandy gave offense to Harve Allen—which as I have told you, was no hard thing to do—bumped into him by accident maybe or didn't get out of the road brisk enough to suit Harve. And Harve without a word, up and hauled off and smacked him down as flat as a flinder. He laid there on the ground a minute, sort of stunned, and then up he got and surprised everybody by making a rush for Harve. He mixed it with him but it was too onesided to be much fun, even for those who'd had the same dose themselves and so enjoyed seeing Harve taking it out of somebody else's hide. In a second Harve had him tripped and thrown and was down on him bashing in his face for him. At that, Singin' Sandy's cub of a boy ran in and tried to pull Harve off his dad, and Harve stopped pounding Sandy just long enough to rear up and fetch the cub a back handed lick with the broad of his hand that landed the chap ten feet away. The cub bounced right up and made as if to come back and try it again, but some men grabbed him and held him, not wanting to see such a little shaver hurt. The boy was sniveling too, but I took notice it wasn't a scared snivel—it was a mad snivel, if you all know what I mean. They held him, a couple of them, until it was over.

"That wasn't long—it was over in a minute or two. Harve Allen got up and stood off grinning, just as he always grinned when he'd mauled somebody to his own satisfaction, and two or three went up to Singin' Sandy and upended him on his feet. Somebody fetched a gourd of water from the public well and sluiced it over his head and face. He was all blood where he wasn't mud—streaked and sopped with it, and mud was caked in his hair thick, like yellow mortar, with the water dripping down off of it. He didn't say a word at first. He got his breath back and wiped some of the blood out of his eyes and off his face onto his sleeve, and I handed him his old skin cap where it had fallen off his head. The cub broke loose and came running to him and he shook himself together and straightened up and looked round him. He looked at Harve Allen standing ten feet away grinning, and he said slow, just as slow and quiet:

"'I'll be back agin Mister, one month frum today. Wait fur me.

"That was all—just that 'I'll be back in a month' and 'wait fur me.' And then as he turned around and went away, staggering a little on his pins, with his cub trotting alongside him, I'm blessed if he didn't start up that little humming song of his; only it sounded pretty thick coming through a pair of lips that were battered up and one of them, the upper one, was split open on his front teeth.

"We didn't then know what he'd meant, but we knew in a month. For that day month, on the hour pretty nigh, here came Singin' Sandy tramping in by himself. Harve Allen was standing in front of a doggery that a man named Whitis ran—he died of the cholera I remember years and years after—and Singin' Sandy walked right up to him and said: 'Well, here I am' and hit out at Harve with his fist. He hit out quick, like a cat striking, but he was short armed and under sized. He didn't much more than come up to Harve's shoulder and even if the lick had landed, it wouldn't have dented Harve hardly. His intentions were good though, and he swung out quick and fast. But Harve was quicker still. Singin' Sandy hit like a cat, but Harve could strike like a moccasin snake biting you. It was all over again almost before it started.

"Harve Allen bellowed once, like a bull, and downed him and jumped on him and stomped him in the chest with his knees and pounded and clouted him in the face until the little man stretched out on the ground still and quiet. Then, Harve climbed off of him and swaggered off. Even now, looking back on it all, it seems like a shameful thing to admit, but nobody dared touch a hand to Singin' Sandy until Harve was plumb gone. As soon, though, as Harve was out of sight behind a cabin, some of them went to the little man and picked him up and worked over him until he came to. If his face had been dog's meat before, it was calf's liver now—just pounded out of shape. He couldn't get but one eye open. I still remember how it looked. It looked like a piece of cold gray quartz—like the tip of one these here gray flint Indian darts. He held one hand to his side—two of his ribs were caved in, it turned out—and he braced himself against the wall of the doggery and looked around him. He was looking for Harve Allen.

"'Tell him for me,' he said slow and thick, 'that I'll be back agin in a month, the same as usual.'

"And then he went back out the road into the oak barrens, falling down and getting up and falling some more, but keeping right on. And by everything that's holy, he was trying to sing as he went and making a bubbling noise through the blood that was in his throat.

"They all stood staring at him until he was away off amongst the trees, and then they recalled that that was what he had said before—that he'd be back in a month; and two or three of them went and hunted up Harve Allen and gave him the message. He swore and laughed that laugh of his, and looked hard at them and said:

"'The runty varmint must love a beatin' a sight better than some other folks I could name,' and at that they sidled off, scenting trouble for themselves if Harve should happen to take it into his head that they'd sided with Singin' Sandy."

Cap'n Jasper stopped to taste of his toddy, and the other older men stirred slightly, impatient for him to go on. Sitting there on the top step of the porch, I hugged my knees in my arms and waited breathlessly, and Singin' Sandy and Harve Allen visualized themselves for me there before my eyes. In the still I could hear the darkies singing their Sweet Chariot hymn at their little white church beyond the orchard. That was the fourth time that night they had sung that same song, and when they switched to "Old Ark A'Movin'" we would know that the mourners were beginning to "come through" and seek the mourners' bench.

Cap'n Jasper cleared his throat briskly, as a man might rap with a gavel for attention and talked on:

"Well, so it went. So it went for five enduring months and each one of these fights was so much like the fight before it, that it's not worth my while trying to describe 'em for you boys. Every month, on the day, here would come Singin' Sandy Riggs, humming to himself. Once he came through the slush of a thaw, squattering along in the cold mud up to his knees, and once 'twas in a driving snow storm, but no matter what the weather was or how bad the road was, he came and was properly beaten, and went back home again still a-humming or trying to. Once Harve cut loose and crippled him up so he laid in a shack under the bank for two days before he could travel back to his little clearing on the

Grundy Fork. It came mighty near being Kittie, Bar the Door with the little man that time. But he was tough as swamp hickory, and presently he was up and going, and the last thing he said as he limped away was fur somebody to give the word to Harve Allen that he'd be back that day month. I never have been able to decide yet in my own mind, whether he always made his trips a month apart because he had one of those orderly minds and believed in doing things regularly, or because he figured it would take him a month to get cured up from the last beating Harve gave him. But anyhow, so it was. He never hurt Harve to speak of, and he never failed to get pretty badly hurt himself. There was another thing—whilst they were fighting, he never made a sound, except to grunt and pant, but Harve would be cursing and swearing all the time.

"People took to waiting and watching for the day—Singin' Sandy's day, they began calling it. The word spread all up and down the river and into the back settlements, and folks would come from out of the barrens to see it. But nobody felt the call to interfere. Some were afraid of Harve Allen and some thought Singin' Sandy would get his bellyfull of beatings after awhile and quit. But on the morning of the day when Singin' Sandy was due for the eighth time—if he kept his promise, which as I'm telling you he always had—Captain Braxton Montjoy, the militia captain, who'd fought in the war of 1812 and afterwards came to be the first mayor of this town, walked up to Harve Allen where he was lounging in front of one of the doggeries. I still remember his swallowfork coat and his white neckerchief and the little walking stick he was carrying. It was one of these little shiny black walking sticks made out of some kind of a limber wood, and it had a white handle on it, of ivory, carved like a woman's leg. His pants were strapped down tight under his boots, just so. Captain Braxton Mont-joy was fine old stock and he was the best dressed man between the mouth of the Cumberland and the Mississippi. And he wasn't afraid of anything that wore hair or hide.

"'Harvey Allen,' he says, picking out his words, 'Harvey Allen, I am of the opinion that you have been maltreating this man Riggs long enough.'

"Harve Allen was big enough to eat Captain Braxton Montjoy up in two bites, but he didn't start biting. He twitched back his lips like a fice dog and blustered up.

"'What is it to you?' says Harve.

"'It is a good deal to me and to every other man who believes in fair play,' says Captain Braxton Montjoy. 'I tell you that I want it stopped.'

"'The man don't walk in leather that kin dictate to me what I shall and shall not do,' says Harve, trying to work himself up, 'I'm a leetle the best two handed man that lives in these here settlemints, and the man that tries to walk my log had better be heeled for bear. I'm half hoss and half alligator and,—'

"Captain Braxton Montjoy stepped up right close to him and began tapping Harve on the breast of his old deer skin vest with the handle of his little walking stick. At every word he tapped him.

"'I do not care to hear the intimate details of your ancestry,' he says. 'Your family secrets do not concern me, Harvey Allen. What does concern me,' he says, 'is that you shall hereafter desist from maltreating a man half your size. Do I make my meaning sufficiently plain to your understanding, Harvey Allen?'

"At that Harve changed his tune. Actually it seemed like a whine came into his voice. It did, actually.

"'Well, why don't he keep away from me then?' he says. 'Why don't he leave me be and not come round here every month pesterin' fur a fresh beatin'? Why don't he take his quittances and quit? There's plenty other men I'd rather chaw up and spit out than this here Riggs—and some of 'em ain't so fur away now,' he says, scowling round him.

"Captain Braxton Montjoy started to say something more but just then somebody spoke behind him and he swung round and there was Singin' Sandy, wet to the flanks where he'd waded through a spring branch.

"'Excuse me, Esquire,' he says to Captain Montjoy, 'and I'm much obliged to you, but this here is a private matter that's got to be settled between me and that man yonder—and it can't be settled only jist one way.'

"'Well sir, how long do you expect to keep this up, may I inquire?' says Captain Braxton Montjoy, who never forgot his manners and never let anybody else forget them either.

"'Ontil I lick him,' says Singin' Sandy, 'ontil I lick him good and proper and make him yell 'nuff!'

"'Why you little spindley, runty strippit, you ain't never goin' to be able to lick me,' snorts out Harve over Captain Braxton Montjoy's shoulder, and he cursed at Sandy. But I noticed he hadn't rushed him as he usually did. Maybe, though, that was because of Captain Montjoy standing in the way.

"'You ain't never goin' to be big enough or strong enough or man enough to lick me,' says Harve.

"'I 'low to keep on tryin', says Singin' Sandy. 'And ef I don't make out to do it, there's my buddy growin' up and comin' along. And some day he'll do it,' he says, not boasting and not arguing, but cheerfully and confidently as though he was telling of a thing that was already the same as settled.

"Captain Braxton Montjoy reared away back on his high heels—he wore high heels to make him look taller, I reckon—and he looked straight at Singin' Sandy standing there so little and insignificant and raggedy, and all gormed over with mud and wet with branch water, and smelling of the woods and the new ground. There was a purple mark still under one of Sandy's eyes and a scabbed place on top of one of his ears where Harve Allen had pretty nigh torn it off the side of his head.

"'By Godfrey,' says Captain Braxton Montjoy, 'by Godfrey, sir,' and he began pulling off his glove which was dainty and elegant, like everything else about him. 'Sir,' he says to Singin' Sandy, 'I desire to shake your hand.'

"So they shook hands and Captain Braxton Montjoy stepped one side and bowed with ceremony to Singin' Sandy, and Singin' Sandy stepped in toward Harve Allen humming to himself.

"For this once, anyhow, Harve wasn't for charging right into the mix-up at the first go-off. It almost seemed like he wanted to back away. But Singin' Sandy lunged out and hit him in the face and stung him, and then Harve's brute fighting instinct must have come back into his body, and he flailed out with both fists and staggered Singin' Sandy back. Harve ran in on him and they locked and there was a whirl of bodies and down they went, in the dirt, with Harve on top as per usual. He licked Singin' Sandy, but he didn't lick him nigh as hard as he'd always done it up till then. When he got through, Singin' Sandy could get up off the ground by himself and that was the first time he had been able to do so. He stood there a minute swaying a little on his legs and wiping the blood out of his eyes where it ran down from a little cut right in the edge of his hair. He spit and we saw that two of his front teeth were gone, broken short off up in the gums; and Singin' Sandy felt with the tip of his tongue at the place where they'd been. 'In a month,' he says, and away he goes, singing his tuneless song.

"Well, I watched Harve Allen close that next month—and I think nearly all the other people did too. It was a strange thing too, but he went through the whole month without beating up anybody. Before that he'd never let a month pass without one fight anyhow. Yet he drank more whiskey than was common even with him. Once I ran up on him sitting on a drift log down in the willows by himself, seemingly studying over something in his mind.

"When the month was past and Singin' Sandy's day rolled round again for the ninth time, it was spring time, and the river was bankfull from the spring rise and yellow as paint with mud and full of drift and brush. Out from shore a piece, in the current, floating snags were going down, thick as harrow teeth, all pointing the same way like big black fish going to spawn. Early that morning, the river had bitten out a chunk of crumbly clay bank and took a cabin in along with it, and there was a hard job saving a couple of women and a whole shoal of young ones. For the time being that made everybody forget about Singin' Sandy being due, and so nobody, I think, saw him coming. I know I didn't see him at all until he stood on the river bank humming to himself.

"He stood there on the bank swelling himself out and humming his little song louder and clearer than ever he had before—and fifty yards out from shore in a dugout that belonged to somebody else, was Bully Harve Allen, fighting the current and dodging the drift logs as he paddled straight for the other side that was two miles and better away. He never looked back once; but Singin' Sandy stood and watched him until he was no more than a moving spot on the face of those angry, roily waters. Singin' Sandy lived out his life and died here—he's got grandchildren scattered all over this county now, but from that day forth Harve Allen never showed his face in this country."

Cap'n Jasper got up slowly, and shook himself, as a sign that his story was finished, and the others rose, shuffling stiffly. It was getting late—time to be getting home. The services in the darky church had ended and we could hear the unseen worshippers trooping by, still chanting snatches of their revival tunes.

"Well, boys, that's all there is to tell of that tale," said Cap'n Jasper, "all that I now remember anyhow. And now what would you say it was that made Harve Allen run away from the man he'd already licked eight times hand running. Would you call it cowardice?"

It was Squire Buckley, the non committal, who made answer.

"Well," said Squire Buckley slowly, "p'raps I would—and then agin, on the other hand, p'raps I wouldn't."

X. BLACK AND WHITE

OVER night, it almost seems, a town will undergo radical and startling changes. The transition covers a period of years really, but to those who have lived in the midst of it, the realization comes sometimes with the abruptness of a physical shock; while the returning prodigal finds himself lost amongst surroundings which by rights should wear shapes as familiar as the back of his own hand. It is as though an elderly person of settled habits and a confirmed manner of life had suddenly fared forth in new and amazing apparel—as though he had swapped his crutch for a niblick and his clay pipe for a gold tipped cigarette.

It was so with our town. From the snoreful profundities of a Rip Van Winkle sleep it woke up one morning to find itself made over; whether for better or worse I will not

Back Home

presume to say, but nevertheless, made over. Before this the natural boundaries to the north had been a gravel bluff which chopped off sharply above a shallow flat sloping away to the willows and the river beyond. Now this saucer-expanse was dotted over with mounds of made ground rising like pimples in a sunken cheek; and spreading like a red brick rash across the face of it, was a tin roofed, flat-topped irritation of structures—a cotton mill, a brewery, and a small packing plant dominating a clutter of lesser industries. Above these on the edge of the hollow, the old warehouse still stood, but the warehouse had lost its character while keeping its outward shape. Fifty years it resounded to a skirmish fire clamor of many hammers as the negro hands knocked the hoops off the hogsheads and the auctioneer bellowed for his bids; where now, brisk young women, standing in rows, pasted labels and drove corks into bottles of Dr. Bozeman's Infallible Cough Cure. Nothing remained to tell the past glories of the old days, except that, in wet weather, a faint smell of tobacco would steam out of the cracks in the floor; and on the rotted rafters over head, lettered in the sprawling chirography of some dead and gone shipping clerk, were the names and the dates and the times of record-breaking steamboat runs—*Idlewild*, Louisville to Memphis, so many hours and so many minutes; *Pat Cleburne*, Nashville to Paducah, so many hours and so many minutes.

Nobody ever entered up the records of steamboat runs any more; there weren't any to be entered up. Where once wide side-wheelers and long, limber stern-wheelers had lain three deep at the wharf, was only a thin and unimpressive fleet of small fry-harbor tugs and a ferry or two, and shabby little steamers plying precariously in the short local trades. Along the bank ran the tracks of the railroad that had taken away the river business and the switch engines tooted derisively as if crowing over a vanquished and a vanished rival, while they shoved the box cars back and forth. Erecting themselves on high trestles like straddle bugs, three more railroads had come in across the bottoms to a common junction point, and still another was reliably reported to be on its way. Wherefore, the Daily Evening News frequently referred to itself as the Leading Paper of the Future Gateway of the New South. It also took the Associated Press dispatches and carried a column devoted to the activities of the Women's Club, including suffrage and domestic science.

So it went. There was a Board of Trade with two hundred names of members, and half of them, at least, were new names, and the president was a spry new comer from Ohio. A Republican mayor had actually been elected—and that, if you knew the early politics of our town, was the most revolutionary thing of all. Apartment houses—regular flat buildings, with elevator service and all that—shoved their aggressive stone and brick faces up to the pavement line of a street where before old white houses with green shutters and fluted porch pillars had snuggled back among hack berries and maples like a row of broody old hens under a hedge. The churches had caught the spirit too; there were new churches to replace the old ones. Only that stronghold of the ultra conservatives, the Independent Presbyterian, stood fast on its original site, and even the Independent Presbyterian had felt the quickening finger of progress. Under its gray pillared front were set ornate stone steps, like new false teeth in the mouth of a stem old maid, and the new stained glass memorial windows at either side were as paste earrings for her ancient virginal ears. The spinster had traded her blue stockings for doctrinal half hose of a livelier pattern, and these were the outward symbols of the change.

But there was one institution among us that remained as it was—Eighth of August, 'Mancipation Day, celebrated not only by all the black proportion of our population—thirty-six per cent by the last census—but by the darkies from all the lesser tributary towns for seventy-five miles around. It was not their own emancipation that they really celebrated; Lincoln's Proclamation I believe was issued of a January morning, but January is no fit time for the holidaying of a race to whom heat means comfort and the more heat the greater the comfort. So away back, a selection had been made of the anniversary of the freeing of the slaves in Hayti or San Domingo or somewhere and indeed it was a most happy selection. By the Eighth of August the watermelons are at their juiciest and ripest, the frying size pullet of the spring has attained just the rightful proportions for filling one skillet all by itself, and the sun may be reliably counted upon to offer up a satisfactory temperature of anywhere from ninety in the shade to one hundred and two. Once it went to one hundred and four and a pleasant time was had by all.

Right after one Eighth the celebrants began laying by their savings against the coming of the next Eighth. It was Christmas, Thanksgiving, and the Fourth of July crowded into the compass of one day—a whole year of anticipation packed in and tamped down into twenty-four hours of joyous realization. There never were enough excursion trains to bring all those from a distance who wanted to come in for the Eighth. Some, travelers, the luckier ones, rode in state on packed day coaches and the others, as often as not, came from clear down below the Tennessee line, on flat cars, shrieking with nervous joy as the engine jerked them around the sharp curves, they being meantime oblivious alike to the sun shining with midsummer fervor upon their unprotected heads, and the coal cinders, as big as buttons, that rained down in gritty showers. There was some consolation then in having a complexion that neither sun could tan nor cinders blacken.

For that one day out of the three hundred and sixty-five and a fourth, the town was a town of dark joy. The city authorities made special provision for the comfort and the accommodation of the invading swarms and the merchants wore pleased looks for days beforehand and for weeks afterward—to them one good Eighth of August was worth as much as six Court Mondays and a couple of circus days. White people kept indoors as closely as possible, not for fear of possible race clashes, because we didn't have such things; but there wasn't room, really, for anybody except the celebrants. The Eighth was one day when the average white family ate a cold snack for dinner and when family buggies went undrivered and family washing went unwashed.

On a certain Eighth of August which I have in mind, Judge Priest spent the simmering day alone in his empty house and in the evening when he came out of Clay Street into Jefferson, he revealed himself as the sole pedestrian of his color in sight. Darkies, though, were everywhere—town darkies with handkerchiefs tucked in at their necks in the vain hope of saving linen collars from the wilting-down process; cornfield darkies whose feet were cramped, cabin'd, cribb'd and confined, as the saying goes, inside of stiff new shoes and sore besides from much pelting over unwontedly hard footing; darkies perspiry and rumpled; darkies gorged and leg weary, but still bent on draining the cup of their yearly joy to its delectable dregs. Rivers of red pop had already flowed, Niagaras of lager beer and stick gin had been swallowed up, breast works of parched goobers had been shelled flat, and blade forests of five cent cigars had burned to the water's edge; and yet here was the big night just getting fairly started. Full voiced bursts of laughter and yells of sheer delight assaulted the old Judge's ears. Through the yellowish dusk one hired livery stable rig after another went streaking by, each containing an unbleached Romeo and his pastel-shaded Juliet.

A corner down town, where the two branches of the car lines fused into one, was the noisiest spot yet. Here Ben Boyd and Bud Dobson, acknowledged to be the two loudest mouthed darkies in town, contended as business rivals. Each wore over his shoulder the sash of eminence and bore on his breast the badge of much honor. Ben Boyd had a shade the stronger voice, perhaps, but Bud Dobson excelled in native eloquence. On opposite sidewalks they stood, sweating like brown stone china ice pitchers, wide mouthed as two bull-alligators.

"Come on, you niggers, dis way to de-real show," Ben Boyd would bellow unendingly, "Remember de grand free balloon ascension teks place at eight o'clock," and Ben would wave his long arms like a flutter mill.

"Don't pay no 'tention, friends, to dat cheap nigger," Bud Dobson would vociferously plead, "an' don't furgit de grand fire works display at mah park! Ladies admitted free, widout charge! Dis is de only place to go! Tek de green car fur de grand annual outin' an' ball of de Sisters of the Mysterious Ten!"

Back it would come in a roar from across the way:

"Tek de red car—dat's de one, dat's de one, folks! Dis way fur de big gas balloom!"

Both of them were lying—there was no balloon to go up, no intention of admitting anybody free to anything. The pair expanded their fictions, giving to their work the spontaneous brilliancy of the born romancer. Like straws caught in opposing cross currents, their victims were pulled two ways at once. A flustered group would succumb to Bud's blandishments and he would shoo them aboard a green car. But the car had to be starting mighty quick, else Bud Dobson's siren song would win them over and trailing after their leader, who was usually a woman, like blade sheep behind a bell wether they would pile off and stampede over to where the red car waited. Some changed their minds half a dozen times before they were finally borne away.

These were the country darkies, though—the town bred celebrants knew exactly where they were going and what they would do when they got there. They moved with the assured bearing of cosmopolitans, stirred and exhilarated by the clamor but not confused by it. Grand in white dresses, with pink sashes and green headgear, the Imperial Daughters of the Golden Star rolled by in a furniture van. The Judge thought he caught a chocolate-colored glimpse of Aunt Dilsey, his cook, enthroned on a front seat, as befitting the Senior Grand Potentate of the lodge; anyhow, he knew she must be up front there somewhere. If any cataclysm of Providence had descended upon that furniture van that night many a kitchen beside his would have mourned a biscuit maker par excellence. Sundry local aristocrats of the race—notably the leading town barber, a high school teacher and a shiny black undertaker in a shiny high hat—passed in an automobile, especially loaned for the occasion by a white friend and customer of the leading barber. It was the first time an automobile had figured in an Eighth of August outing; its occupants bore themselves accordingly.

Further along, in the centre of the business district, the Judge had almost to shove a way for himself through crowds that were nine-tenths black. There was no actual disorder, but there was an atmosphere of unrestrained race exultation. You couldn't put your hand on it, nor express it in words perhaps, but it was there surely. Turning out from the lit-up and swarming main thoroughfare into the quieter reaches of a side street, Judge Priest was put to it to avoid a collision with an onward rush of half grown youths, black, brown, and yellow. Whooping, they clattered on by him and never looked back to see who it was they had almost run over.

In this side street the Judge was able to make a better headway; the rutted sidewalk was almost untraveled and the small wholesale houses which mainly lined it, were untenanted and dark. Two-thirds of a block along, he came to a somewhat larger building where an open entry way framed the foot of a flight of stairs mounting up into a well of pitchy gloom. Looking up the stairs was like looking up to a sooty chimney, except that a chimney would have shown a dim opening at the top and this vista was walled in blankness and ended in blankness. Judge Priest turned in here and began climbing upward, feeling the way for his feet, cautiously.

Once upon a time, a good many years before this, Kamleiter's Hall had been in the centre of things municipal. Nearly all the lodges and societies had it then for their common meeting place; but when the new and imposing Fraternity Building was put up, with its elevator, and its six stories and its electric lights, and all, the Masons and the Odd Fellows and the rest moved their belongings up there. Gideon K. Irons Camp alone remained faithful. The members of the Camp had held their first meeting in Kamleiter's

Back Home

Hall back in the days when they were just organizing and Kamleiter's was just built. They had used its assembly room when there were two hundred and more members in good standing, and with the feeble persistency of old men who will cling to the shells of past things, after the pith of the substance is gone, they still used it.

So the Judge should have known those steps by the feel of them under his shoe soles, he had been climbing up and down them so long. Yet it seemed to him they had never before been so steep and so many and so hard to climb, certainly they had never been so dark. Before he reached the top he was helping himself along with the aid of a hand pressed against the plastered wall and he stopped twice to rest his legs and get his breath. He was panting hard when he came to the final landing on the third floor. He fumbled at a door until his fingers found the knob and turned it. He stood a moment, getting his bearings in the blackness. He scratched a match and by its flare located the rows of iron gas jets set in the wall, and he went from one to another, turning them on and touching the match flame to their stubbed rubber tips.

It was a long bare room papered in a mournful gray paper, that was paneled off with stripings of a dirty white. There were yellow, wooden chairs ranged in rows and all facing a small platform that had desks and chairs on it, and an old fashioned piano. On the wall, framed uniformly in square black wooden frames and draped over by strips of faded red and white bunting, were many enlarged photographs and crayon portraits of men either elderly or downright aged. Everything spoke of age and hard usage. There were places where gussets of the wall paper had pulled away from the paste and hung now in loose triangles like slatted jib sails.

In corners, up against the ceiling, cobwebs hung down in separate tendrils or else were netted up together in little gray hammocks to catch the dust. The place had been baking under a low roof all day and the air was curdled with smells of varnish and glue drawn from the chairs and the mould from old oil cloth, with a lingering savor of coal oil from somewhere below. The back end of the hall was in a gloom, and it only lifted its mask part-way even after the Judge had completed his round and lit all the jets and was reaching for his pocket handkerchief. Maybe it was the poor light with its flickery shadows and maybe it was the effect of the heat, but standing there mopping his forehead, the old Judge looked older than common. His plump figure seemed to have lost some of its rotundness and under his eyes the flesh was pouchy and sagged. Or at least, that was the impression which Ed Gafford got. Ed Gafford was the odd jobs man of Kamleiter's Hall and he came now, and was profuse with apologies for his tardiness.

"You'll have to excuse me, Judge Priest," he began, "for bein' a little late about gettin' down here to light up and open up. You see, this bein' the Eighth of August and it so hot and ever'thing, I sort of jumped at the conclusion that maybe there wouldn't be none of your gentlemen show up here tonight."

"Oh, I reckin there'll be quite a lot of the boys comin' along pretty soon, son," said Judge Priest. "It's a regular monthly meetin', you know, and besides there's a vacancy to be filled—we've got a color bearer to elect tonight. I should say there ought to be a purty fair crowd, considerin'. You better make a light on them stairs,—they're as black as a pocket."

"Right away, Judge," said Gafford, and departed.

Left alone, the Judge sat down in the place of the presiding officer on the little platform. Laboriously he crossed one fat leg on the other, and looked out over the rows of empty wooden chairs, peopling them with the images of the men who wouldn't sit in them ever again. The toll of the last few months had been a heavy one. The old Judge cast it up in his mind: There was old Colonel Horace Farrell, now, the Nestor of the county bar to whom the women and men of his own State had never been just plain women and men, but always noble womanhood and chivalric manhood, and who thought in rounded periods and even upon his last sick bed had dealt in well measured phrases and sonorous metaphor in his farewell to his assembled children and grandchildren. The Colonel had excelled at memorial services and monument unveilings. He would be missed—there was no doubt about that.

Old Professor Lycurgus Reese was gone too; who was principal of the graded school for forty-odd years and was succeeded a mercifully short six months before his death by an abnormally intellectual and gifted young graduate of a normal college from somewhere up in Indiana, a man who never slurred his consonant r's nor dropped his final g's, a man who spoke of things as stimulating and forceful, and who had ideas about Boy Scout movements and Native Studies for the Young and all manner of new things, a remarkable man, truly, yet some had thought old Professor Reese might have been retained a little longer anyhow.

And Father Minor, who was a winged devil of Morgan's cavalry by all accounts, but a most devoted shepherd of a struggling flock after he donned the cloth, and old Peter J. Galloway, the lame blacksmith, with his impartial Irish way of cursing all Republicans as Black Radicals—they were all gone. Yes, and a dozen others besides; but the latest to go was Corporal Jake Smedley, color bearer of the Camp from the time that there was a Camp.

The Judge had helped bury him a week before. There had been only eight of the members who turned out in the dust and heat of mid-summer for the funeral, just enough to form the customary complement of honorary pallbearers, but the eight had not walked to the cemetery alongside the hearse. Because of the weather, they had ridden in hacks. It was a new departure for the Camp to ride in hacks behind a dead comrade, and that had been the excuse—the weather. It came to Judge Priest, as he sat there now, that it would be much easier hereafter to name offhand those who were left, than to remember those who were gone. He flinched mentally, his mind shying away from the thought.

Ten minutes passed—fifteen. Judge Priest shuffled his feet and fumed a little. He hauled out an old silver watch, bulky as a turnip, with the flat silver key dangling from it by a black string and consulted its face. Then he heard steps on the stairs and he straightened himself in his chair and Sergeant Jimmy Bagby entered, alone. The Sergeant carried his coat over his arm and he patted himself affectionately on his left side and dragged his feet a little. As Commander of the Camp, the Judge greeted him with all due formality.

"Don't know what's comin' over this here town," complained the sergeant, when he had got his wind back. "Mob of these here crazy country niggers mighty near knocked me off the sidewalk into the gutter. Well, if they hadn't been movin' tolerable fast, I bet you I'd a lamed a couple of 'em," he added, his imagination in retrospect magnifying the indignant swipe he made at unresisting space a good half minute after the collision occurred. The Sergeant soothed his ruffled feelings by ft series of little wheezing grunts and addressed the chair with more composure:

"Seems like you and me are the first ones here, Judge."

"Yes," said the Judge soberly, "and I hope we ain't the last ones too—that's what I'm hopin'. What with the weather bein' so warm and darkies thick everywhere"—he broke off short. "It's purty near nine o'clock now."

"You don't say so?" said the Sergeant. "Then we shorely oughter be startin' purty soon. Was a time when I could set up half the night and not feel it scarcely. But here lately I notice I like to turn in sort of early. I reckin it must be the weather affectin' me."

"That must be it," assented the Judge, "I feel it myself—a little; but look here, Sergeant, we never yet started off a regular meetin' without a little music. I reckin we might wait a little while on Herman to come and play Dixie for us. The audience will be small but appreciative, as the feller says." A smile flickered across his face. "Herman manages to keep younger and spryer than a good many of the boys."

"Yes, that's so too," said the Sergeant, "but jest yestiddy I heared he was fixin' to turn over his business to his son and that nephew of his and retire."

"That's no sign he's playin' out," challenged Judge Priest rather quickly, "no sign at all. I reckin Herman jest wants to knock round amongst his friends more."

Sergeant Bagby nodded as if this theory was a perfectly satisfactory one to him. A little pause fell. The Sergeant reached backward to a remote and difficult hip pocket and after two unsuccessful efforts, he fished out what appeared to be a bit of warped planking.

"They're tearing away the old Sanders place," he confessed somewhat sheepishly, "and I stopped in by there as I come down and fetched away this here little piece of clapboard for a sort of keepsake. You recollect, Judge, that was where Forrest made his headquarters that day when we raided back into town here? Lawsy, what a surprise old Bedford did give them Yankees. But shucks, that was Bedford's specialty—surprises." He stopped and cocked his whity-gray head toward the door hopefully.

"Listen yonder, that must be Herman Felsburg comin' up the steps now. Maybe Doctor Lake is with him. Weather or no weather, niggers or no niggers, it's mighty hard to keep them two away from a regular meetin' of the Camp."

But the step outside was too light a step and too peart for Mr. Felsburg's. It was Ed Gafford who shoved his head in.

"Judge Priest," he stated, "you're wanted on the telephone right away. They said they had to speak to you in person."

The Sergeant waited, with what patience he could, while the Judge stumped down the long flights, and after a little, stumped back again. His legs were quivering under him and it was quite a bit before he quit blowing and panting. When he did speak, there was a reluctant tone in his voice.

"It's from Herman's house," he said. "He won't be with us tonight. He—he's had a kind of a stroke—fell right smack on the floor as he was puttin' on his hat to come down here. 'Twas his daughter had me on the telephone—the married one. They're afraid it's paralysis—seems like he can't move one side and only mumbles, sort of tongue tied, she says, when he tried to talk. But I reckin it ain't nowhere near as serious as they think for."

"No suh," agreed the Sergeant, "Herman's good for twenty year yit. I bet you he jest et something that didn't agree with him. He'll be up and goin' in a week—see if he ain't. But say, that means Doctor Lake won't be here neither, don't it?"

"Well, that's a funny thing," said the old Judge, "I pointedly asked her what he said about Herman, and she mumbled something about Doctor Lake's gittin' on so in life that she hated to call him out on a hot night like this. So they called in somebody else. She said, though, they aimed to have Lake up the first thing in the momin' unless Herman is better by then."

"Well, I'll say this," put in Sergeant Bagby, "she better not let him ketch her sayin' he's too old to be answerin' a call after dark. Lew Lake's got a temper, and he certainly would give that young woman a dressin' down."

The old Judge moved to his place on the platform and mounted it heavily. As he sat down, he gave a little grunting sigh. An old man's tired sigh carries a lot of meaning sometimes; this one did.

"Jimmy," he said, "if you will act as adjutant and take the desk, we'll open without music, for this onc't. This is about the smallest turn-out we ever had for a regular meetin', but we can go ahead, I reckin."

Back Home

Sergeant Bagby came forward and took a smaller desk off at the side of the platform. Adjusting his spectacles, just so, he tugged a warped drawer open and produced a flat book showing signs of long wear and much antiquity. A sheet of heavy paper had been pasted across the cover of this book, but with much use it had frayed away so that the word "Ledger" showed through in faded gilt letters. The Sergeant opened at a place where a row of names ran down the blue lined sheet and continued over upon the next page. Most of the names had dates set opposite them in fresher writing than the original entries. Only now and then was there a name with no date written after it. He cleared his throat to begin.

"I presume," the Commander was saying, "that we might dispense with the roll call for tonight."

"That's agreeable to me," said the acting adjutant, and he shut up the book.

"There is an election pendin' to fill a vacancy, but in view of the small attendance present this evenin'—"

The Judge cut off his announcement to listen. Some one walking with the slow, uncertain gait of a very tired or a very feeble person was climbing up the stairs. The shuffling sound came on to the top and stopped, and an old negro man stood bareheaded in the door blinking his eyes at the light and winking his bushy white tufts of eyebrows up and down. The Judge shaded his own eyes the better to make out the new comer.

"Why, it's Uncle Ike Copeland," he said heartily. "Come right in, Uncle Ike, and set down."

"Yes, take a seat and make yourself comfortable," added the Sergeant. In the tones of both the white men was a touch of kindly but none the less measurable condescension—that instinctive turn of inflection by which the difference held firmly to exist between the races was expressed and made plain, but in this case it was subtly warmed and tinctured with an essence of something else—an indefinable, evasive something that would probably not have been apparent in their greetings to a younger negro.

"Thanky, gen'l'men," said the old man as he came in slowly. He was tall and thin, so thin that the stoop in his back seemed an inevitable inbending of a frame too long and too slight to support its burden. And he was very black. His skin must have been lustrous and shiny in his youth, but now was overlaid with a grayish aspect, like the mould upon withered fruit. His forehead, naturally high and narrow, was deeply indented at the temples and he had a long face with high cheek bones, and a well developed nose and thin lips. The face was Semitic in its suggestion rather than Ethiopian. The whites of his eyes showed a yellow tinge, but the brown pupils were blurred by a pronounced bluish cast. His clothes were old but spotlessly clean, and his shoes were slashed open along the toes and his bare feet showed through the slashed places. He made his way at a hobbling gait toward the back row of chairs.

"I'll be plenty comfor'ble yere, suhs," he said in a voice which sounded almost like an accentuated mimicry of Judge Priest's high notes. He eased his fragile rack of bones down into a chair and dropped his old hat on the matting of the aisle beside him, seemingly oblivious to the somewhat puzzled glances of the two veterans.

"What's the reason you ain't out sashaying round on the Eighth with your own people?" asked the Judge. The old negro began a thin, hen-like chuckle, but his cackle ended midway in a snort of disgust.

"Naw suh," he answered, "naw suh, not fur me. It 'pears lak most of de ole residenters dat I knowed is died off, and mo' over I ain't gittin' so much pleasure projectin' round 'mongst all dese brash young free issue niggers dat's growed up round yere. They ain't got no fitten respec' fur dere elders and dat's a fac', boss. Jes' now seen a passel of 'em ridin'

119

round in one of dese yere ortermobiles." He put an ocean of surging contempt to the word: "Huh—ortermobiles!"

"And dis time dar wam't no place on de flatform fur me at de festibul out in dat Fisher's Gyarden as dey names it, do' it taint nothin' 'ceptin' a grove of trees. Always befoah dis I set up on de very fust and fo'most row—yas suh, always befoah dis hit wuz de rule. But dis yeah dey tek and give my place to dat 'bovish young nigger preacher dat calls hisse'f de Rev'rund J. Fontleroy Jones. His name is Buddy Jones—tha's whut it tis—and I 'members him when he wam't nothin' but jes' de same ez de mud onder yore feet. Tha's de one whut gits my place on de flatform, settin' there in a broadcloth suit, wid a collar on him mighty nigh tall nuff to saw his nappy haid off, which it wouldn't be no real loss to nobody ef it did.

"But I reckin I still is got my pride lef ef I ain't got nothin' else. My grandmaw, she wuz a full blood Affikin queen and I got de royal Congo blood in my veins. So I jes' teks my foot in my hand and comes right on away and lef' dat trashy nigger dar, spreadin' hisse'f and puffin' out his mouf lak one of dese yere ole tree frogs." There was a forlorn complaint creeping into his words; but he cast it out and cackled his derision for the new generation, and all its works.

"Dey ain't botherin' me none, wid dere airs, dat dey ain't. I kin git long widout 'em, and I wuz gwine on home 'bout my own business w'en I seen dese lights up yere, and I says to myse'f dat some of my own kind of w'ite folks is holdin' fo'th and I'll jess drap up dar and set a spell wid 'em, pervidin' I'se welcome, which I knows full well I is.

"So you go right ahaid, boss, wid whutever it 'tis you's fixin' to do. I 'low to jes' set yere and res' my frame."

"Course you are welcome," said Judge Priest, "and we'll be mighty glad to have you stay as long as you're a mind to. We feel like you sort of belong here with us anyway, Unde Ike, account of your record."

The old negro grinned widely at the compliment, showing two or three yellowed snags planted in shrunken bluish gums. "Yas suh," he assented briskly, "I reckin I do." The heat which wilted down the white men and made their round old faces look almost peaked, appeared to have a briskening effect upon him. Now he got upon his feet. His lowliness was falling away, his sense of his own importance was coming back to him.

"I reckin I is got a sorter right to be yere, tho' it warn't becomin' in me to mention it fust," he said. "I been knowin' some of you all gen'l'men since 'way back befoah de war days. I wonder would you all lak to hear 'bout me and whut I done in dem times?"

They nodded, in friendly fashion, but the speaker was already going on as though sure of the answer:

"I 'members monstrous well dat day w'en my young marster jined out wid de artillery and Ole Miss she send me 'long wid him to look after him, 'cause he warn't nothin' but jess a harum-scarum boy noway. Less see, boss—dat must be goin' on thutty or forty yeah ago, ain't it?"

It was more than thirty years or forty either, but neither of them was moved to correct him. Again their heads conveyed an assent, and Uncle Ike, satisfied, went ahead, warming to his theme:

"So I went 'long with him jess lak Ole Miss said. And purty soon, he git to be one of dese yere lieutenants, and he act mighty biggotty toward hisse'f wid dem straps sewed onto his cote collar, but I bound I keep him in order—I bound I do dat, suhs, ef I don't do nothin' else in dat whole war. I minds the time w'en we wuz in camp dat fust winter and yere one day he come ridin' in out of de rain, jess drippin' wet. Befoah 'em all I goes up to him and I says to him, I says, 'Marse Willie, you git right down offen dat hoss and come yere and lemme put some dry clothes on you. What Ole Miss gwine say to me ef I lets you set round here, ketchin; yore death?

"Some of dem y'other young gen'l'men laff den and he git red in de face and tell me to go 'way from dere and let him be. I says to him, I says, 'I promised yore maw faithful to 'tend you and look after you and I pintedly does aim to do so.' I says, 'Marse Willie,' I says, 'I hope I ain't gwine have to keep on tellin' you to git down off'en dat hoss.' Dem y'others laff louder'n ever den and he cuss and r'ar and call me a meddlin' black raskil. But I tek notice he got down off'en dat hoss—I lay to dat.

"But I didn't have to 'tend him long. Naw suh, not very long. He git killed de very fust big battle we wuz in, which wuz Shiloh. Dat battery shore suffer dat day. 'Long tow'rds evenin' yere dey come failin' back, all scorified and burnt black wid de powder and I sees he ain't wid 'em no more and I ax 'bout him and dey tells me de Battery done los' two of its pieces and purty near all de hosses and dat young Marse Willie been killed right at de outset of de hard fightin'. I didn't wait to hear no mo'n dat—dat wuz 'nuff fur me. I puts right out to find him.

"Gen'l'men, dat warn't no fittin' place to be prowlin' 'bout in. Everywhahs you look you see daid men and crippled men. Some places dey is jess piled up; and de daid is beginnin' to swell up already and de wounded is wrigglin' round on de bare ground and some of 'em is beggin' for water and some is beggin' for somebody to come shoot 'em and put 'em out of dere miz'ry. And ever onc't in a wile you hear a hoss scream. It didn't sound like no hoss tho', it sound mo' lak a pusson or one of dese yere catamounts screamin'.

"But I keep on goin' on 'count of my bein' under obligations to 'tend him and jess him alone. After while it begin to git good and dark and you could see lanterns bobbin' round whar dere wuz search parties out, I reckin. And jess befo' the last of de light fade 'way I come to de place whar de Battery wuz stationed in the aidge of a little saige-patch lak, and dar I find him—him and two y'others, right whar dey fell. Dey wuz all three layin' in a row on dere backs jes' lak somebody is done fix 'em dat way. His chist wuz tore up, but scusin' de dust and dirt, dar wam't no mark of vilence on his face a t'all.

"I knowed dey wam't gwine put Ole Miss's onliest dear son in no trench lak he wuz a daid hoss—naw suh, not wile I had my stren'th. I tek him up in my arms—I wuz mighty survig'rous dem times and he wam't nothin' but jes' a boy, ez I told you—so I tek him up and tote him 'bout a hundred yards 'way whar dar's a little grove of trees and de soil is sort of soft and loamy; and den and dere I dig his grave. I didn't have no reg'lar tools to dig wid, but I uses a pinted stick and one of dese yere bay-nets and fast ez I loosen de earth I cast it out wid my hands. And 'long towo'ds daylight I gits it deep nuff and big nuff. So I fetch water frum a little branch and wash off his face and I wrop him in a blanket w'ich I pick up nearby and I compose his limbs and I bury him in de ground."

His voice had swelled, taking on the long, swinging cadences by which his race voices its deeper emotions whether of joy or sorrow or religious exaltation. Its rise and fall had almost a hypnotizing effect upon the two old men who were his auditors. The tale he was telling was no new one to them. It had been written a score of times in the county papers; it had been repeated a hundred times at reunions and Memorial Day services. But they listened, canting their heads to catch every word as though it were a new-told thing and not a narrative made familiar by nearly fifty years of reiteration and elaboration.

"I put green branches on top of him and I bury him. And den w'en I'd done mark de place so I wouldn't never miss it w'en I come back fur him, I jes' teks my foot in my hand and I puts out fur home. I slip through de No'thern lines and I heads for ole Lyon County. I travels light and I travels fast and in two weeks I comes to it. It ain't been but jes' a little mo'n a year since we went 'way but Gar Almighty, gen'l'men, how dat war is done change ever'thing. My ole Miss is gone—she died de very day dat Marse Willie got killed, yas

Back Home

suh, dat very day she taken down sick and died—and her brother, ole Majah Machen is gone too—he's 'way off down in Missippi somewhars refugeein' wid his folks—and de rest of de niggers is all scattered 'bout ever'whars. De Fed'ruls is in charge and de whole place seem lak, is plum' busted up and distracted.

"So I jedge dat I is free. Leas'wise, dar ain't nobody fur me to repote myse'f to, an' dar ain't nobody to gimme no ordahs. So I starts in follerin' at my trade—I is a waggin maker by trade as you gen'l'men knows—and I meks money and saves it up, a little bit at a time, and I bury it onder de dirt flo' of my house.

"After 'while shore-nuff freedom she come and de war end, soon after dat, and den it seem lak all de niggers in de world come flockin' in. Dey act jess ez scatter-brained as a drove of birds. It look lak freedom is affectin' 'em in de haid. At fust dey don't think 'bout settlin' down—dey say de gover'mint is gwine give 'em all forty acres and a mule apiece—and dey jess natchelly obleeged to wait fur dat. But I 'low to my own se'f dat by de time de gover'mint gits 'round to Lyon County my mule is gwine be so old I'll have to be doctorin' him 'stid of plowin' him. So I keeps right on, follerin' my trade and savin' a little yere and a little dar, 'tell purty soon I had money nuff laid by fur whut I need it fur."

There was a crude majesty in the old negro's pose and in the gesturing of his long arms. It was easy to conceive that his granddam had been an African Chieftainess. The spell of his story-telling filled the bare hall. The comb of white that ran up his scalp stood erect like carded wool and his jaundiced eyeballs rolled in his head with the exultation of his bygone achievement. In different settings a priest of ancient Egypt might have made such a figure.

"I had money nuff fur whut I needs it fur," he repeated sonorously, "and so I goes back to dat dere battle-field. I hires me a wite man and a waggin and two niggers to help and I goes dar and I digs up my young marster frum de place whar he been layin' all dis time, and I puts him in de coffin and I bring him back on de railroad cyars, payin' all de expenses, and actin' as de chief mourner. And I buries him in de buryin' ground at de home-place right 'longside his paw, which I knowed Ole Miss would a wanted it done jes' dat way, ef she had been spared to live and nothin' happened. W'en all dat is done I know den dat I is free in my own mind to come and to go; and I packs up my traps and my plunder and leave ole Lyon County and come down yere to dis town, whar I is been ever since.

"But frum dat day fo'th dey calls me a wite folks' nigger, some of 'em does. Well, I reckin I is. De black folks is my people, but de wite folks is always been my frends, I know dat good and well. And it stands proven dis very night. De black people is de same ez cast me out, and dat fool Jones nigger he sets in my 'pinted place on de flatform,"—a lament came again into his chanting tone, and he took on the measured swing of an exhorter at an experience meeting—"Dey cast me out, but I come to my wite friends and dey mek me welcome."

He broke off to shake his wool-crowned head from side to side. Then in altogether different voice he began an apology:

"Jedge, you and Mistah Bagby must please suh, s'cuse me fur ramblin' on lak dis. I reckin I done took up nuff of yore time—I spects I better be gittin' on towo'ds my own home."

But he made no move to start, because the old Judge was speaking; and the worn look was gone from the Judge's face, and the stress of some deep emotion made the muscles of his under jaws tighten beneath the dew-laps of loose flesh.

"Some who never struck a blow in battle, nevertheless served our Cause truly and faithfully," he said, as though he were addressing an audience of numbers. "Some of the bravest soldiers we had never wore a uniform and their skins were of a different color from our skins. I move that our comrade Isaac Copeland here present be admitted to membership in this Camp. If this motion is regular and accordin' to the rules of the organization, I make it. And if it ain't regular—I make it jest the same!"

"I second that motion," said Sergeant Jimmy Bagby instantly and belligerently, as though defying an unseen host to deny the propriety of the step.

"It is moved and seconded," said Judge Priest formally, "that Isaac Copeland be made a member of this Camp. All in favor of that motion will signify by saying Aye!"

His own voice and the Sergeant's answered as one voice with a shrill Aye.

"Contrary, no?" went on the Judge. "The Ayes have it and it is so ordered."

It was now the Sergeant's turn to have an inspiration. Up he came to his feet, sputtering in his eagerness.

"And now, suh, I nominate Veteran Isaac Copeland for the vacant place of color bearer of this Camp—and I move you furthermore that the nominations be closed."

The Judge seconded the motion and again these two voted as one, the old negro sitting and listening, but saying nothing at all. Judge Priest got up from his chair and crossing to a glass cabinet at the back of the platform, he opened the door and drew forth a seven foot staff of polished wood with a length of particolored silk wadded about its upper part and bound round with a silken cord.

"Unde Ike," he said, reverently, "You are our color-sergeant now in good and proper standin'—and here are your colors for you."

The old negro came shuffling up. He took the flag in his hands. His bent back unkinked until he stood straight. His long fleshless fingers, knotted and gnarled and looking like fire-blackened faggots twitched at the silken square until its folds fell away and in the gas light it revealed itself, with its design of the starred St. Andrew's cross and its tarnished gold fringe.

"I thanky suhs, kindly," he said, addressing the two old white men, standing at stiff salute, "I suttinly does appreciate dis—and I'll tell you why. Dey done drap me out of de Cullid Odd Fellers, count of my not bein' able to meet de dues, and dis long time I been feared dat w'en my time come to go, I'd have to be buried by de co'pperation. But now I knows dat I'll be laid away in de big stylish cemetary—wid music and de quality wite gen'l'men along and ker'riges. And maybe dar'll be a band. Ain't dat so, gen'l'men—ain't dar goin' to be a band 'long too?"

They nodded. They were of the same generation, these two old white men and this lone old black man, and between them there was a perfect understanding. That the high honor they had visited upon him meant to their minds one thing and to his mind another thing was understandable too. So they nodded to him.

They came down the steep stairs, the Judge, and the Sergeant abreast in front, the new color bearer two steps behind them, and when they were outside on the street, the Judge fumbled in his pocket a moment, then slipped something shiny into the old negro's harsh, horny palm, and the recipient pulled his old hat off and thanked him, there being dignity in the manner of making the gift and in the manner of receiving it, both.

The Judge and the Sergeant stood watching him as he shuffled away in the darkness, his loose slashed brogans clop-lopping up and down on his sockless feet. Probably they would have found it hard to explain why they stood so, but watch him they did until the old negro's gaunt black shadow merged into the black distance. When he was quite gone from sight, they faced about the other way and soberly and silently, side by side, trudged away, two stoutish, warm, weary old men.

At the corner they parted. The Judge continued alone along Jefferson Street. A trolley car under charter for the Eighth whizzed by him, gay with electric lights. On the rear platform a string band played rag time of the newest and raggedest brand, and between the aisle and on the seats negro men and women were skylarking and yelling to friends and strangers along the sidewalk. The sawing bleat of the agonized bass fiddle cut through the onspeeding clamor, but the guitars could hardly be heard. A little further along, the old Judge had to skirt the curbing to find a clear way past a press of roystering darkies before a moving picture theatre where a horseshoe of incandescent glowed about a sign reading *Colored People's Night* and a painted canvas banner made enthusiastic mention of the historic accuracies of a film dealing with The Battle of San Juan Hill, on exhibition within. The last of the rented livery rigs passed him, the lathered horse barely able to pluck a jog out of his stiff legs. Good natured smiling faces, brown, black, and yellow showed everywhere from under the brims of straw hats and above the neckbands of rumpled frocks of many colors. The Eighth of August still had its last hours to live and it was living them both high and fast.

When Judge Priest, proceeding steadily onward, came to where Clay Street was brooding, a dark narrow little thoroughfare, in the abundant covert of many trees, the tumult and the shouting were well dimmed in the distance behind him. He set his back to it all and turned into the bye-street, an old tired man with lagging legs, and the shadows swallowed him up.

Made in the USA
San Bernardino, CA
30 June 2015